THE BONE QUEEN

THE BONE QUEEN

A Novel

Will Shindler

MINOTAUR
BOOKS
NEW YORK

This is a work of fiction. All of the characters, organizations, and events portrayed in this novel are either products of the author's imagination or are used fictitiously.

First published in the United States by Minotaur Books, an imprint of St. Martin's Publishing Group

EU Representative: Macmillan Publishers Ireland Ltd, 1st Floor, The Liffey Trust Centre, 117–126 Sheriff Street Upper, Dublin 1, D01 YC43

 Printed in the United States of America. For information, address St. Martin's Publishing Group, 120 Broadway, New York, NY 10271.

www.minotaurbooks.com

Designed by Omar Chapa

The Library of Congress Cataloging-in-Publication Data is available upon request.

ISBN 978-1-250-39331-9 (hardcover)
ISBN 978-1-250-39332-6 (ebook)

First Edition: 2026

10 9 8 7 6 5 4 3 2 1

For my mum, who did not live long enough to see my books,
but who told me I'd get there . . .

Reality is merely an illusion, albeit a very persistent one.

—ALBERT EINSTEIN

THE BONE QUEEN

Prologue

The rain lashes across her face like a whip. She's running into the night and even the trees feel like they're conspiring against her, their gnarled branches twisting like the interlocked fingers of old men. These woods are dense, and she has no idea which direction to even head for. All she knows is her pursuer is gaining ground and what's ahead can't be worse than what's behind. The earth beneath is wet and leafy and she can taste the salt on her lips from the sea which is rolling and roaring somewhere close.

Panic forces her to quicken her pace. Her Nikes, bought with such pride in another time and place, are coming apart and she stumbles on a root sending her tumbling. For a second, she remains down, feeling the stitch in her chest mercifully subside a little. She considers staying put—hiding in the shadows. Then she hears it—hears *her*—that hint of cold laughter caught on the night air and knows it's not an option. With a whimper, she forces herself back up onto her feet and starts running again.

She tries to imagine a road on the other side of the trees and that thought gives her renewed hope. In her mind's eye, she sees a car with its headlights cutting through the darkness like laser beams. A kind stranger leaning across to open the passenger door. An escape back to a world she should never have left, to people she should never have hurt. Behind her the urgent rush of her pursuer is getting louder, wood snapping underfoot as it scrabbles after her. If she's caught, there won't be any mercy shown.

The tears streaming down her face are a distraction. The only thing that matters is getting away and she's starting to lose faith that it's even possible now—that the reach of what's chasing her is too long. It feels like these woods have been waiting for her all her life and that this is where everything surely ends.

She skids on some moss and crashes against something hard. There's immediate sharp pain in her side. Something's cut through her jeans into her thigh. She sees a huge fallen branch, jagged spikes of wood jutting out of it randomly, cloaked by the darkness. Swearing under her breath she reaches down and can feel the blood leaking through her fingers. She can't stop herself from crying out—more in despair than pain. That's a mistake and she knows it straightaway.

She hears it stop, imagines its head turning now, craning to listen before changing direction. There's a pitter-patter as the rain begins to get heavier. Just as it has for the last week it quickly starts pounding down, the noise increasing with a rumble. She takes advantage of it and begins moving again. There's a bank in front and she hauls herself up and over with a desperate heave. The woods seem to be thinning out now but everything's a blur. She's not sure what's on the other side of these trees but is hoping for a break. Something, anything.

She finds herself on open ground and runs raggedly across the long grass, but not fast enough. And then her heart stops as it dawns on her where she is. There's a short, battered fence in the middle distance, and on the other side of it she can hear the sea pounding against the rock face far below. There's sheer terror now as she realizes there's nowhere left for her to run, and she turns to face what's coming.

It's her—of course it is. The thing she's been running from for so long, and everything seems to coalesce at that moment. All she can hear now is a roaring in her ears and the cold seems to go right through her. The rain is sheeting down and the terrible cowled figure slowly, jerkily, raises an arm and holds it out towards her accusingly.

Her nerve breaks. She turns and sprints towards the cliff edge, not looking back. Climbing the short fence she stands for a moment, pressing her back against its rotting wood. The jagged rocks glint below, showing her the way—and without hesitation, she leaps into the abyss.

Chapter 1

Today

The first thing that hit her was the sound of the place. Seagulls—lots of them circling overhead, crying and squalling as the ferry inched closer. Some people enjoy traveling like this, but Jenna Tipton knew she definitely wasn't one of them. The whole process was laborious and tiring and she felt sick. But that wasn't because of the choppy waters—she'd been living with the nausea for days and was almost getting used to it. Almost. She knew there was only one thing that was going to make that go away. In her early forties, the last week had aged her badly. Her mousy brown hair had turned frizzy, her lips were dry and chapped, and her skin felt like battered old leather. But none of that mattered, not in the way they normally would.

She'd been told Athelsea Island was stunning but now that they could see it properly, there was nothing that stood out about it. A small rock tucked thirty miles or so off the Cornish coast. In the summer months, it was overrun by tourists—but in the cold blast of February, the huddle of white-brick buildings clustered around the harbor looked more like the death of hope.

"Nearly there, Jen. Are you okay?" said a voice behind her and she turned to see her sister Hattie fiddling with her phone trying to get some sort of signal on it. Much as she loved her, Jenna hoped it wasn't because she wanted to upload a picture of the bloody island onto her Insta. Then she felt bad for having the thought because without her she'd never have made it even this far.

"I'm fine," she said, answering the question with a dirty fat lie.

Hattie was three years younger. Wearing a navy fur-lined puffa jacket, she looked impossibly glamorous, which was standard. Long black locks cascaded around her neck, tousled from the wind, which made her seem even more stunning than usual. It was all the more impressive given how much she hated the sea. A city girl by nature, she'd had a phobia about water since childhood and had done a decent job of covering it since they'd set off. Jenna turned back to face the island, which was getting ever closer.

"Have we made a mistake coming here?" she said, but Hattie shook her head.

"We're following the breadcrumb trail, aren't we? And from what we know this is the likeliest option, isn't it?" She said it as if explaining the search for a misplaced set of keys.

"What if I'm wrong though?" said Jenna, wincing as yet another blast of cold wet wind swept across them. "What if we're wasting valuable time? What if this is just a self-indulgence and we miss something important back home because of it?"

The questions had been tormenting her all day and Hattie had already heard them several times over.

"And what if the moon's made of green cheese? More to the point—what if she *is* here? That's why we've come, isn't it? To bring her home?"

Jenna nodded—there was that.

She could see the bay a bit more clearly as the ferry got closer and its attractions were becoming a little more obvious now. There were boarded-up seafront cafés and restaurants which presumably did a roaring trade fleecing tourists during the summer. Pretty cobbled streets divided them, and old-fashioned-style signposts pointed the way to attractions such as the Athelsea Lighthouse and the Haunted Coves.

"It looks dead," said Hattie and she was right. It also had that superficiality that all these kinds of places possessed which crowds and fine weather helped mask. In ordinary circumstances, it wouldn't take Jenna more than an hour to get bored here, but these weren't ordinary circumstances.

"Who lives here?" she said. "And why would you live here? I mean—it's like this during the winter, then gets overrun by drunken twenty-somethings in the summer. I can't see the attraction."

Hattie smiled. "That's because you're middle-aged."

"Thanks, mate. Don't get too cocky—you're not that far behind me."

The dynamic between them sometimes felt like it had been frozen in aspic from when they were teenagers. The passing of time didn't seem to affect them. It felt as if it would always be like that.

"You know what I mean, Jen. I imagine the population here is largely retired. It's not meant for people like us, is it?"

"So why in the world would she come here?"

And for that, her sister had no answer.

The ferry finally eased to a halt, and after a few minutes they began to disembark, both glad to be on dry land once again. They were each dragging small cases on wheels which rattled noisily as they walked off the wooden jetty and out onto the gray, cobbled thoroughfare.

"Jenna Tipton?"

The voice was rich and fruity, and she turned to see a hearty-looking man in his mid-forties wearing a thick Aran jumper walking towards them. He had ruddy red cheeks, wiry brown hair, and was wearing a warm, friendly smile. Jenna wondered if he had a bag of Fisherman's Friend in his pocket too, to complete the ensemble.

"That's me," she said and extended a hand.

"Ben Markham—from the B&B?"

"You're our taxi driver?"

His smile widened and there seemed to be a twinkle in his eye. "You can call me that if you like. You won't get your Uber working around here though." He said the word "Uber" as if it were a substitute for "Martian." "I run the place with my wife, so I'm used to picking up guests from the harbor. I'm parked up just around the corner. They've pedestrianized this bit because it gets so congested during the summer. Bloody stupid if you ask me when it's like this most of the year."

He gestured at the deserted marina before turning and striding away. Even the locals seemed to share her assessment of the place and Jenna shot Hattie a look that said "I told you so." Her sister rolled her eyes and they both trailed after him.

As they turned the corner, it became obvious that the harbor was much larger than just the small area where their ferry had docked. There were actual signs of life now with more people milling around and even one or two shops open doing business. Hattie was right though; the vast majority seemed to be much older. This was a retirement home set on a tourist trap, not a natural place for young people.

"So, what brings you to Athelsea out of season?" he said as they walked on.

"This," said Jenna, stopping. She fumbled in her handbag for a sheaf of slightly crumpled papers, plucked one free and handed it to him. "I'm looking for my daughter, Chloe. She's sixteen, though I think she probably comes over as a bit younger than that. She disappeared about a week ago."

"Disappeared?" he replied uncertainly. "As in ran away, or . . ."

The question hurt like a needle under a fingernail, and she shrugged helplessly. Awkwardly, Ben focused on the flyer. At the center was a large color photo of a teenage girl sitting around a kitchen table. It was a particular favorite of Jenna's—a good one of her daughter actually smiling. She had bright pink dyed hair with a low fringe, alabaster skin, and milky blue eyes that she'd inherited from her mother. Underneath, together with contact details were written the words *"Missing: Have you seen this girl?"* Ben held the piece of paper with both hands and ran his eyes over the image. The extended amount of time he spent examining it briefly raised Jenna's hopes, but then he shook his head.

"No . . . I'm, sorry, I haven't seen her. She'd have stood out a mile here with hair that color."

It was just one man, the first person they'd even asked, but it still felt like a hammer blow.

Jenna was becoming increasingly aware of how cold it was, far fresher on land than it had been on the ferry. Now that they were here it seemed even more extraordinary to her that Chloe would, could, have made this journey. Her daughter bellyached if the house was anything below greenhouse temperature in the autumn. Jenna shook her head in bemusement. Why has she done this? Why is she doing this to me? Where the hell is she? The same old questions. And she tried not to think of all the worst-case scenarios because she couldn't let herself go there.

She was about to delve into her bag again for some tape to attach the flyer to a nearby lamppost when something caught her eye. A workman in blue overalls was clambering out of a manhole onto one of the cobbled streets. He was wearing thick industrial gloves and had the look of someone who'd like to be just about anywhere else than here. In his hands was a dark round mound of something. At first glance, it looked a bit like a wreath, and she thought it was maybe a collection of moldy leaves but then the smell hit her, and she gagged. It was like death itself had just climbed up her nostrils.

They all looked more closely at the object which he was now carefully placing down on the ground. It was a collision of matted wet black hair, razor-sharp white teeth, flashes of pink flesh, and thick wiry white lengths knotted randomly together like spaghetti. Rats, Jenna realized with horror, lots of them, dead and intertwined. She could feel the bile rising in her throat as multiple sets of glassy eyes stared up at her.

"What is that?" she said.

The man saw her looking and gave her an appalling grin.

"It's a rat king," he said.

"A what?" said Hattie, who usually couldn't handle a spider in the bathtub.

"I thought they were just urban legends?" said Ben, who seemed equally hypnotized by the sight. The man shook his head.

"No, they're more common than people think. I'm clearing them out of the harbor bay sewers all the time."

Hattie looked like she was about to throw up there and then, and Jenna was praying she didn't because she knew she wouldn't be too far behind. The stench coming from it was almost too much to bear.

"It's what happens when a nest of rats gets their tails entwined together," he continued. "They can't free themselves and eventually end up starving to death. But not before they've taken a few chunks out of each other in the process."

It sounded like nonsense to Jenna but then she saw the agonized look on the face of one of the dead creatures and wasn't arguing. Ben's attention had now been caught by something in the middle distance and she followed his gaze, glad to look away from the putrefying heap on the ground.

On the far side of the harbor, a small crowd of people had gathered. There was a police car there too and they seemed to be waiting for a small fishing boat which was crawling its way towards them.

"What's that all about?" said Ben. "Isn't that the Hanway's boat?"

The man in the manhole nodded, busy now loosening up some green industrial-strength waste disposal bags.

"Yes. There's a rumor going round that they found a body in the water this morning."

Jenna's stomach instantly heaved at the words, and she didn't even notice the smell of the rats anymore. Blood was rushing to her ears, and it felt like her whole world was about to collapse.

Chapter 2

The wait was agonizing. They stood watching with the rest of the small crowd as the fishing boat bobbed on the waves like a child's rubber duck in the bath. To Jenna's eyes, it didn't seem to be progressing and yet simultaneously was somehow inching forward through the frothy water.

"It's not her," whispered Hattie into her ear.

"How the hell do you know that?" thought Jenna. Groundless reassurances were more irritating than helpful. She was a journalist by trade, so she knew a thing or two about the importance of staying dispassionate. Hattie was also smart enough to understand that it *could* be Chloe, which made the words even more unhelpful.

Jenna could see a police officer cast straight from every TV cop drama she'd ever watched, standing at the head of the queue waiting to greet the vessel. Frowning in a long brown raincoat, he was a tall, mixed-race man with sharp features, probably in his late thirties—and attractive with it, she found herself observing randomly. She assumed she was noticing details like that because she was on the verge of hysteria now. Ben caught her staring and leant across.

“That’s Liam Tandy. Detective Inspector Tandy, I should say. This must be important—he’s the most senior officer on the island.”

The boat had finally reached the jetty, and Tandy stepped forward to greet its occupants. A craggy-faced man in a woolen bobble hat emerged and he seemed to immediately recognize the policeman. The pair began talking—bobble hat man, gesticulating and pointing at the dark green water behind him. Jenna was watching their faces, looking for any kind of clue but the exchange seemed more businesslike than emotional. Finally, the conversation ended, and both men walked out onto the deck of the small vessel. Bobble hat man bent over and lifted a dark tarpaulin to show the policeman something underneath that Jenna couldn’t see.

She was fighting every impulse to barge her way through the crowd and join them. In her mind’s eye all she could picture was Chloe’s face, bloated and gray from days in the sea and couldn’t stop herself from letting out a small cry of anguish. Hattie’s hand immediately curled around hers in response and the two sisters stood and waited for whatever fate was about to deliver them.

“Do you want me to go and try and find out what’s going on?” said Ben.

“Or, alternatively I could find out for myself,” said Jenna, already deciding she wasn’t going to wait. She began weaving her way through the onlookers. She’d convinced herself of the worst now, bracing her body for the shock—the lightning bolt that was about to strike.

“This is my fault,” she muttered.

“Don’t be ridiculous,” whispered Hattie but the worry was audible in her voice too. Ben had followed them and went straight over to the side of the boat.

“Ross!” He shouted at one of the other fishermen on board. He was a young-looking man with a neat black beard, barely more than a boy, and looked animated as they spoke. Just as before, there was an excruciating wait for them to finish. Ben gave him a pat of thanks on the arm and then walked back over. Jenna knew there was a moment of truth coming and saw a small smile of reassurance spread across his features. From that alone, Jenna knew it wasn't Chloe on the deck of that boat because there's no way of telling a stranger that their daughter was dead which begins with a smile of any kind. She still needed to hear the words said out loud though.

"They've found several human bones," he said. "But they're clearly not recent."

"See . . ." said Hattie and Jenna's tears of relief came thick and hard.

"Come on, let's get away from this circus," said Ben and Jenna nodded as she reached into her bag for a tissue. But even as she wiped her face, she was watching Tandy, now on his radio, and selfishly thought whatever they'd found wasn't helpful to her. Briefly, their eyes met as she caught him staring. He was someone she'd need to talk to, but he was going to have his hands full for the foreseeable future.

Chapter 3

They turned and walked away, heading up a short steep hill that led from the seafront and found Ben's car, which looked like something the 1990s had forgotten to hand back. As they moved off, Jenna felt glad to escape the bay area and refocus her mind. It might not have been Chloe on that fishing boat but the reason they'd come to Athelsea hadn't changed. Ben was taking them to the village of Ravensgate, at the northern tip of the island. Away from the bright sugar confection of the harbor, the road inland wound deep into an oakwood forest. Rich, mint-colored leaves swayed in the wind on either side and the density of the trees seemed to thicken the further in they went.

Jenna sensed the discovery on the boat had shaken Ben and she could guess why. On the mainland, bodies were found every day, but for a place like this, with its relatively small population, the find would be shocking. Word would probably already be filtering around the small network of villages dotted around the island.

"I don't suppose you get too many murder investigations here?" she said and for a moment wondered if he'd even heard her.

"No," he replied eventually. "There's only around two and a half thousand people on Athelsea so major crimes here are rare. And that policeman's only just started—so this is a big test for him too."

"What happened to the guy before?" said Jenna, assuming it was a man. Randomly she pictured a bewhiskered old copper from an old Victorian sketch, drinking whisky from a teacup at his desk. It seemed to fit this place.

"He had a heart attack a few months back," said Ben as they emerged from the woods into a stretch of open road.

"He retired?" said Jenna, but Ben simply shook his head, and they realized what he meant.

The landscape had become considerably more rugged now. Short, cropped stone walls lined the winding roads.

"Where have you come from?" said Ben, seemingly keen to change the subject.

"London," replied Jenna.

He nodded.

"And what makes you think your daughter has traveled all the way out here?"

Jenna exchanged a glance with Hattie.

"This," she said, fishing into her bag again. She pulled out a crumpled piece of paper and Ben glanced across at it. "It's a printout of train and ferry timetables. It was quite clear where she was planning to go. There were a few other things on her laptop and phone too about Athelsea."

Ben nodded. "I don't have kids myself, but I didn't think teenage girls could be separated from their gadgets?"

"Not as a rule and certainly not my daughter. I think she left them behind deliberately so that she couldn't be traced electronically." She shook her head with frustration. "I just don't understand *why*—it makes no sense to me."

Even as she said the last sentence she heard the echo of the words in her mind. She'd been repeating them for days now.

"But you must have some rough idea why she would want to come here specifically?" said Ben. Again, Jenna looked over at Hattie, who simply shrugged.

"Over the last few weeks something seemed to take hold of her, something I just couldn't cut through—and whatever that was . . . I think it's connected to this island somehow."

The drive to Ravensgate took about another ten minutes and Jenna's first view of the place took her by surprise. They were deep into the woods, and the village was nestled amidst towering trees almost peering over it with a polite interest. Quaint cottages adorned with climbing vines dotted the landscape and she could see a picturesque brook winding its way through the center. Sunlight, filtered through the canopy of trees, cast dappled patterns onto the cobblestone pathways and Jenna exchanged a surprised glance with Hattie. It was as if they'd traveled from a Cornish fishing village to the heart of the Bavarian countryside in the space of half an hour.

The B&B was a small white-painted detached house set in a small street close to the brook. Ben parked up before taking their luggage inside. It was genuinely idyllic, but Jenna tried to blot the feeling out; they weren't here on holiday. She wanted this visit to be as short and as swift as possible.

"Let's check in," she said briskly and pulled up the handle of her bag.

"Hold on," said Hattie. She walked down towards the stream and turned. "Just take a moment—it'll do you good. Come on . . ."

Jenna looked out at the picture-book setting and surrendered to it. She followed her sister to the water's edge and realized Hattie was right—it wouldn't hurt to take a second and reset. They both stood and breathed in the air; fine, clear, and fresh. For the first time in days, Jenna felt her thoughts separate out with a semblance of clarity.

"We'll find her," she whispered, and Hattie gave her a small smile back. They turned and walked through to the open door of the guesthouse and found themselves in a neat hallway that smelt of cleaning fluid. A lean-looking woman in a jumper and jeans, roughly the same age as Ben, greeted them. She had an oval face with shoulder-length black hair and there was a natural warmth to her smile.

"I'm Katrina," she said, leading them through into a small reception. "My husband's just taking your bags up to your room—let me get you checked in." She turned to a grid of keys mounted on a board behind her, plucked a set off its hook, and handed them over to Jenna. "The front door's locked after eleven p.m. but the big silver key will let you in if you need it. Breakfast is served in the dining room from seven." She frowned for a second and then found a piece of paper on the desk in front of her which she handed across. "And this is the Wi-Fi password—do you need any local information? I've got pamphlets for some of the best walks on the island, and there are several restaurants we can recommend," she said, with well-rehearsed practice. Jenna smiled politely and then explained why they were there and why the tourist attractions were of little interest. Katrina's expression immediately changed to one of concern as Jenna reached into her bag and passed her one of the flyers she'd brought. She studied it closely and then shook her head.

"No, I'm sorry I haven't seen anyone like that. But that doesn't mean she's not here. For a relatively small island, there's still plenty of places she could have got to. Have you spoken to the police about her yet?"

Jenna shook her head. "Only the ones at home and they weren't that interested. Chloe's sixteen and they're saying she left of her own volition so there's not much they can do. If she is here have you any idea where she might have gone—who she might have sought out or where she might be staying?"

Katrina thought about it for a moment. "It depends what she's come here for—"

Before she could develop the point Ben came through holding his phone in one hand with a deep-set frown on his face.

"There's a rumor going around that those bones they found may belong to Adam Nicks. Apparently, off the record, the dental records look a decent match."

Something seemed to pass between Ben and Katrina.

"Who's Adam Nicks?" said Jenna.

She felt herself shiver, this felt important without even knowing why yet. Ben saw her expression and turned to her.

"He was a young man who used to live here in Ravensgate. His girlfriend was found dead a couple of decades back—he and their little boy vanished at the same time. The police thought he'd killed her and escaped to the mainland. Most people assumed he'd started a new life somewhere. If those bones are his then it looks like we were all wrong."

Chapter 4

Two weeks ago

"Your mum's going to go mental," said Evie.

Chloe stood outside the hairdresser's and grinned. She could see her hair reflecting in the glass window. Frankly, the shade of neon pink she'd just had it dyed would be visible to anyone half a mile down the street. And her friend was right, Jenna would indeed go spare when she saw it.

"I love it," said Chloe with a wide grin.

"I wish I had your balls," said Evie. They were the same age, but Chloe had always felt senior even if Evie was mathematically the older of the two by a couple of months. The difference was she'd never had to watch her parents go through a divorce.

"Mum will make a lot of noise but what's she going to do? I know her—give it a week and she'll be saying it suits me."

Evie laughed, and they began meandering down the street. "What about school?"

"I asked last week if it would be all right. Miss Alcock checked with the head and she said as long as my parents were okay with it, then they wouldn't have a problem."

"And what did you say?"

Chloe looked at her reflection again, this time in the window of a parked car. "What do you think?"

Evie shook her head in mock despair. "Clo—you're terrible."

"Oh come on, they're worse than Mum. They'll do exactly the same thing. Maybe a bit of noise when they first see it, but it's not like I didn't warn them. I can't wait to go in on Monday, it's going to be brilliant." She delved into her pocket and took out her phone. She unlocked it and passed it over. "Here, take a picture. I need to get it up on my Insta." Evie took the handset and began to frame her up. Chloe's face clouded over.

"There's only going to be one problem."

"What?" said Evie.

Chloe posed and beamed for the camera.

"My dad."

"Are you deliberately trying to provoke us?" roared her father.

Tom had seen the pictures online and immediately hit the roof. In his mid-forties, with prematurely graying hair, his well-moisturized cheeks tended to turn pink when he got angry. Chloe had anticipated the extent of his fury because he hadn't even tried to text or call. Instead, he'd driven straight to Jenna's house and was waiting with her when she got home in a rare joint show of unity. It was fascinating to see how wound up they both got when she stepped out of line, how much noise they made and how badly they wanted her to know when they were upset. But when things were just muddling along it was a different story—like she didn't exist. And they couldn't even see the irony of that.

"Of course not and what's the problem, anyway? It's just hair. I checked it out at school and they're fine with it."

Chloe had decided to adopt a line of patient shrugging with them both; the old people making a silly noise about something that no one reasonable would be bothered about. *I'll gaslight the gaslighters,* she'd thought.

"We'll find out next week what your school really thinks," said her mother. "But I'm guessing you were a little economical with the truth when you told them what you were planning?"

"And more to the point you didn't think to check this out with either of us first. Don't you think we deserve a little bit more respect than that?" snapped Tom.

The angrier he got, the more pompous he got too. Her mum had shared that insight with Chloe more than once and it was never more obvious than now. *Prissy,* she thought watching him, and she reckoned her mother was probably thinking the same. There were times she really couldn't see what DNA she shared with either of them.

"How much did it even cost you?" said Jenna, turning her gaze on her like a laser beam. Chloe shrugged again.

"I've been saving for it."

"I'm working my socks off for us both just to keep the lights switched on and the taps running here and this is what you do," her mother continued.

"Oh come on, that's an exaggeration," said Chloe with deliberately added snark. It wasn't the first time Jenna had used that expression and frankly, it *was* a bit over the top.

"Again, some respect would be nice," said her father backing up his ex-wife.

The sustained hostility was starting to get to Chloe. It wasn't as if she'd stolen something. All she ever saw from either of them these days was *this.* She'd had a growing sense for a while that she was just a giant pain in the arse to them that they were both forced to tolerate. It was a feeling that had only increased since her father had moved out of their small semidetached house. She stared at them both defiantly for a moment.

"It's just hair and I love it. In a few months, I'll probably get bored with it and dye it black. Get over yourselves," she shouted at them and then stomped from the living room before either of them could see her eyes reddening. Their own eyes were already rolling but she didn't care.

"Maybe she's seeing a boy," she heard her dad say a few minutes later. Predictably, now that she'd removed herself from the equation, they were starting to turn on each other.

"Oh, for God's sake is that the best you can offer?" Jenna shouted back. It was as if they thought the door to her bedroom had some sort of magical soundproofing properties when in truth it might as well have been made out of cardboard. There was a silence as he tailed off, and Chloe could imagine the scene in the kitchen, knowing exactly the crossed-arm, pissed-off glare her mum was giving him. She knew too what the look on her dad's face in response would be: the suppressed frustration at not having any easy answers put on a plate for him. The silence was protracted, and she wondered if they'd finally figured out that she could hear them.

"Do we always have to argue?" said Tom, in the weary voice he tended to use before properly losing it. "Maybe she's right and we are overreacting. It's no biggie, she's a teenage girl; shit happens, get over it."

"No biggie? She could get *expelled* for this. I looked at the school's website—hair color is at their discretion—I don't think they're going to be impressed with neon-sodding-pink. And that's not even what's pissing me off," shouted Jenna, on a roll now. "She's done this as a screw-you to the pair of us as punishment for the last year—for putting her through the divorce."

"Don't be so dramatic," she heard Tom say, but Chloe thought her mother was actually making a reasonable point. Guilty as charged, really. A splash of pink was the *least* she could pay them back with.

"I'm sorry," Jenna replied, her voice laced with heavy sarcasm. "Getting a bit difficult is it for you? Going beyond the skin-deep and actually trying to understand your daughter?"

Even from the distance of her bedroom, Chloe could hear her dad's next words said through gritted teeth.

"She's like a lot of kids I come across these days. She probably just saw some influencer that she wanted to copy."

"Sorry, am I missing something—*all these kids* you come across? You're a commercial lawyer who spends every hour on God's earth in his office, so when exactly does that happen?"

There was another silence. Chloe gave the conversation five more minutes because she knew what her dad's patience levels were like.

"Lauren has a teenage son, remember?"

Lauren was her father's girlfriend and Chloe seemed to have a better recall of the current state of his love life than her mother. Jenna had made it quite clear she wasn't interested in a new relationship for the foreseeable future and Chloe was beginning to wish that she would reconsider that; it might make her slightly more pleasant to live with.

Later, her father came up for a quiet word. That too she'd seen coming a mile off. He wasn't going to just leave without one last nibble. The quiet heart-to-heart, the *"I just want to understand"* approach. She almost felt like telling him that it was okay and that he didn't need to put them both through this. A brief, slightly patronizing chat was interrupted by a phone call from Lauren, and he'd left shortly afterwards with a casual offer to take her to the cinema the following weekend if she fancied it. The usual journey from fury, through finger-wagging, to trying better to connect with her, now complete. Her earlier bet with Evie that her mum would quickly let this go still stood too, she reckoned.

Chloe went over to her bed and sat cross-legged on it looking at her reflection once more in the mirror on her dressing table. She liked the new look, it made her feel strangely more adult, she thought. She reached for her phone and tapped out a message to Evie.

"Mum and Dad exactly as expected." She added a rolled-eyes emoji for good measure.

Evie responded with a smiley and then sent a link followed by the words:

"Don't become like this girl."

She clicked on the link, and it took her to a videoclip. She watched a Japanese schoolgirl shouting at what appeared to be her mother. She didn't understand a word they were saying and laughed as the row escalated into a full-on screaming war, and it was hard to work out which of the pair had become the more frenzied. Underneath the clip were comments from all over the world.

"Bruh—if I ever raised my voice to my mum like that, I'd see stars quicker than a bullet travels," said *Gamer245*.

"Treat your mother with respect. She's the one person who will always love you no matter what you do, or who you become," offered *Darius90* sagely. Chloe stopped reading for a moment, she could hear Mum doing the hoovering downstairs now. Unlike her father, she wouldn't be coming up to try and make peace. When they fell out it tended to be a war of attrition that thawed pretty slowly. She looked down at her phone again, tempted to play the clip again.

The next comment said simply:

#UnderHerRule followed by another URL. It had been posted by someone called *Athelsea100*. Without much thought, Chloe idly tapped on the link. Her phone's screen immediately turned dark.

An image, in stark black-and-white, slowly took form staring malevolently up from the display. There was an accompanying sound too, a scream, sonorous and guttural, and it seemed to be in the air around her rather than coming from her phone. The image hypnotized her, right there and then. It was a highly detailed sketch of a cowled figure, half its face hidden in shadow, while the other half appeared to be that of a young woman. But the features that were visible were distorted and scarred, a single eye blazing with almost contemptuous hate. It was hard not to feel that it was a fury being projected by the hand that had drawn it. The figure was holding something too, wielding it like a spear and as she looked more closely Chloe realized it was meant to be a bone of some sort, spindly and long like a skeleton's arm or leg.

Chapter 5

Jenna's room was small and comfortable with a view across the woods. Initially, she'd just stood looking out of the window trying to remember what her plan of action was. She'd done her research before leaving London, had known what to expect in Ravensgate, but now she was here felt disoriented. It was the same sense of dislocation she'd experienced after Chloe had first run away. There had been a plan. She'd wanted to speak to the local police and now could even put a face and name to the officer in charge. She'd wanted to flood the village with flyers, speak to the locals, and start building a picture of where her daughter might be. She'd wanted to do all that in the first few hours on the island. Instead, she felt paralyzed, almost overwhelmed by the size of her task. The discovery of those bones at sea had thrown her and she needed to recalibrate.

She also badly wanted a drink and looked longingly over at the cupboard containing the small fridge. Inside were mini bottles of whisky and vodka, a small bottle of Merlot too. The pull of it was strong, but she'd been sober for a long time now and this wasn't the moment to fall apart. It hadn't stopped her looking at the selection though, from almost the moment she'd set foot in the room.

Quashing the feeling, she went over to her travel bag and unzipped it. Almost reverently she lifted out a metallic pink object and placed it on the small desk beneath the window. Chloe's laptop was battered and scratched and coated in a variety of colorful stickers and the sight of it made her sad. There were too many memories of her daughter sitting cross-legged on sofas or beds frowning at the screen.

Between them, she and Tom knew the passwords to both her laptop and phone. Chloe had given her dad the one to the computer because she trusted *him* not to go snooping in it. The phone's code, Jenna had seen her tapping in enough times to have picked up. After she'd gone missing the first thing they'd done was pool information so that they could thoroughly search through their daughter's electronic life.

She desperately wished now she'd paid more attention to precisely what Chloe had been doing. By and large she felt they had a good relationship, one that had come through the trauma of her divorce—and her drinking. When they fell out, it tended to be childish—like mother, like daughter, she grudgingly thought. A period of mutual sulking would follow and then they'd invariably make up again. They'd never *really* fallen out—not properly—and that cord between them was Jenna's most valuable possession. But in recent weeks, there'd been something new in the mix, a more lasting, deeper distance that she hadn't encountered before. She'd assumed it was just another phase of her teenager's adolescence, but now in hindsight she wondered if she hadn't missed something important right under her nose. As ever work had got in the way.

Jenna was a freelance journalist who was employed mainly by press agencies these days to hammer out copy. In her heyday, she'd had a decent career as an investigative reporter with several national newspapers but more recently, ambition had given way to simply trying to stay afloat. There was nothing glamorous about it—most of her time was spent sitting in empty newsrooms at unsociable hours. Being a single mother was tough, being a single mother with no guaranteed income during an economic downturn meant every penny counted. No offer of work could be turned down, no shift—whatever its hours—could be refused and Chloe had undoubtedly suffered as a consequence.

Jenna tapped in the laptop's password and watched as it booted up. The desktop picture was a close-up of their cat, a tabby called Ginger who was currently on extended leave at a West London cattery. The timetables she'd found in her daughter's bedroom had pointed her to Athelsea, but it had been the internet search history on this device that had directed Jenna to Ravensgate. She was somewhere here, in this small community. She was sure of it and now she had to find out where and with who.

She opened up an internet browser and automatically glanced through her daughter's social media again. She'd looked through it many times over the last few days, but still had a sneaking feeling there was something she'd missed. Something that might just kick-start her now. There was a reason Chloe had come to this island and this particular village.

She scrolled through the same old photos and videos—mainly of Ginger, one or two from some holidays they'd taken together. In the main though, her daughter wasn't prone to sharing too much of herself online. Jenna sighed with frustration. She looked again through the list of things Chloe had "liked" over the last few weeks. Amusing cat videos, some incomprehensible rants from an American rapper Jenna had never heard of, and some memes doling out life advice like *"Never reply when you're angry or make decisions when you're sad."*

"Ain't that the truth," Jenna muttered under her breath.

There was another below that. A link with just a string of letters to it. She hadn't noticed it before because it was easy to miss amongst the pictures and videos. Jenna automatically clicked on it and watched as the slow guesthouse Wi-Fi took her to a new page. Her eyes widened at the image that stared out of the screen at her.

"What the hell's that?" said Hattie, breaking Jenna's train of thought, and she turned to see her sister standing in the doorway. She'd freshened up and changed, looking immaculate in a beige leather jacket, dark green top, and smart black trousers. Jenna turned back to the screen. There was an image of a face, female with a cowl that shrouded much of it. The eyes were sunken and piercing, the lips thin and cracked. Jenna realized she'd assumed it was of an old woman, but it wasn't. She was young, the visible skin cracked and wrinkled from scars of some sort. There were some words underneath, but they were foreign—Russian or Greek by the look of them. A single word in English was legible—*Athelsea*. Jenna took a deep breath.

"I don't know but I think it might be important."

The guesthouse had a small alcove with a PC and printer on the ground floor, and Jenna printed off a copy of the picture. It wasn't much to work with, but it was something.

"You think Chloe came here for *that*?" said Hattie, motioning at the picture as Jenna tucked it into her bag.

"I've no idea, we don't know enough about any of this. Until we have more information, we're just guessing about why she left." For a moment her mind flashed back to that bottle of Merlot in her fridge. She could almost taste the velvety liquid in her mouth.

"Come on, we won't learn anything in here."

As they stepped out onto the street the first thing that crossed her mind was that poverty didn't seem to be a problem on Athelsea. All the houses appeared to have had work done in some form, smart new extensions with gleaming glass ceilings and expensive-looking cars parked on the street outside. She could see large gardens too, hidden by high spotless white walls. But this was a picture-book village, and she wondered, just as on the mainland, whether there was a less attractive underbelly elsewhere.

“Where are we going?” said Hattie.

Jenna looked up and saw a building in the middle distance. A colorful sign was hanging out of the front, and she could see a small blackboard in the street offering a variety of local ales. She smiled wryly at her sister.

“For a drink . . .”

Chapter 6

The Black Horse Inn looked and felt comfortable from the moment they stepped inside. It seemed to Jenna the kind of place that was aiming to tread a line between keeping the locals happy in the winter and drawing in the tourist trade during the summer. The bar area had a traditional style with dark cherrywood chairs and tartan-covered stools and benches. As they walked through she could also see a light and airy restaurant space, its tables laid with sparkling clean wineglasses which caught the light.

"What are we doing in here?" said Hattie.

"If you want to know what's happening—where better than the local pub?" said Jenna. Behind the counter, a tall jowly middle-aged man with a shaven head looked up and smiled pleasantly at them.

"What can I get you?" he said before they'd even reached the bar. Once again, Jenna explained why they were there and riffled in her bag for one of the flyers. He shook her hand with a meaty grip and introduced himself as Frank Archer, before reaching into the top pocket of his shirt and pulling out a pair of reading glasses. He slipped them on and looked at the picture of Chloe carefully. Jenna's heart began to thump, just as it had earlier when they'd been in the harbor waiting to see what that fishing boat had brought back.

"No," he said finally. "I've not seen her. On an island like this, I'd have *heard* about a girl with bright pink hair, trust me. People have pretty conservative tastes around here." He looked at her slightly awkwardly. "Not me, I hasten to add; I think it really suits her."

Jenna nodded glumly. She'd only asked three people so far and they'd only been here for a matter of hours, but each negative response felt like a stab to the heart. A thought occurred to her as she remembered her conversation with Hattie on the ferry about the island's aging population.

"I haven't seen too many teenagers around the place. Where do they all tend to hang out?"

Frank rolled his eyes and gestured at the lounge. "*Here,* to be honest. It's a different thing in the summer when the tourists come and the weather's warmer, but at this time of the year we don't have too many troublemakers knocking about. They sit in the corner drinking sensibly and chatting amongst themselves and that's about it."

"So where would a sixteen-year-old on her own go to? There must be somewhere—a youth hostel for example?"

He shook his head. "There isn't anything like that on Athelsea. There's just half a dozen very small villages and the harbor. I'd say it was more likely if your daughter is here then she's staying with someone."

That was what was worrying Jenna, and she could see Hattie was having a similar thought. That sense that someone had got to Chloe, lured her here.

"If you hear anything, I'm staying at the B&B, just up the street," she said and Frank nodded.

"Ben and Katrina are old friends. I'll keep my ear to the ground and if something comes up, I'll find you."

"Thank you. There's one more thing," said Jenna. She pulled out the picture of the strange witch-like creature she'd found earlier. "Do you recognize this?"

Frank's face was as inscrutable as Ben's had been earlier. Not contemptuous or curious or even dismissive, just unreadable and she wondered for a moment if that was in itself significant.

"An old Athelsea legend," he said finally. Jenna looked up with interest. "I don't really know the backstory," he continued. "What it looks like—a witch. Children dress up as her at Halloween," he said with a shrug and handed it back as if he'd got his hands dirty by simply touching it. "Sorry, I don't know much more."

"It's more than I knew before," she said with a smile and then exchanged the picture for the flyer of Chloe. "Would you mind pinning this up in here? Just in case it jogs anyone's memory. I'd really appreciate it."

He smiled revealing slightly yellowing teeth. "Of course. Kids, eh? Makes me kind of grateful I haven't got any."

Jenna frowned.

"One more question if that's okay. When the ferry arrived, there were a lot of police in the harbor. A fishing boat found some human remains out at sea. Ben thought they might belong to someone called Adam . . ."

Frank's affable smile froze at the name. "*Adam?* As in Adam Nicks?"

He sounded genuinely surprised and Jenna nodded.

"That's who Ben thought they might belong to."

Frank leant against the counter for a second, visibly trying to make sense of the information. "I haven't heard that name in a long time."

Jenna and Hattie exchanged a glance.

"Did you know him?" said Jenna.

Frank rubbed the back of his neck. "He disappeared years ago—2002, maybe 2003, somewhere around then. It surely has nothing to do with your daughter?"

Jenna shrugged off a wave of tiredness, the long journey suddenly catching up with her.

"Maybe I'm overthinking it because I'm overthinking *everything* right now. But if Adam Nicks was killed and no one knew about that until today—then someone got away with murder once, didn't they?" she said and again his face hardened into something she couldn't read.

The sun had gone in, and the sky had turned white, its palette smeared with streaky gray clouds as they left the pub.

"Nice one Jen, I think you set the mood for lunch in there, just perfectly," said Hattie.

"It doesn't make me wrong though, does it? said Jenna as they made their way down the street. She could feel tiredness hitting her again as they set off. She was beginning to think she needed hot food and a decent night's sleep before starting the search properly in the morning. Then she felt a surge of self-loathing at her own weakness. Her daughter could be here in one of these houses, locked up in a cold cellar, and she banished the thought of rest.

"You know what this place reminds me of?" she said, and Hattie nodded immediately.

"I'm way ahead of you."

The two sisters had been raised in a small village in Kent, within range of the London commuter belt. Ravensgate in many ways didn't feel that different. Already, from the brief conversations they'd had, Jenna was getting a sense of a very familiar type of community. One where everyone knew each other, where stories from the past like Adam Nicks were the stuff of local legend.

She stopped next to a lamppost and pulled out another of the flyers from her bag together with a roll of sticky tape. Biting the tape off with her teeth she attached the poster to the lamppost and looked at her daughter smiling cheerfully back at her. Fear coursed through her once more, the terror she'd never see that face in the flesh again.

"Good Lord, I'm so sorry. It's usually a lost pet or something people are pinning up," said a voice, earthy and warm. Jenna spun round and saw a middle-aged woman with rust-colored hair in a red coat peering at the picture. Jenna shook her head and briefly went through what was now becoming a well-rehearsed speech.

"I don't suppose you've seen her, have you? She's very distinctive—" But the woman—who introduced herself as Ruth O'Brien—shook her head before she could finish the sentence.

"No, I'm so sorry. What makes you think she's come to Athelsea?"

Again, Jenna went through what little she knew.

"You must be worried sick," said Ruth. "Have you really no clue at all why she would have traveled all the way out here?"

"Show her the picture," muttered Hattie and Jenna reached into her bag again.

"Only this. I don't know what it is, but it seems to have some sort of link to Athelsea."

Jenna held up the printout of the witch, and like Frank before her Ruth studied it carefully. She was quiet, her eyes absorbing every detail.

"That's quite the piece of art," she said.

"Can you tell me anything?" said Jenna. "*Who* it is? It's all I've got to go on."

"Yes," she said and pointed to some trees in the middle distance overlooking the street. "Let me show you."

Ruth led them through a path that separated two of the houses and up into a small patch of woodland. As they passed through, Jenna saw what looked like the remains of a gray stone wall. There was more of it scattered around and she realized the woods had grown around it—the foundations of some vast and old building.

"What is this place?" she said.

"Part of what used to be Ravensgate Jail," replied Ruth. "It's not even a tourist attraction really, there's not enough of it left—just some of the stonework. But three hundred years ago, the whole of the village was centered around here. Those expensive houses below were built over the remains of where the prison staff and their families used to live."

Hattie looked around unimpressed.

"So what are we looking for? Surely Chloe didn't come here for this?"

Ruth pointed over at a large Scots pine tree that dominated the center of the clearing. "That's what I wanted you to see. What you're standing on is Gallows Hill and that is the tree where they used to hang the convicts from."

Jenna stared up. The thing itself wasn't evil, obviously—just a tree. But there was something about it for sure. Tall, and surprisingly thin with thick gray-brown bark. At the top, the wind whistled through short blue-green leaves. She turned and looked out over the village. It was the last thing those who were brought here would have ever seen, the view more or less untouched by time.

"Go take a look at it more closely," said Ruth. Jenna exchanged a look with Hattie and slowly walked towards it. As they got nearer Jenna could see the trunk was covered in carvings. Words, images, and sigil-like designs that had been etched in over the years. It was easy to tell which were the older ones, they were darker, the writing more elaborate and the phrasing more biblical. She read one or two at random: *"The eyes of God are watching"* and *"The last enemy that shall be destroyed is death itself."* Had it been one of the prisoners or the staff of the jail who'd added that one? she wondered.

"Dean loves Lucy," she read out and Hattie stifled a laugh. Ruth shrugged.

"Believe it or not, this is a popular night spot for some of the younger tourists in the summer. I'll leave it to your imagination what kind of things they get up to here."

Jenna turned back to the tree and slowly walked around it, surveying some more of the markings. Ruth pointed at one in particular.

A small circular image carved at almost head height. It was a rudimentary face, or half a face to be accurate, one eye staring out above a crooked smile.

"That is *her* mark," she said. Jenna looked at the crumpled piece of paper again and then glanced back at the carving. "She comes for the bones of children, so the legend goes," said Ruth. The wind blew through them for a moment, and it had been a long time since Jenna had felt this cold. Her eyes alighted again on the crude face that seemed to be smirking at her from the bark of the tree. "Do you know why they stopped using this island as a jail?" continued Ruth. "Because all the prison staff's children died. A plague of some sort. They say she came for them in retribution and took their bones."

"Retribution for what?" said Jenna. "Who is she?"

Jenna couldn't take her eyes off that face now, all the other carvings on the tree seemed to have become invisible.

She walked up to the tree and examined it closely. There was another version of the round half-face and beneath it was what looked like a small stanza. Judging by its shading and the spidery writing it looked old. Jenna leant in and read the words out loud:

In shadows deep the Bone Queen sleeps,
Beware the night when shadows creep,
For in her gaze the lost bones weep.

Chapter 7

"I don't like it—it doesn't make any sense at all," said Ben Markham. He was sitting on a stool in the Black Horse Inn as Frank Archer poured him a pint of cloudy-looking beer from one of the taps. Frank placed the glass on a coaster and then leant forward pressing his hands down on the counter as he considered what his friend was saying.

"No one knows anything for sure yet," growled the publican. "It's all hearsay and rumor, which let's face it, is ninety percent of what this island is built on. Those bones were found at sea, and they could be anyone's. A suicide or even someone who just fell off a boat somewhere and washed up here."

Ben nodded and took a sip of the beer, wiping his top lip as he swallowed it.

"It can't be Adam, it just *can't* be. There's no logic to it. Why now?"

There was a momentary flash of fear in his eyes which Frank caught.

"If his bones have been in the water for that long then I'd hate to think what condition they're in," Frank said pointedly, and Ben nodded slowly.

"But what if it *is*. What if—"

"Don't," said Frank, cutting him off.

"What are you two gossiping about like old washerwomen?" said a crisp Essex accent, interrupting them. Frank's wife, Debbie, a heavily made-up woman with prematurely gray-black hair, had entered the lounge and walked over to join her husband behind the bar. As usual she was dressed ever so slightly more glamorously than the day demanded.

"Nothing and everything—you know us," said Frank quickly and she smiled.

"Leave us here long enough and we'll gossip for England," added Ben.

She looked at them both suspiciously. "I know that. Thick as thieves, you two."

"No different to you and Katrina when you get going," Frank responded.

"Cheeky," she replied. "Some of the barrels need changing. Don't let a bit of work get in the way of your chitchat though." Frank sighed as Ben chuckled and lifted his glass again. "And you can wipe that smile off your face, Ben Markham. I'm sure Kat could use a hand back at the guesthouse. Does she know you've slipped down here for a quick one?"

"How do you put up with this all day long," said Ben to his friend, pretending to ignore her.

"Our marriage works on one simple principle," Frank replied solemnly. "I do precisely as I'm instructed when I'm instructed and that keeps her in her place." They all laughed, and he raised his hands in mock surrender. "Okay, I'm going to change the barrels." But as he passed Ben, a look, if not an understanding, passed between them.

By the time he'd reached the pub's cellar, any pretense of warm affability had given way to cold concern. There was no way those bones *could* belong to Adam Nicks. The rumors were premature—they had to be. He looked down at the stack of metal barrels on the floor and saw the familiar cartoon outline of the island on a consignment of Athelsea IPA. Leaning forward to lift it, something stopped him. A feeling, a slight constriction around his throat. He raised a hand to his Adam's apple and tried to take a breath but found himself struggling for air. He couldn't swallow either and felt a wave of panic rising. Something jerked his head back and there was a strange sensation of heat in his throat and then it all stopped as quickly as it had started. He stood still panting for air and tried to recover his composure. What the hell had that been? He was sweating too he realized and wiped his brow.

"Are you all right down there?" shouted Debbie. "Anytime today would be good."

"I'm fine," he yelled, trying and just about succeeding in matching the levity of her tone. But he was feeling anything but fine. He shook his head—it was just his aging body giving him a reminder to go for a run later, that was all. Steadying himself, he bent down and lifted the barrel.

Chapter 8

Two weeks ago

It started in the night with a dream about a room with no doors. Chloe was with Evie, and they were laughing about something. Some of the others from school were with them. She couldn't quite identify what was so funny, but it was cruel—they were laughing *at* someone, but she couldn't see who it was or why they were doing it. She was scared they were laughing at her, which didn't make sense because she was joining in. One by one everyone melted away until Chloe was alone in a white void. Her own laughter seemed to magnify, booming until it didn't seem to even sound like her and then there was just silence.

"Is anyone there?" she called out, but her voice just echoed around her.

As she listened again, she thought she could hear a sound. A hum so distant that at first she wasn't sure it was even there. It was getting louder though, almost like white noise, and then she recognized it. It was a *howl* of raw despair. Now it was loud, really loud—almost unbearable, the screech cutting right through her. She put her hands over her ears and began to scream.

Mercifully, it began to fade and then she became aware something was in there with her. She lifted her hands away from her head as the thing solidified into shape. She saw herself staring, standing in the void. The girl with pink hair was looking at her with the same terrified curiosity she could feel in her own expression.

"Who are you?" said Chloe.

"Who are *you*?" responded the newcomer.

They locked eyes and then the girl smiled. Her face began to melt until it split in half, her skin wrinkling and dissolving as if acid had been poured upon it. A new face began to appear, the flesh rotten and burnt. A cowl seemed to grow out of the shadows around her, and she began walking towards Chloe.

"Who are you?" repeated the creature, but this time the voice was different, harsh and sibilant.

Before Chloe could respond, she woke.

She was ice-cold and pulled her duvet around her. It took her a moment to remember and then she grabbed her phone from her bedside table and retrieved the picture she'd found the previous night. *That's* where she'd heard that scream before. She stared at the image again in fascination and then swiped it away.

If she thought the lingering unease of a bad night would pass quickly she was wrong. It stayed with her all day as did the constant shivering. At home, at school, on the journeys in between, the chill was relentless and sapping. Even more strange there'd been a sense of sound and smell that had accompanied the dream which didn't fade either. As her history teacher droned on that afternoon about some medieval war in Europe, it had come back to her. The drag of something ominous heaving itself slowly across wet ground, the accompanying smell of burning meat, like lamb chops that had been left under the grill too long.

The itching had started that morning too. A light irritation at first on her arm that she didn't think too much of. But as the day went on, it had got progressively worse. She'd sat in a toilet cubicle manically clawing at her skin, savoring the strange combination of relief and pain it brought. She'd put it all down to a bad day that had begun with a nightmare and that was all. But as it turned out, that was only the start.

That night she'd locked herself in her bedroom and gone looking again for more information on the internet. The dream and that soul-wrenching howl hadn't left her. The memory of it was worse than fingers down a blackboard or metal grating on metal and she couldn't stop herself from conjuring it. She didn't want to go to bed again that night, because she'd already convinced herself what she would see once her eyes closed.

She found the link on her laptop that she'd followed on her phone before, brought up that picture and heard the scream once again. She did a reverse image search and immediately a list of very similar images spread out in front of her. What was this thing? She clicked on the first one and her breath caught as she stared at this new larger portrait. It was clearly the same thing—the same putrefying skin, the lone eye glowing with malevolent intensity. There were three words underneath and even though it was the first time she'd read them, it felt like she'd always known them:

The Bone Queen

Chapter 9

One week ago

"Have I done something to upset you?" said Jenna.

She'd barely got a word out of Chloe for the best part of a week and enough was enough. She felt like she was being punished for something but hadn't got a clue what it was. At first, she'd thought it was some lingering resentment about her new hair color, but they'd put that one to bed a while ago. There hadn't been any major problem at school about it and rather irritatingly it had even grown on Jenna. But since that row, her daughter hadn't been the same and she was beginning to sense the change in mood wasn't connected to that at all. Now, as they sat over the breakfast table, Chloe in her school uniform, Jenna in her work clothes ready for another ten-hour shift, she was genuinely shocked not just by her demeanor but by her appearance too.

Her face was ashen, and her skin was bad, and not just with the usual adolescent problems. She smelt too, unwashed and unhealthy. Even the bright new hair seemed to have faded and dulled prematurely. It was as if she'd stopped bothering. She was also scratching herself periodically, a nervous compulsive action that was increasingly as distressing as it was irritating to watch.

"You haven't done anything, Mum," said Chloe. She was sipping at a cup of tea and staring at the back of a cereal packet on the kitchen table as if it contained the secret to life itself.

"Aren't you hungry? Are you sure I can't get you something? It wouldn't take me five minutes to scramble up some eggs?" offered Jenna.

"I'm fine," said Chloe, slurping on her tea, still avoiding her gaze. Jenna sighed. Enough was enough, she thought. Again.

"What's the matter, love? Is it some boy?" Her daughter gave her a death stare. "All right then, are you being bullied? I know what school can be like. You can tell me if there's a problem. There's nothing you're going through I didn't go through once either. You just don't seem like yourself and if it isn't me that's the cause then I'd like to know what is."

Chloe just looked pissed off with her now.

"I don't want eggs," she said and pawed at her arm again.

"And what is with that scratching? Have you got a rash or something?" snapped Jenna.

Chloe looked desolate, and Jenna instantly regretted her tone. It was ironic, she thought; she'd give anything right now for a bit of the snark or backchat that normally drove her mad. "What is it, just tell me?"

There was another long silence and finally the teenager met her gaze.

"You wouldn't understand."

It was the classic teenage response but there seemed to be a desperation to it, as if she wanted to share something but couldn't. Instead, she stood, grabbed her coat from behind her chair, and tugged it on.

"I'll see you tonight," she said, before reaching for her schoolbag, clearly keen on bringing the inquisition to an end. Jenna's head was already in her hands as she heard the front door shutting with a thud.

Chloe stood outside and took a deep breath because she really didn't want to go through with this, didn't want to go to the bus stop and didn't want to spend the day in school. She looked around nervously. The quiet suburban street in West London where they lived looked the same as it always did, but that didn't mean anything anymore. She scratched her arm and winced. Checking that her mother wasn't watching through the window, she rolled up her sleeve, looked at the exposed flesh and saw a chaotic network of red welts spread across it. She *really* didn't want to go to school.

The dreams hadn't stopped—if anything they'd got worse. She'd even got used to the permanent shivering and itching. Something had happened to her from the moment she'd set eyes on that picture, she was sure of it. All this had started then. There'd been a change that she couldn't articulate or explain but could *feel*. Reality itself felt like it had been bending ever since.

She'd done some initial searching on the internet but hadn't liked what she'd found. A short video on YouTube, an American girl around her own age who spoke with a Texan drawl:

"The moment you know about the Bone Queen, she knows about you."

The words had kept repeating themselves in Chloe's mind.

At school, she couldn't concentrate. Both the lessons and her friends just became background noise, everything overshadowed by that ever-present sense of foreboding. During break time she couldn't help looking over her shoulder. The gray corridors seemed to stretch endlessly now, filled with hushed whispers and the distant shuffle of footsteps—that sense of reality bending again.

"Are you ill?" Evie asked her. They were in one of the corridors of the science block because Chloe had refused to go outside. Of all the people in her life, Evie was the one Chloe most wanted to confide in.

But now they were alone she found herself paralyzed, unable to properly articulate how she was feeling. The idea of being dismissed or misunderstood by her best friend was too much.

"I think I've got myself into trouble, Eves," she whispered.

"What kind of trouble?"

"I'm not sure," said Chloe uncertainly. "But I think something might happen soon and I'm scared."

She could hear it in her voice, the absurdity of the words, matched only by her total belief in them.

"What's going to happen?" said Evie, nonplussed.

She tried again to express herself but couldn't and just shook her head helplessly.

By the time the day ended, she felt sick and empty. As she gathered up her stuff, she could see Evie eyeing her at the back of the room. There was a strange stiffness between them as they walked to the school gates. Evie, aware something was wrong, but still at a loss at how to help. As they parted, Chloe felt a strong surge of emotion. She couldn't even identify whether it was sadness, anger, or something else completely, but she just wanted to retreat to the sanctuary of her bedroom.

"Clo . . ." began Evie but she was already gone.

When she got home, she found a note on the kitchen table reminding her that Jenna wouldn't be back from work until late and that there was a lasagna in the fridge that she could warm up for dinner. Chloe ignored it and went straight to her room. She sat on her bed, and let the tears come. She'd been holding them at bay all day. With the house to herself, she didn't have to worry about making any noise either. Her body trembled with the intensity of it and the worst feeling was that she didn't have anyone she could talk to about it. At least, not someone who'd understand.

She went over to her dressing table and powered up her laptop, going back to the webpage she'd found before.

"The moment you know about the Bone Queen, she knows about you."

Below the video posted by *Athelsea100* was a comment. It simply said, "Do you need answers?" There was an email address next to it: *eyeofthequeen@uk.mail.com*. Chloe's finger hovered over the keyboard. She wasn't sure what she wanted to ask or even say, but she *did* need answers and began to type. She described what she'd been going through and how she felt. The reply was waiting for her there the next morning. Just three words:

"You've been marked."

Chapter 10

Today

"It's better than just sitting at home," bellowed Jenna into her phone. It was early evening now, and the village was shrouded in darkness. The air carried a hint of dampness and the distant sounds of birds whistling and trilling echoed around them. Jenna had been on her way back to the guesthouse when Tom had called. He was now mansplaining from his office in central London about why traveling to Athelsea had been a fundamental mistake on Jenna's part.

"I'm just saying—it's a bit of a leap, to take a few bits of paper from Chloe's bedroom and some random stuff in her internet search history and assume she's gone to some island in the arse end of nowhere because of it."

His voice had gone up an octave. Jenna had a brief flashback to the countless other arguments they'd had over the years which had followed the same pattern. Her, deploying blunt-force common sense, him, responding with measured patronizing stupidity.

"You didn't see what I saw over the last few weeks. She *changed,* Tom."

There was a pause and she heard him gulp down some water, which she pictured coming from an over expensive metallic bottle on his desk.

"What you've done is like going up to Loch Ness because she mentioned the monster once when she was a kid. It's absurd and I'm more concerned that this is about someone she met online. Surely you must have had some idea of *who* she was talking to?"

Despite the provocation, Jenna felt an unexpected moment of pure calm. As she stared out at the strip of cottages in front and heard the wind blowing through a thick mass of trees nearby, she was more certain than ever that she'd made the right decision to come here.

"You have to admit there was something different about her before she left," she said.

There was a silence as he considered it.

"She *had* become more withdrawn," Tom said. "I thought she was just going through a phase and that's what the pink hair was all about."

"It was more than that, she changed. She was *scared,* Tom—really scared. And that's why I keep beating myself up about this because I didn't get it. I thought she was just being stupid and now . . ." She felt her eyes begin to sting. "I'm wondering if it's something I'll regret for the rest of my life."

"You need to stop beating yourself up, Jen . . ."

He said the words quietly and she knew what he was referring to, the period immediately after their divorce when she'd started drinking again. There was a lot to feel guilty about—some people were amusing when they were drunk, others become confused—she was an ugly drunk. She'd get loud and aggressive and lash out, the worst of her would come to the surface. The strange thing was that she'd suffer memory loss the morning after, but then the scenes and images of what had happened would slowly filter back over the next few days and weeks. The most painful part was the sound of her own voice raging, blaming the world for her troubles, and also the sight of her daughter, tear-strewn and terrified of her mother.

She shivered at the memory and thought about all the times she'd boasted that Chloe had *turned out so well, despite everything I put her through.* Now she was wondering if she'd been a bit premature with that and whether the seeds of what was happening now had been laid back then. It didn't feel fair because she'd been through a lot, and the divorce was by no means even the worst of it. She'd first discovered solace in a bottle of wine when she'd been much younger, and it had always been her easiest place of retreat.

"Now that you're there you might as well carry on with what you're doing. Just in case there's something in it," said Tom gruffly. "I'll speak to the police again here and see if they'll do a bit more. It's been almost a week. Let's stay in touch."

That was Tom, infuriating, yet supportive and decent too—all in the same short conversation. She ended the call and stuffed the phone back into her bag.

The boost she'd taken from talking to Ruth and identifying the picture she'd found had been balanced out by the irritating row with Tom. They'd only been on Athelsea for a few hours but there was already plenty to think about and Jenna's concentration was all over the place. She was grateful Hattie had gone ahead to the hotel, giving her a moment alone.

But Ravensgate village looked different in the half-light of dusk. The first thing Jenna noticed was that it was a bit larger than she'd initially thought. There was a cluster of small houses dotted around in the forest above. It was only when you started walking through the woods that—one by one—they became visible. It was a strange community, she thought. Self-contained away from the rest of the island's residents, but not too tightly knit. She knocked on a few of the doors and although people weren't rude, neither were they helpful. No one had seen Chloe or to Jenna's frustration seemed to take the time to think about the question too deeply.

As she tried to navigate her way back down to the village center, the woodland paths began to crisscross with one another and in the growing murk were taking on a maze-like quality. Without anything to use as a reference point, she was starting to feel literally and metaphorically lost. Looking around she didn't have a clue where she was now. Hattie was probably sitting in her room with a steaming cup of tea and Jenna didn't know whether to laugh, cry, or simply scream.

It was starting to get seriously cold as well and as she hugged herself, heard a noise behind her. It sounded like a footstep, followed by a breath, and she stopped to listen. She waited to allow a gust of wind to blow through and then heard it again, though this time it seemed more like a sharp intake of breath.

"Hello?" she called out. "Is there someone there?"

She peered into the gloom and could vaguely make out a tall silhouette in the trees and she stepped forward to get a better look.

A shape dissolved into existence—a skeleton, the usual bone grin of the skull twisted into a shriek. With horror, she realized that's because it *wasn't* completely bone. As its head turned, she could see pink-brown rotting flesh hanging off in strands from one side, a single eyeball stuck in the bloody mucus of its socket. It seemed to be in agony too—the lone eye, screaming silently at her—and just as quickly as it appeared, the wind gusted again, and it was gone.

Chapter 11

"Am I cracking up, Hat?" said Jenna, in the guesthouse's dining room. She was sipping a mug of hot tea, staring down at a flaccid plate of scrambled eggs on toast. Out of season, the place wasn't doing much business and frankly, Jenna was grateful for that this morning. Not surprisingly she'd slept appallingly. She was still recovering from her experience in the woods the previous night. She'd instinctively turned and fled and more by luck than design had found her way back down to the village.

"You're just wrung out," said Hattie. "You're worried sick about Chloe, you're exhausted, and it was freezing cold out in those hills. I'm not surprised you . . ."

". . . started hallucinating?" said Jenna finishing the sentence for her.

"Are struggling," corrected Hattie. "I'd be more concerned if all of this *wasn't* having some effect on you."

"It seemed so real, the detail of it—almost like it was pleading with me. Where did my brain even pull that from?"

"That's easy enough to understand. From those bones that they dragged up from the sea yesterday. They obviously lodged in your subconscious," said Hattie. "It *wasn't* real though, forget it happened."

Easier said than done, thought Jenna. She could still see the thing so vividly, even *smell* the rotting flesh—like meat that had been left out in the sun.

"I wanted a drink last night when I got in," she said looking down.

"And did you?" asked Hattie. Jenna shook her head.

She was underselling it—she'd *really* wanted a drink and had got as far as opening the minibar fridge and staring hard at its contents. What stopped her was the knowledge that if she'd started then she'd never have stopped.

She took an unenthusiastic bite of her breakfast and shook the pepper pot over it in an effort to give it some flavor. The incident had shaken her. It was her guilt over Chloe made manifest, and it felt as if her self-confidence was unraveling like a loose thread on a jumper. She just wanted to go back to bed and sleep. She'd been feeling that way a lot, that this situation was *so* upsetting, minute by minute, that she simply didn't want to be conscious until it was over.

"So, what are we going to do with the day?" said Hattie.

Jenna refocused.

"We know what that picture was. Now, I want to know *who* the Bone Queen is." She rose to her feet.

"Where are you going?" said Hattie.

"I've got an idea about how we might find that out. I'll meet you back here in ten minutes," she said, taking one last look at her half-eaten breakfast before heading for the door.

Frank Archer mopped the lounge floor of the inn vigorously and then squeezed out the dirty water into a bucket. He was about to go again when he heard his phone ping from where he'd left it on the counter. Simultaneously, there was a tap at the window. He picked up the handset and saw a message from Ben on the display.

"We need to talk—all of us."

Even as he read the words, he could see Jenna Tipton standing outside smiling pleasantly at him. The pub wasn't open yet and she made a hand motion suggesting she wanted to come in. He swiped the message away and composed himself. This woman was trouble he thought, and her timing was terrible. He took a deep breath and opened the door.

"I'm so sorry to bother you this early," said Jenna. She saw the mop in his hand and smiled apologetically at him. "I can see that you're busy, but I just wondered if I could pick your brain for a moment?"

His mind was still on Ben's text message, but he forced himself to concentrate.

"Of course, how can I help?"

"I'm looking for someone. I just don't know who yet and I thought you might be able to point me in the right direction." She looked up and saw the flyer of Chloe pinned up behind the bar. "And thank you so much for that, by the way, I really appreciate it," she said, pointing at the picture.

"I only hope it helps," he replied. "So, who is it you're after?"

"Someone who *really* knows the history of Athelsea. I'm trying to figure out what Chloe was looking for here and I want someone who can color in the detail for me."

Frank felt a twinge of relief. That was, at least, an easy one to answer. "You should talk to Sheelagh Deeney then. There isn't anything about the place she doesn't know. Give me a second . . ."

He went back to the counter and picked up his phone. Cross-checking with Jenna's number which was on the flyer, he sent her the contact details she needed.

"You're a star, thank you," she said as it flashed up on her screen.

He smiled, watched as she walked out, and as the door closed behind her his face hardened, and he typed out a reply to the message he'd received from Ben.

"Here—tonight. 8 pm."

Chapter 12

One week ago

Jenna was sitting at her desk eating a jacket potato and baked beans from a polystyrene container. LPC News, better known as London Press Corporation News, wasn't the most prestigious of the UK's press agencies, or the best payer for that matter, but they were a source of regular income and that's all that mattered. It was eight o'clock in the evening and she was alone in the large open-plan office.

Most of the management and journalists who populated the place during the day left on the dot of six which was how Jenna preferred it. She had zero interest in the petty office politics of the place and just wanted to earn her wage in as uncomplicated a way as possible. She was a scavenger, she often thought—someone who mopped up the unsociable shifts that no one else wanted to do. A ghost no one noticed who kept her head down and did the job as efficiently as possible. The people who employed her rarely passed comment on her efforts, which she took as a tacit approval that they were happy with it.

Once she'd had driving ambition, but she'd messed her career up with her drinking which had returned with a vengeance during her

divorce. It started with the small stuff; occasionally arriving late for work and lunch breaks lasting longer than they should. As someone who'd built a strong reputation for her professionalism it attracted attention. They knew she was going through a difficult time, so initially they were sympathetic. Then the issues started creeping into her work, small errors in her copy, forgetting to attend interviews with people she'd arranged for stories she was writing. By then people had noticed there was a problem, the after-work drinks that turned into something longer and more concerning, the hangovers the next morning. Finally, she'd made the cardinal mistake of any journalist—she'd left a factual error in a story that had gone live which had then led to a lawsuit against the paper.

They'd made her redundant and she found herself unemployed for the first real stretch in her life. She'd even had to accept the humiliation of financial assistance from her ex-husband to get her and Chloe through that spell. Even now, she could remember the burning desire she'd once possessed about her career, and the way she'd thrown all that away still burnt. So much had been lost because of her drinking, and now she was simply grateful to be earning—even from dead-end shifts like this.

She was staring at a Metropolitan Police press release on her screen. It was the story of a murder reduced to the harsh cold-speak of police business:

"An investigation has been launched after a teenage girl was stabbed in Lewisham. Police were called at around 04:30 hrs on Monday, 16 January to Catford Broadway, SE6, to reports of a stabbing. Officers attended the scene along with London Ambulance Service and discovered a girl with stab wounds. She was sadly pronounced dead at the scene. We are in the process of informing next of kin."

Someone's daughter reduced to one paragraph and a few lines of copy. There was a story behind that paragraph too—a moment of terror, agonizing pain, and then a lonely death on a cold London street. Jenna forked some tepid, mushy potato into her mouth as she thought about how best to write it up and then, not for the first time, found herself distracted by her own daughter.

The world was not a safe place, and Chloe was at a dangerous age. Old enough to be willful and disobedient, too young to understand just how hazardous it could truly be. Jenna knew though and had firsthand experience of it. She'd suffered loss in her time and understood the cavernous feeling it left behind . . . the things you did to fill that hole. The idea that one day someone might be sitting in a room like this one, writing up a press release detailing her daughter's final moments, was the stuff of nightmares. The consolation that *every* parent felt that way was no consolation at all.

It felt like Chloe was slipping away from her. She'd talked about it with the few friends she had these days. It wasn't that she didn't have any significant friendships, but her life was so busy just navigating from one day to the next that she'd let too many of them slide. Most of the superficial ones had disappeared during her drinking years. She didn't miss them in the slightest. The ones that mattered were still there, even if they were slightly more distant than they had been in the past. What they all collectively agreed was that *"this is just a phase"* and *"she's a teenager—get used to it"* but it didn't feel that way to Jenna.

This wasn't a pubescent rebellion, nor was it sulkiness, or just plain rudeness. It was like the life had drained out of Chloe. Even the most badly behaved of teenagers simply transferred their emotions into something else: going out with friends, drinking, sex, drugs even—but that wasn't what Jenna was seeing. The performance that morning over breakfast had been a good example. Was it depression? That was the nearest thing she could see that matched the behavior. Nothing seemed to motivate or interest Chloe, and she was spending more and more of her time alone in her bedroom. It was hard not to think that it was there that the damage was being done somehow.

Jenna pushed the tray of now cold jacket potato to one side and began to type up the story of the dead girl in Lewisham. She'd done this so many times over the years that it almost came to her automatically.

"A woman's been murdered in south London . . ."

But her mind was still on Chloe as she typed, and alone in this big soulless newsroom, paranoia was setting in. Was it someone in her online world who'd got to her? She'd written up those stories too—the ones about teenage girls found hanging in their bedrooms because they'd been bullied at school. She remembered the famous words of American secretary of defense Donald Rumsfeld: *"There are known knowns; there are things we know we know. We also know there are known unknowns."*

What *didn't* she know? Because she was increasingly sure there was something and if she didn't get a grip on this, it had the potential to get worse and then who knew where it would go? The one thing she certainly didn't want was to look back on nights like this, when she'd had the chance to address it but hadn't acted.

She shivered, the room suddenly feeling cold. All of this would have to wait. She was good with words—she'd find the right ones, use them to get through to her daughter because she genuinely believed that at heart Chloe was a decent girl. She'd never do something truly stupid. She did have the option of talking this over with Tom but as he'd proven with the argument over the pink hair dye, he was about as useful in these situations as a chocolate teapot. He treated everything as if it were a minor problem that would eventually blow over. Underestimating things was his superpower and one day he'd get horribly caught out.

When she got home that evening she glanced up as she put the front door key into the lock and saw the light on in Chloe's room. She pondered whether to go up and talk to her. It was nearly midnight, and she really should be in bed given that it was a school night. The lateness of the hour might be an advantage though, thought Jenna. The fact that they were both tired could help open the conversation up and stop it from becoming fractious. As she pondered it, she checked the fridge and saw the lasagna she'd left for Chloe was still there in its tin foil covering and she beat down a wave of irritation.

The decision made for her, she climbed the stairs and knocked on Chloe's door.

"Are you still up, love?" she called. There was no reply, and she opened the door anyway. Chloe was sitting on her bed, hugging herself, her laptop open next to her and she greeted Jenna with a wild-eyed stare which took her mother aback for a moment.

"You really should be in bed," said Jenna gently, deliberately trying to keep her tone nonconfrontational.

"I'm not tired," said Chloe in a monotone voice.

"Or hungry, apparently?"

Chloe didn't reply. She didn't just look jittery, she looked *hunted*.

"What is it, love? Please—you look terrible. Can't you just tell me what it is?"

Chloe sniffed. "Nothing. There's nothing wrong," she said but Jenna knew then that she was lying, she just didn't know what more she could do. She couldn't wring the truth out of her, much as she felt like doing exactly that. She sighed and produced the warmest smile she was able to find.

"I'm your best friend, Clo. Whatever else is happening, try and remember that, eh?"

She looked her daughter in the eye as she said the words as if trying to inject them into her. Half an hour later, Jenna was lying in bed, staring up at the ceiling and for the first time in many years, felt utterly alone under her own roof.

Chapter 13

Today

It had developed into a beautifully crisp winter morning as Jenna and Hattie walked through the village. As ever it seemed deserted with few people out on the streets, which seemed odd given the number of properties in and around Ravensgate. It had only been hours since they'd arrived and yet it already felt like they'd been there for days. Jenna checked the address that Frank had given her against the map app on her phone and pointed behind them.

"That way, I think," she said.

Hattie seemed hypnotized by the small brook that divided the village. A quaint footbridge adorned with vines connected the two halves, while crystal-clear water glistened in the sunshine, its gentle trickling providing a soothing background soundtrack. Or at least, Jenna thought so.

"I hate the water," said Hattie, almost inaudibly.

"I know," said Jenna. "Thanks for coming with me, Hat. You know I appreciate it," she added.

"What else was I going to do today?" said her sister, visibly brightening.

Jenna pulled a face. "I meant to the island. You didn't have to drop everything and do this."

"I wasn't going to leave you on your own," said Hattie and they began to walk again.

As ever, Hattie looked stunning, wearing an emerald-green coat with smart black trousers this morning. Jenna glanced down at her own rather tatty jeans and not for the first time wondered how her sister constantly managed to look so impressive.

"How are you holding up?" said Hattie.

Jenna stock-checked herself for a moment, properly considering the question given the last twenty-four hours.

"Truthfully? I'm still worried sick. What if Chloe doesn't *want* to come back home? We can't force her to, can we?"

She'd played that scenario out a few times in her head already and not once had it gone well.

"No, she'll definitely need handling with some care," Hattie agreed. "You're not going to start blaming yourself again though, are you?"

"Probably. I'm a bad mum and a bad sister for that matter."

"Now you're being stupid."

"Am I?" The two stopped and faced each other. "I'm sorry for a few things, Hat. One day we'll have that conversation properly."

Hattie smiled tightly. "Yeah, but not today, eh?"

At first, Jenna thought the address Frank had given her for Sheelagh Deeney had been wrong. When they reached their destination, they found themselves outside the village Rectory, a large clay-brick building with a thatched roof, surrounded by a colorful array of well-tended plants and bushes. As she looked around, Jenna was puzzled as to where the actual church itself was. But then she saw the tip of the spire poking up through the russet brown woodland in the hill above. It looked a bit of a hike up there, but now that she could see it, the relationship between the two buildings seemed oddly protective. The church peeking down over at its custodian.

Jenna rang the bell, and after a few moments the door opened to reveal a middle-aged woman with a short brown bob. She was wearing a light lavender blouse with a knee-length navy skirt. A silver cross pendant hung around her neck.

"Sheelagh Deeney?" said Jenna cautiously.

The woman smiled. "The Very Reverend Sheelagh Deeney if I was being particular, which I'm not," she added disarmingly. "How can I help?"

Jenna quickly got the explanations out of the way.

"Frank Archer suggested we come and talk to you. What I really need is some local knowledge and he thought you might be able to help me," she said.

"Did he now?" said Sheelagh with a slight ambivalence that might have indicated either irritation or affection. "Come on in, and I'll do my best to try," she said motioning at them to enter.

There was something innately peaceful about the interior—it had the same musty smell as a secondhand bookshop. They were led through to a large messy living room which had a log fire burning in a large black wrought iron fireplace. The heat was welcome as the sisters took a seat together on a large sofa. Even that broke Jenna a little inside. If she was that cold, then what kind of state was her daughter in right now? For what seemed the thousandth time she suppressed the feeling and focused on her surroundings.

"Can I get you a cup of tea or coffee?" said Sheelagh. "I've only got instant I'm afraid, but I could put the kettle on?" They declined and she went over to a small desk in the corner of the room to retrieve a pair of gold-framed glasses which she slipped on before joining them on the sofa opposite. Jenna passed her one of the flyers and she took a long, hard look at it before placing it gently on the coffee table in front.

"I'm sorry, I wish I could give you some good news, but I haven't seen anyone like this recently."

Again, Jenna tried and failed to hide her disappointment. She explained why she thought Chloe had come to Athelsea and Sheelagh listened with considered interest.

"I don't mean to be rude—but why did Frank point you my way?"

"Because of this," said Jenna pulling the now slightly crumpled picture of the Bone Queen from her bag and passing it to Sheelagh. Just for a moment, she thought she detected a change in the other woman's expression, almost a flinch at the sight of the image. It vanished almost as quickly as it had appeared. "My daughter seems to have taken an interest in the Bone Queen. I'd never heard of her until I came here, but I think it might be something to do with what brought her here."

Sheelagh nodded like a doctor, humoring a worried patient as she listened. For a moment she said nothing as she considered her response, the only sound the cries and calls of the crows outside.

"It's a particularly nasty story," said Sheelagh. "Come with me," she added unexpectedly and rose to her feet. She led them through into the hallway and then up a flight of narrow stairs. Paintings lined the linen-white wall of the staircase, and she pointed at an elaborately gold-framed one halfway up. It depicted a terrified-looking young woman running in fear from a group of leering men against the backdrop of the familiar Athelsea birch trees. If the image was disturbing, then the artwork was breathtaking. The fine brushstrokes conveyed every bit of the woman's petrified emotion, the men captured perfectly in their casual cruelty.

"What's happening here, what am I looking at?" said Jenna, fascinated. Sheelagh frowned, as if slightly uncomfortable at having to explain the story behind the painting.

"The wife of one of the original prison guards back in the 1700s was a woman called Eleanor Aubney. So, the legend goes she came home and found her husband had killed their three children in a drunken rage. Driven mad by grief she ended up homeless." Sheelagh pointed at the woman in the picture. "She was tortured and set alight by a group of her husband's friends who then threw her into the lake to drown. So, the story goes, she rose to take vengeance and took the bones of her murderers' children."

"The Bone Queen?" said Hattie slowly, unable to remove her gaze from the stricken expression on the woman's face. Jenna was equally absorbed. She'd found what she was looking for, she could sense it. There was a direct connection between the woman in the painting and the picture on the internet—she now knew the *reason* behind that cruel expression, why that face seemed scarred. She remembered her vision in the woods too, that smell of rotting meat that had accompanied it. Surely, it wasn't the same thing?

"Why would Chloe have become obsessed with that?" said Hattie.

"Dead children again . . ." murmured Jenna. Sheelagh looked at her quizzically.

"How do you mean?"

Jenna turned to look at her.

"It seems to be a running theme here. Someone in Ravensgate told me yesterday about how the children of the old prison staff all died here once." Jenna realized what she was saying as she said it. "Wouldn't that have been around the same time as this?"

Sheelagh nodded. "You're right—there is a dark history on Athelsea concerning young people. A family picnic in 1805 where a young boy drowned close to the spot which that picture depicts," she said pointing up at the painting again. "A scullery maid who was found in 1893 with her throat cut. The fisherman's son who disappeared without a trace in Ravensgate in 1915, and so on. The Admiralty established Athelsea as a base of operations against possible invasion between the two world wars. Later, people feared something supernatural during the black-outs. And do you know why?" She paused, knowing full well that Jenna didn't. "Because of a serviceman who was found with a broken neck in 1937."

"It's all around Ravensgate too," mused Jenna. "But there's nothing supernatural about any of those incidents. These are all just unpleasant fatalities. Pick just about any anywhere and you'll find a history like that if you go back far enough."

"Perhaps, but there's something else, another *aspect* of the legend if you like," said Sheelagh.

Was it Jenna's imagination, or was this woman getting more and more uncomfortable the longer they talked about this? Reluctant, even.

"What?" said Hattie, glancing at Jenna. This felt important.

"Part of the legend is that before she comes for them, the Bone Queen puts her mark on her victims."

"Her *mark*?" said Jenna. "How? In what way?"

"I don't think it's a literal mark, more a sensibility. A foreboding. The various tales tell it differently. Night terrors, cold shivers, loss of appetite—that sort of thing."

Jenna felt the blood drain from her face.

"What about a rash, an itch that won't go away?"

"Possibly, but those deaths I mentioned—if you look into the accounts, the recorded histories . . . all the victims experienced *something* in the days before."

"It doesn't mean a thing," whispered Hattie. "Just because they all had a cold, or some bad dreams doesn't mean this creature actually exists. It's like a horoscope saying you'll be lucky in love—say it enough times and you'll probably be right."

Jenna shook her head with irritation.

"If Chloe read about this somewhere, came to believe she'd been marked, then that would explain all of this."

Sheelagh nodded politely.

"Supernatural legends often gain strength over time due to a combination of cultural storytelling, societal fascination, and our natural tendency to embellish. Where better for all that to flourish than on the internet?"

Jenna wasn't interested in a lecture. At last, she had a foothold into what her daughter had been thinking.

"How do you remove this mark?"

Sheelagh shook her head.

"As far as I'm aware—you can't."

Chapter 14

Five days ago

"You've been marked."

Chloe hadn't been able to stop thinking about those three words. The person she'd emailed—whoever they were behind the alias *Athelsea100*—hadn't responded to her follow-up questions so she'd been left hanging, worse still, left to brood. Deep down she knew though—could *feel* their meaning. It explained perfectly what she'd been going through, the constant cold, the itching skin, and the nightmares. It was all a prelude to *something*. But what?

She'd gone looking on the internet again for more answers and hadn't liked what she'd found. There wasn't a huge amount, but it was clear that there were stories about the Bone Queen dating back years from all over the world and none of them ended well. There was a village in Peru where an entire nursery school of children had been lost in a fatal landslide in 1952. A grieving teacher had blamed *"La Reina de Los Huesos."* She'd claimed the entire school had been cursed by her in the weeks before the disaster, that the children had all been acting strangely. There was a French family who'd spent a summer's afternoon in 1967 by Lake Annecy and lost their teenage son there. The father had been arrested for murder despite the fact a body had never been found. There were whispers of domestic abuse, but the mother had sworn blind that the boy had been marked by *"La Reine des Os."*

There were forums too, dedicated to the supernatural which mentioned the phenomenon. One long post written by someone in Toronto claimed she was a spirit of retribution punishing children for the sins of their parents. That, in particular, had made Chloe stop and think. She could remember nights when she'd been younger, and her mother had been drinking alone. She'd tried to blot those memories out. Jenna wasn't a good drunk—when she'd been through a bottle of red wine, fury and bitterness overtook her.

She'd said things to her young daughter that no child should ever hear. *"Don't ever put your faith into another person because they'll only let you down."* When Chloe tried to speak, she'd shout her down. Worse than that, she'd laugh at her. It was a strange sound, cruel and mocking, and she only ever heard her mother do it when she was drunk. She'd never forget that laughter though.

Later Jenna would be mortified, ashamed of herself, and would apologize profusely. In many ways, she'd never stopped apologizing. The drinking had eventually ended but you couldn't roll back time and erase those memories. Chloe could still remember just how confused and hurt she'd felt, hurt too that her dad hadn't done more to help. Is this why she'd been singled out by the Bone Queen? As punishment for her useless parents?

The person on the same forum had also put up some statistics. The truth was out there hiding in plain sight, and it was amazing how blind people were to it. Children and young people went missing every day, in every country across the globe and in numbers. There were other stories too—people complaining of fevers and nightmares who'd been posting on their social media about it and then suddenly *stopped.* Each time Chloe found someone who thought they'd been marked, there was only one common outcome—they disappeared with no further online trace of them. The link seemed clear even if it wasn't spelt out; once you'd been marked by the Bone Queen it didn't take long before she came for you.

The idea was terrifying and the more it sank in the more it became clear that she couldn't go on living the way she was. She'd told her mum that she was ill and made sure she'd done it just before Jenna left for work so that there wasn't time for an argument. Alone now in her bedroom she opened up her laptop and fired off another email to *Athelsea100*, repeating her previous unanswered question.

"How do I remove the mark? Please—I don't know what to do."

She stared at the screen as if expecting an instant response, but it didn't come. She was trying hard not to panic but it was difficult. She might just be able to avoid going back to school the next day, but she wouldn't be able to keep doing that. The Bone Queen could take her at any time and Chloe didn't want to be one of those kids that just blinked out of existence.

She heard a noise from the corner of the room and thought something had fallen off a shelf. It started as a whisper—or rather two whispers talking over each other, and she listened, unsure if it was her imagination or not. She looked around in mounting horror as a third voice, female this time, seemed to join them, and it grew into a chorus of hushed muttering. She looked again at the picture on her phone and that single malignant eye seemed different this time, almost as if it was sneering at her now. The noise stopped, and the room was quiet again. Simultaneously a message flashed up on her laptop, and with shaking hands she opened the email and saw a brief message.

"The only way you can remove the mark is to make a sacrifice. Blood for blood."

Chapter 15

Today

Progress was a deceptive feeling, Jenna thought. She now had a good idea what had drawn Chloe to Athelsea, knew a little bit about the Bone Queen and what her daughter had been feeling in the weeks before she left. In some ways there was relief—it was something Jenna couldn't have guessed. She'd suspected depression, bullying perhaps from some of the other kids at school, and in a worst-case scenario that a predator had been getting into her head from afar.

But she couldn't have imagined that Chloe had believed herself to be marked by a supernatural creature from an island on the other side of the country. When she remembered the fear on her daughter's face, the jitteriness, the scratching . . . it all made a strange sort of sense now. But what had brought her to Athelsea? Had she thought there was some sort of solution to be found here? But what or how? Worst of all, she still had no idea where Chloe was. She had a basic sense of the island's geography—knew that there were just a handful of villages together with the harbor area. That didn't mean much in itself though; in the short space of time they'd been here she'd seen how many random cottages and homes were dotted around the isolated spots in between.

She and Hattie had now returned to the harbor. The police station was based here, and she'd wanted to catch up with DI Liam Tandy. It probably wouldn't do much good, but she reasoned the police should know that there was a missing teenager on their island, and he might just be able to give her steer about where Chloe might have gone.

As they got closer to the waterfront, Jenna could hear the distant sound of clinking rigging once more, and as they turned the corner they saw a small crowd gathered there again. The scene was remarkably familiar to the one they'd witnessed shortly after arriving the previous day. Jenna recognized DI Tandy, talking to a uniformed police constable by the water's edge. This time though it wasn't a fishing boat they were waiting for. Jenna could see a noisy police vessel slowing down on its approach and she exchanged a glance with Hattie.

An old woman carrying a shopping bag in each hand was shuffling towards them and she produced a toothy grin as she passed.

"It's all coming to the surface now," she announced with a cackle. "They've found more bones out there."

The sisters watched as a very similar series of events unfolded in front of them for the second time in twenty-four hours. Liam Tandy boarded the police boat as soon as it docked and then emerged minutes later with the same grim expression he'd worn the day before. Men and women in blue gowns—forensic officers, Jenna assumed—were busy on the boat, talking animatedly amongst themselves. Tandy's body language was revealing though. He looked fed up, and from a distance it seemed to be a mixture of frustration and bewilderment. A nasty thought went through Jenna's head. She'd made an assumption about what was on that boat, but nothing had actually changed. It was still entirely possible that they'd found Chloe out there.

"Jen . . ." said Hattie, anticipating what she was thinking, but Jenna was already moving.

"Sorry miss, can you stay back please," snapped one of the constables but she ignored him.

"DI Tandy?" she called out and he turned with a look of surprise when he saw the stranger in front of him.

"My name's Jenna Tipton, my teenage daughter's missing, and I need to know she's not on that boat," she said, getting the words out quickly. The burly officer who'd barked at Jenna was already moving to intercept her, but Tandy waved him back. His expression softened into a reassuring smile as her question penetrated.

When he spoke, it was with an unexpectedly gentle Irish accent. Cork, or thereabouts if Jenna wasn't mistaken.

"No, those are bones we've found—not a body—and they're old by the looks of them. A fishing boat found some human remains yesterday and we've had divers out looking to see if there were any more in the same area. It's too early to say for certain, but I suspect these are from the same body."

Despite herself, Jenna couldn't stop the relief from showing on her face. She'd known that was probably the explanation, but she'd still needed to hear it again all the same.

"Thank you," she said, feeling slightly embarrassed now of the fuss she'd made.

"How long has your daughter been missing?" asked Liam.

She went through her now well-rehearsed speech and gave him one of the flyers from her bag. He analyzed it carefully and then pocketed the piece of paper.

"I'll enter this into the system when I get back to my desk and make sure every officer on the island has her description."

"Thank you, I appreciate it," she said, watching the ongoing activity behind him on the police boat. "At the village where I'm staying everyone seems to already know who those bones belong to," she said. "Somebody called Adam?"

Liam smiled wryly. There was something of the bashful schoolboy about him that she found quite endearing. For a police officer, he seemed almost shy.

"You get used to that on Athelsea, trust me. I spent years working for the Met Police in London and it's a bit of a step change here. Everybody seems to know everything almost as soon as it's happened, but you get used to it." He looked behind him and watched what was going on for himself and then seemed to arrive at a decision. "I don't suppose I can buy you a cup of coffee, can I? You can tell me some more about Chloe and I'll see what more we might be able to do to help you."

Jenna glanced round at Hattie, who mouthed silently *"I'll see you later,"* and then she turned back to Liam, who was watching the exchange. "Thank you," she said.

The skies seemed almost white as they walked along the waterfront. In the distance, Jenna could see a small line of people queuing to reach a retro chrome stand where an overworked barista was busy serving lattes and cappuccinos. The ferry was now departing back to the mainland, and Jenna watched it slowly moving out with a sad pang. She'd already had quite enough of island life.

"I came to the harbor to find you anyway," Jenna said, and explained what she knew so far.

"I'll do what I can, but I don't have a very large team I'm afraid. Hopefully a girl with pink hair would stand out though—it's not a very big island. I'm surprised she hasn't been spotted by anyone yet."

Jenna frowned. "Are you saying she's *not* here?"

"No, but the options are limited, which is a positive. If no one in Ravensgate has seen her then maybe you should try the other villages?"

Jenna shook her head. "From what I found, Ravensgate was the reason she came here."

Before Liam could respond his phone rang. He briefly checked the display and then pocketed it without answering. "I'm keeping you," she said with concern, and he shook his head dismissively.

"The world can wait another ten minutes."

They'd reached the front of the queue now and he bought them cappuccinos. Jenna clasped her hand around the small cardboard cup as he passed it to her, enjoying the warmth it was generating before taking a sip.

"Do you mind me asking, but who is Adam Nicks?" she said. "And why is everyone in Ravensgate so familiar with his name?"

He took a breath. "Because that's where it happened back in 2003. Adam and a few of his mates were partying in the woods above the village on a hot summer's day."

"Why?" said Jenna.

"It was someone's birthday. They were doing what young people do. Drinking, smoking, fooling around a bit, away from prying eyes. Nicks drank too much and got into an argument with his girlfriend—a young woman called Lily Yates who was the mother of his three-year-old son, Josh. A short while later Lily was found dead from what the postmortem report said was a blunt force trauma to the head. Nicks and the boy disappeared and were never seen on the island again. The presumption was that he'd slipped on a ferry to the mainland. Most people assumed he'd started a new life somewhere."

Jenna was beginning to understand now.

"Except now it looks like he never left. If those are his bones, then he's been here all along. What about Josh though, what happened to him?"

At the back of her mind, something important was flagging. Josh Nicks was yet another child who'd met an uncertain fate on Athelsea. Liam's jaw tightened and Jenna recognized the same look of frustration she'd seen after he'd stepped off the police boat.

"He's still missing; those weren't children's bones we found in the sea—they were too big."

"And you really think they're Adam's?" said Jenna.

He looked at her guardedly and then nodded. "The early forensic work is leaning that way," he said.

"Then perhaps they both fell in while they were escaping, and Josh is still out there somewhere?"

Liam shook his head.

"Maybe. There was extensive damage to the top of the skull we found yesterday, but I'm not ruling out the possibility that occurred *before* the body ended up in the water, given what happened to Lily."

Jenna pursed her lips and stared out at the choppy waters beyond.

"What?" said Liam, seeing her expression. "You can't think this has any connection to your daughter—it was years ago."

Jenna tried to assemble her thoughts into some sort of order.

"This happened in Ravensgate—where the local vicar just told me there's a history of young people dying unexpectedly, all connected to the Bone Queen. And then there's . . ." She gestured at the sea. ". . . these *bones* you've just found."

Liam rolled his eyes. "Bodies decompose over time. There's nothing supernatural about that."

"Maybe, but it all seems a bit coincidental," she faltered, unable to explain any further what she meant. "Do Lily's family still live here?"

"Her mother's the only surviving one, but she's old and lives in a care home now. To be fair she never thought her grandson ever left Athelsea."

"It sounds messy," said Jenna.

"Very," agreed Liam, nodding. "And those friends Adam was with that day—they all still live there. Ben and Katrina Markham, Frank Archer, Sheelagh Deeney, and Ruth O'Brien. I'll need to be catching up with all of them."

Jenna froze, the significance of what he was saying dawning on her. Not just that she'd met all of these people, but also the possibility that one of them could be a killer in the very place she was looking for her lost daughter.

Chapter 16

Five days ago

The room is sparse with dirty white-bricked walls, one small rickety table, and two red plastic chairs facing each other. There's a single, fixed camera angle pointing down at the two people sitting on the chairs and the color of the image is washed out. One of them is a middle-aged man wearing thick black glasses with a clipboard perched on his lap. Sitting opposite is a schoolgirl, perhaps around fourteen, looking every inch the moody teenager. You can't quite see her face because of a shroud of long dark blond hair and because she's staring down at the floor as if there's something important happening there.

"Se på meg, Emilie," says the man in Norwegian with a lilting accent. After a pause, a slightly stilted English voice-over translates on the soundtrack.

"Look at me, Emilie."

She doesn't seem to hear, and he repeats it. Reluctantly, she tilts her head towards him, and he asks her politely to sit up straight.

"Soren is going to be okay—I thought you'd want to know that." She doesn't respond to the words and runs a finger along the table instead. "He's going to be in hospital for some time though. Do you want to tell me why you did it?" She looks at the dust she's collected on the tip of her finger for a moment. "Emilie?" he says more firmly.

For another second or two it seems like she's going to ignore him again and then she swings her legs around and looks at him shyly.

"I didn't want to, but I was afraid of what would happen if I didn't."

Her tone is matter-of-fact.

"And what was it you thought *would* happen?"

"That she'd come for me."

"Who'd come for you?"

Even without the translation, it's possible to hear the neutrality in the interviewer's voice and the slight sense of urgency underpinning it.

"The Bone Queen," she says.

The man isn't expecting that, and it takes him a moment to readjust.

"Who is the Bone Queen, Emilie?"

She doesn't respond and he repeats the question, but still she doesn't answer.

"What will happen to me?" she asks.

"I'm afraid this is serious, and you won't be going home anytime soon. You stabbed Soren five times and then left him for dead. He's only eight years old and you're very lucky he was found before he bled out."

"Jeg vet," she replies in her singsong accent and Chloe knows what it means before the translation comes. *"I know."*

She swiped the image up and away from her phone's screen and shivered. But Emilie's face and the musical tone of her voice weren't so easily dismissed. Her arm was itching ferociously again like tiny, relentless ants were raging beneath her skin, and she rubbed it hard with four fingers of her hand. The last message from *Athelsea100* had been very clear. If Chloe wanted to remove the mark of the Bone Queen, then she needed to offer up someone in her place just like Emilie had tried to do—*"Blood for blood."*

She searched online some more and found a newspaper article from a small town in Oregon in the United States. The headline was:

"Teenage girl slays parents following divorce"

Erin Henderson had stabbed both her parents in one crazy morning. She'd killed her mother as she lay sleeping in bed and then knifed her unsuspecting father in the back of the neck after calling him over in an apparent state of distress. However, it was the reporting of the subsequent court case that Chloe had found particularly interesting. There was so much in Erin's story that resonated with her. Under interview, she'd claimed her parents had stopped caring about her since their divorce and that they'd frequently been short-tempered and irritable with her. But that wasn't why she'd done it. She'd said something had been stalking her in the weeks leading up to the killings. Chloe took a sharp intake of breath as she read the final sentences of the article.

"The Bone Queen was real to Erin Henderson, and this was the only way she believed she could protect herself from her," said Hood River Deputy District Attorney Ted Schillaci.

There were more stories like it from all over the world. The death of a teenage boy near Lake Tahoe that had originally been treated as a suicide but was now being investigated as a possible homicide. These things were always near water, Chloe had noticed. There was Emilie and Soren in Oslo close to Lake Randsfjorden. Even Erin hadn't lived too far from Goose Lake in Oregon. There'd also been a Canadian news report on YouTube of a mother whose daughter had strangled a school friend on their way home from a night out close to Lake Ontario. Only the intervention of a passer-by had prevented a fatality there.

"I don't think there were any obvious signs that she was ill," said the woman in dark glasses, almost forcing herself to find the words. Chloe felt sorry for her, knew she wouldn't have seen any signs, because her daughter wasn't ill. *"She's receiving treatment, and she does understand the gravity of what she's done. I'm sure about that,"* she said, those final words sounding anything but sure. Chloe was determined that *she* wasn't going

to be receiving treatment anytime soon, nor was her mother going to end up like that—a broken curiosity on the net. There had to be another way. It was later that afternoon that *Athelsea100* emailed her again and she discovered that there was.

"Are you going back to school tomorrow?" asked Jenna that evening, glancing across from the hob where she was desperately trying to prevent a hastily thrown together pasta sauce from sticking to the pan while decanting a pot of spaghetti into a colander. Chloe peered up at her uncertainly from the kitchen table and Jenna glanced round, raising an expectant eyebrow.

"Yes," came the answer finally, without much conviction.

Jenna eyed her suspiciously.

"You've made a recovery then?" she said, not hiding her cynicism. "From whatever it was that you had?"

"I'm feeling better if that's what you mean," Chloe lied.

Jenna mixed the pasta with the sauce then split two portions evenly between a couple of bowls and brought them over. She collapsed into her seat and brushed her hair out of her eyes.

"I don't know what's been going on with you but we're going to have to have a proper conversation at some point," she said wearily. "I've been giving you some space and hoping that you'll work this through. But I'm not going to keep doing that forever, do you understand?" she continued and then determinedly began to fork some food into her mouth.

Chloe didn't react. There was only one way out of this now as far as she could see.

"Come to Athelsea and we can protect you," the last email had said, boiling her options down to a simple binary choice; spill some blood or find sanctuary on an island miles away. The only certainty she felt was that things couldn't continue the way they had been.

"Say something. Anything," said her mother, mistaking her silence for resistance. "Call me some names, tell me I wouldn't understand, I don't mind—just *communicate* with me, because I can't deal with this silence anymore."

She was trying to be tough but there was an element of pleading in her voice too. For a microsecond, Chloe contemplated making the same choice as Erin, Emilie, and the others. Taking the fork she was using to twirl her spaghetti with, and plunging it into her mother's chest, just to be free of this. She shook her head and in that moment her mind was made up.

"Really?" said Jenna watching her. "That's all you can do?"

Chloe stood up.

"Where are you going?" said Jenna.

"I'm not hungry, I'm sorry."

"Chloe, don't you dare."

But her daughter had already left the room.

In her bedroom, she started thinking through the reality of what she was intending to do. There was a way out of this, a place of sanctuary where she could go—she knew that now. It was one thing making the decision, but it was a whole other matter acting upon it. She emailed *Athelsea100* again to confirm she would be coming to the island the following day. This time the reply was almost instantaneous with a list of clear concise instructions on what to do. She felt her heart pound as she read them through and then steeled herself. Every doubt, every obstacle, every fear was dwarfed by what would happen if she *didn't* go through with this.

She plotted out the journey, making notes on a piece of paper next to her laptop of the relevant train and ferry times. She had enough cash for the ferry, but not the train so she'd have to deal with that somehow in the morning. Her mind was racing as she shed the torpor that had been dragging her down for the past two weeks. She had at least found a way out, a way that she could avert the inevitable and also now a name to go with it.

"Stella."

She had no idea who was behind *Athelsea100*. They could literally be anyone, but she had no choice but to trust them. Each message they'd sent had been honest. It wasn't like she'd been asked for money or anything else dodgy for that matter and everything they'd told her so far had turned out to be true. The rest of the world was sleeping but it felt to Chloe like she'd just woken up. She grabbed some clothes and underwear and began stuffing them into her backpack. She knew she should think about this for a bit longer and not rush into it but there simply wasn't the time.

The email specified that she couldn't take her phone or laptop with her because they could be used to track her. It had also instructed her to buy a burner phone on her way so that they could communicate when she reached the island. She didn't like the idea of being parted from her own phone, but it made sense, and she certainly didn't want either of her parents following her to Athelsea. After it was all over, she'd come back and explain herself to both of them.

She looked around her room and at her bulging backpack. Downstairs, she could hear her mum watching TV. By the time she was out of bed the next morning Chloe would be long gone. There was just one last thing she needed to do before she tried to get some sleep. She found her phone and FaceTimed Evie. Her friend connected with a smile and then reacted immediately as she saw the expression on Chloe's face.

"What's happened?" she said.

"I've had a row with Mum. I've made up my mind and I'm leaving tomorrow," she said, and Evie stared back at her with astonishment.

"What do you mean you're *leaving*?"

"Remember I said I thought I was in danger? There's somewhere I can go where I'll be safe."

And then she saw it, the look in her friend's eye, the one that said she didn't believe her.

"I don't understand . . . where?"

Chloe felt the tears of frustration beginning to well.

"I live five minutes' walk from the River Thames. If I don't do something about this—" she faltered. She knew she probably shouldn't be having this conversation—the email had stressed that too, but she'd needed to talk to *someone.*

"Why are you doing this?" said Evie and now it was her friend who looked tearful.

"I don't have any choice, Eves."

"What about your mum?"

"She'll be fine. Once things have settled down, I'll contact her and let her know where I am. But you can't tell her—you can't tell *anyone.* I'll call you tomorrow when I'm on my way."

Chapter 17

Today

Liam gave Jenna a lift back to Ravensgate and as they got out of his car, she couldn't resist glancing at the dense woods in the hills above which overlooked the village. They'd taken on a new significance now that she'd learnt more about the history of the area. It was hard to picture the horror that had taken place up there once. A direct line connecting that quiet piece of landscape with the bones that she'd seen hauled from the sea. Given how small the community was here she could only imagine the impact those events must have had at the time.

"Is your sister staying with you here?" said Liam as they entered the guesthouse's hallway. Jenna thought guiltily about Hattie and her last sight of her at the harbor. There was a lot they needed to catch up on, but before she could respond, Katrina bustled through from the lounge. Her smile of welcome froze when she saw who was with Jenna. Liam produced his warrant card and introduced himself, even though it was clear Katrina knew exactly who he was and why he was there.

"Is your husband about too? It would be great to talk to you both together," said Liam as if suggesting a quiet spot of lunch between friends. Katrina walked towards the stairs and called out Ben's name and a moment or two later he descended, greeting them all with a carefully curated smile. Jenna suspected he'd already overheard the conversation from upstairs.

"I won't take up too much of your time," said Liam, before explaining why he wanted to talk with them.

"We were half expecting a call." Ben motioned at Liam to come on through to the lounge and the policeman turned to smile at Jenna.

"I meant what I said earlier—we'll circulate Chloe's description across the island and if I hear anything at all I'll be straight in touch."

Jenna thanked him and walked out into the corridor. She was about to head up to her room but then held back, not quite shutting the door behind her. She hovered just out of view and listened as they settled down in the lounge.

"I can only tell you how I remember that day," said Ben. "Which is what I told the police at the time. Nothing's changed."

"That's okay," said Liam. "I'm relatively new here, remember? So, I'm listening with fresh ears to all this."

Outside, Jenna gently pushed the door a little further open and glanced through. She could see Katrina and got a sense of someone making a real effort to keep her emotions in check. Despite the Markhams' relaxed words, there was a tension in the room too. "Do you really think those bones you found belong to Adam then?" said Katrina. From her position, Jenna could see what looked like the detective's head nodding.

"The dental structure in the skull was extremely well preserved. From the early work we've done, I think I have to work on the assumption that it is him," said Liam. "And that's why we need to have this conversation," he added, his earlier charm morphing into something more professional now.

Katrina nodded, while Ben composed himself and then began to speak.

"Fair enough. But you have to understand, Adam Nicks always was a piece of work. None of us really warmed to him, but he was Lily's boyfriend, and we all loved Lily."

"He was an outsider then?" said Liam.

"Yes, we'd all been to school together over at St. Joseph's. Kat and I, Sheelagh Deeney, Lily, Ruth, and Frank. We always were a tight little group."

"But you'd left school by this point. You must have been in your early twenties?" said Liam, and Katrina nodded. "So where did Adam come from?"

"Lily was working as a barmaid at one of the harborside pubs a few summers earlier. That's where she first met him. He came over for a holiday and never left."

Jenna had a sudden flash of that tugboat and its haul of bones. That last sentence was certainly true.

"So, talk me through what happened, as you remember it?" said Liam. Ben ran a hand through his hair and resumed. He seemed to be making a genuine effort to mine his memories.

"We were celebrating. It was Ruth's birthday, and the weather was good, so we'd gathered some supplies—wine, beer, food—that sort of stuff."

"Was that a regular place you went?" said Liam. "The woods above the village?"

Katrina nodded. "I suppose. It's a huge area and despite how close it is, once you're up there the trees kind of curtain you off from the world. There are some quite large parts where it plateaus out and it's completely private. That day we just went up there to party. To eat, drink, and sunbathe. We had no idea it would turn out the way it did," she said.

Liam nodded politely. "So, what happened?"

Jenna liked the way he asked the question, almost casually. Katrina seemed to blink as if she were in pain and put a hand on her temple and rubbed it.

"Adam was volatile," said Ben picking up. "Always had been and that's what really sparked the whole thing. I was drunk when it all kicked off. We'd been up there for a couple of hours. It was hot, and I'd had way too much." He looked across at Katrina for support and she nodded.

"We heard Adam and Lily arguing. Josh was crying. Lily started shouting at Adam and she slapped him in frustration. He didn't like that and lost his temper," she said.

"It came from nowhere but that was Adam, you never quite knew what you were going to get with him," said Ben.

"And what did Lily do?" said Liam.

"She grabbed Josh and stormed off into the woods and that was the last time we saw her alive," he replied. "We all fell asleep in the sun and when we woke Adam and Josh had disappeared. Ruth went looking for them and she was the one who found Lily. She tried to help her but by then it was way too late. He'd beaten her head in with a rock or something and then must have run away with Josh while we were sleeping."

Jenna was watching Katrina closely through the crack in the door. She'd closed her eyes and was massaging her temples again. It was more than just an aide-mémoire, she thought. The woman looked in real pain.

"And what did you think had happened? Not just then—but over the years—you must have speculated?" said Liam. Ben's head turned towards his wife, and the pause before he answered suggested to Jenna that he'd only just noticed how much pain she seemed to be in.

"The same as before—that they'd argued, and Adam, in the heat, after too much beer, had lost it, *really* lost it this time. The funny thing was how easy it was to believe that. He had it in him, for sure."

Katrina was nodding along now to her husband's account.

"And what did you do when you saw what had happened, realized that Adam and Josh were gone?" said Liam.

Ben shrugged. "Back then the mobile phone coverage on the island was pretty rubbish so he had quite a head start on us. By the time we'd got ourselves back down to the village and told people about it, he may well have already got himself on a ferry to the mainland and from there who knows?"

"No one in the village saw them leave then?"

"No, but that didn't mean anything. Once you're up in those woods there are loads of routes to get across the island without anyone seeing."

"And now what do you think happened, in light of what we found this week?"

Jenna was finding herself almost as intrigued by Katrina as she was by the story her husband was telling. She'd slumped back in her seat and closed her eyes again.

"Probably that he went off into the hills after it sank in what he'd done," continued Ben. "I think he threw himself off a cliff top with guilt and took that poor kid with him." His head turned to look directly at Liam. "How else do you explain it?" The policeman held his gaze.

"Lily's mother always thought something like that must have happened." Neither Ben nor Katrina responded, and Liam looked at them curiously. "What exactly was her view, she must have spoken to you about it?"

"She's been grieving for a long time, and her mind's gone," said Ben.

"What's that supposed to mean?"

Ben shifted uncomfortably in his seat. "She thought the Bone Queen killed Adam and took Josh."

Outside in the corridor, Jenna leant in.

"But presumably you don't?"

"Of course not," said Ben. "It's patently nonsense."

"Are you okay?" said Liam to Katrina; he only just seemed to have noticed the distress she was in. Slowly she shook her head.

"My eyes," she muttered. "There's just this sharp pain behind my eyes. It's agony . . ."

She bent forward, putting a hand on her forehead and then slumped onto the ground.

Jenna quickly rushed up the stairs before any of them could see her, trying to digest what she'd just seen and heard. She found Hattie waiting for her in her room. Jenna updated her with what had been happening, and Hattie shook her head with confusion.

"I don't understand—what's any of this got to do with Chloe?"

"Because they never found Adam Nicks's son."

Hattie looked at her blankly. "It was ages ago, wasn't it?"

"This island has a history of stuff like this. Something's been happening here, and it goes back years."

"The Bone Queen?" said Hattie and Jenna paused, remembering what she'd overheard Ben just say about Lily Yates's mother.

"At least one person thought she was responsible for what happened to Adam Nicks. Chloe is connected to her in some way, and I think she believed she could find some sort of safety here. The question is *where* on this island did she think that was?"

She looked up at Hattie as she said the words and then stopped. Her sister's pallor seemed to have blanched, the color almost drained from it. Her skin looked dry and then began flaking from her face, revealing the skeletal structure underneath. Shadows accentuated the hollow sockets where her eyes had been, now replaced by a black abyss that seemed to swallow the room's light. Jenna tried to speak, but the words died in her throat, and she stood paralyzed by the sight.

"Jen?" said Hattie and Jenna blinked and saw nothing but her sister's normal face, peering back at her with concern. The process had reversed just as quickly, the flesh started to fill out on the bone again, her teeth pinkened with gums and the eye sockets slowly refilled with soft jelly.

Jenna exhaled with a tremble.

"I think I need some air."

Chapter 18

It was now early afternoon and Ravensgate, veiled in the muted hues of winter, smelt of damp earth under what was an increasingly leaden sky. Jenna's stomach rumbled loudly as they began to walk, and she realized she hadn't eaten a thing since breakfast. Food, another of those things that had lost all importance since she'd entered this new world without Chloe. That was probably all it was, she thought uneasily—an empty stomach combined with a lack of sleep and the drip-drip of permanent worry. They stopped at a small shop and bought some stale sandwiches together with a tasteless coffee.

Jenna wolfed it down as they began resuming their walk along the side of the brook, happy to just consume something hot and solid and feeling immediately better for it.

"I wonder what Mum and Dad would say?" she said, suddenly.

"Where did that come from?" said Hattie.

"Dad would blame all this on me; tell me I'm a bad mother."

Hattie gave her a reproachful glare.

"You know that's not true. He'd probably find a way of blaming himself for this instead," she said.

Jenna stopped and looked at her sourly.

"Yeah, that's also true. His fault he raised me so badly to *be* such a bad mother . . ."

Hattie shook her head and began walking again. "Come on, getting maudlin doesn't help."

"You always were their favorite," said Jenna softly.

Hattie nodded slowly. "I'm not sure either of us had much choice about that."

They both looked out across the countryside that lay beyond the village. A grid of dark green fields separated by weathered stone walls was spread out in front of them. There was a nip in the air now too.

"I don't want my daughter to die on this island," said Jenna and as she said the words remembered again what Ben Markham had said to Liam earlier. She turned to Hattie with energy. "And I think there's someone here who might be able to help us . . ."

It was almost as if it had happened yesterday. Even though she was in her late eighties the pain and most of all, the anger, was ferociously clear in Nina Yates's expression. It hadn't been difficult finding her. There were only two care homes on the island and through a mixture of charm and a little white lying Jenna had persuaded the staff at the one Nina was residing in to let them pay a visit.

She hadn't forgotten the details of what had been done to her daughter over two decades before. The news that she'd outlived the man responsible for Lily's death had also brought her visible pleasure.

"If they found Adam Nicks's bones at the bottom of the ocean, then I hope the Bone Queen herself took them and that his death was painful," was her immediate response. That alone intrigued Jenna.

When Lily had died, Nina had been living in Ravensgate with her late husband. There was nothing old or shaky about this woman though, and as they sat on a couple of chairs in her bedroom facing her, Jenna got a sense of the person she'd once been. She had long gray-brown brush-like hair and was wearing a floral-patterned dress with a brown shawl draped over her shoulders, but the fire was most definitely still burning. She must have been formidable in her day; a powerful matriarch, denied the opportunity to be one after fate had intervened.

As Jenna looked around the neatly arranged room, she wondered what effect this news would have on her after such a long time. It was a day she surely must have thought that she'd never live to see, but her eyes were blazing with concentration.

"What's your interest in this again?" she snapped at Jenna.

"My daughter ran away from home, and I think she's come here in search of the Bone Queen." She realized what she'd said and corrected herself. "To be more accurate I think Chloe believed she'd been *marked* by the Bone Queen and thought she could find some sort of answer to that on Athelsea."

An unexpected smile spread across Nina's expressive face exposing sharp yellowing teeth.

"There's no answer once you've been marked."

"How do you mean?" said Hattie.

"What did you do to that girl?" said Nina searching Jenna out with her eyes.

"*Do* to her? Nothing. I don't understand—"

"The Bone Queen comes for the children to punish the parents," said Nina cutting across her.

"The Bone Queen's just a *story,*" said Hattie scornfully but Jenna was now feeling a wave of new guilt. She could still hear the hollow sound of her apologies to Chloe the mornings after she'd drunk herself into the ground. *"Sorry love, you know I didn't mean any of that—it was just the wine talking"* she'd say. She could remember the contempt on her daughter's face when she tried to explain herself, like a mirror to the fear that had been written across it the previous night. It wouldn't have been so bad if they were just isolated incidents, but they hadn't been.

Nina crossed her arms.

"It won't be you or me who decides," she said quietly.

"Don't listen to her—you haven't done anything," said Hattie. Jenna ignored both of them and refocused.

"I was told you believed the Bone Queen was responsible for what happened to your grandson," she lied.

Nina sniffed the air for a moment before responding. "I didn't like Adam from the day I met him, but Lily was besotted. I hoped she'd get bored with him but then she fell pregnant," said Nina tailing off.

"Had he hurt her before?"

Nina looked upset as she remembered. "Yes, and that's what upsets me most. The signs were there, but I ignored them. I remember a bruise on her face one morning. I'd heard them arguing in her bedroom the night before. She swore blind that it was an accident, but I knew she was lying."

"Is that why you think the Bone Queen killed your grandson?" said Jenna. "As punishment for what Adam did?"

Nina's eyes blazed again. "In part. But also because we should have stopped him. *We* allowed it to happen, and she punished us for it."

"We?" said Jenna.

"Me . . . and those young folk who were with Lily when she died. Retribution has no fear or favor—it is what it is."

"But they're all fine," said Jenna, confused. "Frank Archer, the Markhams, Sheelagh Deeney—they've all lived here in peace ever since that day."

Nina smiled wolfishly back at her, and it made Jenna feel uneasy. There was something about it that cut right through.

"They were all *marked* and one day she'll collect," said Nina as if it were indisputable.

Jenna felt the hairs go up on the back of her neck, the implication of that was terrifying as was this woman's absolute conviction.

"Do you really believe that?" said Jenna. "Are you saying that will happen to my daughter too?"

"As I said before, it's not me who'll decide."

"I refuse to give up on Chloe," said Jenna. "Whatever mistakes I've made in the past. You must have some idea where she might be. What did she think she could find in Ravensgate that would protect her?"

Nina was inscrutable. "If she's here, she won't be in the village itself but there are caves all over the island. They say the caverns around Ravensgate are where the Queen buries her victims."

As the taxi drove them back, there was an awkward silence in the car. Jenna already knew what Hattie was thinking, and it was her sister who went first.

"You don't actually believe all that nonsense, do you?"

Jenna smiled almost involuntarily, but it was more a nervous reaction than because she'd found anything about this amusing. The two strange visions she'd had; one in the woods, the other earlier in her room at the guesthouse came into her mind and she banished them. "What I'm trying to do is put myself in the head of a sixteen-year-old girl who *has* bought into all this. What did you take from that conversation?" she said.

The taxi driver swore as a tractor pulled out in front of them. On Athelsea's narrow roads, they were likely to be stuck behind it for a while. Hattie looked out of the window as she considered the question.

"If Chloe thinks she's been marked, she must be scared witless. That old woman looked terrified, and she's lived here all her life. There must be some part of this story we don't know yet, something Chloe found out about that convinced her there was something important here. Find out what that is, and we'll be a lot closer to knowing where she is."

Jenna nodded remembering the look on Nina Yates's face at the end. Beneath all the anger, there'd been a streak of genuine fear.

"But what is it, Hat? We've talked to the local historian, to the police, and now to a woman who believes the Bone Queen killed her grandson and we still don't know what it is."

Hattie turned to her as the taxi driver found a stretch of open road and put his foot down, easing them past the tractor.

"She did tell us one thing—there are caves around Ravensgate."

"Chloe didn't take a sleeping bag or anything like that and the weather's freezing. You know what she's like; she can't handle a London townhouse in the winter without the heating on full blast."

Hattie shrugged helplessly, unable to provide an answer.

"It's all we've got to go on, Jen."

By the time they returned to the village, it was early evening, and the temperature had dropped even further as they walked back to the guesthouse. It only served to reinforce the point Jenna had made in the car. Had her daughter really been living in a cave for the last week; how scared would she have had to be? Then Jenna remembered how Chloe had looked in those final few days—she'd been petrified.

"I suppose you want to go and try and find these caves right now?" said Hattie. The light was going, and it was starting to drizzle.

Jenna nodded. She glanced up at the woodland above the village. The hill continued to rise until it merged with some rougher terrain before eventually forming part of the rock face of a cliff.

"If we're after caves—that way seems likeliest," she said, pointing. It looked a climb through dense forest, in gloomy wet conditions.

Hattie blew through her lips.

"It would be easier when there's more light . . ." she said uncertainly and was probably right. But now that Jenna had got the idea into her head that Chloe might be near, there was no question of waiting.

"It looks worse than it is; fifteen, twenty minutes at most. With me to the end, remember? What do you say?"

Chapter 19

Ben and Katrina Markham entered the Black Horse Inn glad to get out of the rain and were pleased to see a roaring fire burning in the wrought iron fireplace in the lounge. Frank greeted them with a wave from behind the bar and turned to Debbie, who was standing next to him.

"Can you take over for a bit, love? I shouldn't imagine things are going to get too busy tonight."

"How long are you going to be?" she said.

There was genuine irritation in her voice. She knew there was a gathering taking place that evening, but he'd been decidedly unforthcoming about why.

Adam Nicks was all anyone in the village had been talking about for the last twenty-four hours. The blame for Lily Yates's death had always lain squarely with him. The assumption had been that he'd got away with it and was living out a new life somewhere a long way away. But since those bones had been recovered from the seabed, Frank had noticed a change around Ravensgate. People were talking and the pub had been noticeably quieter than it usually was on these cold winter nights. It wasn't just them. The memories of a hot summer's day in 2003 had been flooding back. The discovery of those bones meant something, he was sure of it, and the implication was terrifying. *"Hold your nerve,"* he'd said to himself more than once—but that was proving a lot easier said than done.

Now here they were, all together once again—the group of friends who'd been there when Lily had died. Debbie had been repeatedly asking him about it all day. She was from the mainland and knew the story but hadn't *lived* it the way they all had.

"It's nothing you need to worry about Debs, I promise," he assured her.

"Are you sure, Frank?" she said, fixing him with the stare that she only used when she meant business. He knew what she was telling him—*"I'll let this go for now, but if I find out later that you're lying then there'll be hell to pay."*

"Tonight's just about us supporting each other," he said with a voice that was calmer than he felt.

"Why do you need to support each other if there's nothing to worry about?"

It was a reasonable enough question, but there were things he could tell her, and things he couldn't. The truth was he was protecting her and sometimes ignorance really was bliss.

"Just trust me love, eh?" he snapped. Still unconvinced, she watched him as he grabbed a freshly washed glass and jammed it under a bottle of scotch, drawing a small measure and downing it in one gulp.

Ruth O'Brien came through the door holding a soaking-wet umbrella which she closed and shook before joining the Markhams at a large wooden table in the corner of the room.

"Are you sure this isn't just about making sure your stories are straight?" said Debbie and he turned, looking at her sharply.

"What's that supposed to mean?" he said.

This time she looked less certain, and he slammed the empty whisky glass down on the counter.

Sheelagh Deeney entered next. She was wearing a plastic raincoat with a hood which she lowered, and her glasses immediately steamed up. The other three made space for her and she sat down awkwardly next to Ruth. For a casual catch-up, their body language didn't seem comfortable at all, thought Frank, echoing his wife. They looked tense and scared. Ben was looking over at him now and he held up a hand in acknowledgment.

"Go on, your master's calling," said Debbie.

"We'll talk about everything, and I mean *everything*, later," said Frank.

He lifted the hinged counter but as he strode across the room felt his phone vibrating in his pocket. He read the message on the display: *"Come outside now—Addison Lane."*

Swallowing, he looked over uncertainly at his friends. He didn't recognize the number, but he didn't like it. Everything felt like it was in flux right now, had done ever since those bloody bones had turned up. If there was someone out there who knew something they shouldn't . . .

"Frank," said Ben. "What is it?"

"I'll be back in a moment; I've just got to check on something. Two minutes," he said and went straight to the door, ignoring their reaction and the stare of his wife, boring into the back of his skull like a laser beam.

Outside the rain was driving down but he didn't care. He jogged to the end of the road and heard a rumble of thunder. As he turned into Addison Lane, he stopped. Ahead was a figure standing underneath the yellow beam of a streetlamp, the falling rain illuminated by it. All the fear that had been building in him over the last twenty-four hours coalesced into one moment of primal terror. He wanted to run, but his legs wouldn't obey and there was nowhere to run to. There was a smell too, despite the rain—sour and cloying, like burnt fat. The figure turned sharply; it was cowled, its face obscured by the shadows. Slowly the Bone Queen raised the long human femur bone in her hand and pointed it straight at him.

Chapter 20

It didn't take long for Jenna to feel like she'd made a mistake. Within five or ten minutes, Ravensgate village had disappeared from view. The uphill path through the trees demanded resilience and the incline felt like it was conspiring against them, often leading to foliage so thick it seemed almost unpassable. She'd offered Hattie the option of turning back again, but once more she'd steadfastly refused. They were now in a no-man's-land between the village and the foot of the cliff above, and Jenna's earlier estimate that it wouldn't take more than twenty minutes was looking laughably optimistic.

Just to add to the difficulty the rain was getting heavier by the minute and the wind was picking up too. The conversation between them had given way to silence as they concentrated on battling the elements. Jenna consoled herself with the thought that downhill would at least be easier, and perhaps the rain might have eased off by then. And just maybe, there might be three of them.

Oddly, if she turned off the physical sensation of it—the biting wind on her face, the increasingly wet feel of her socks in her shoes—there was a strange beauty in their surroundings. The air smelt clean and earthy, and the moonlight was now beginning to come through the skeletal branches. The water was hanging off them like diamonds in the white light.

"Come on, Hat," she panted. "Think of the calories we're burning off."

Her sister didn't reply, and Jenna drew to a halt, in need of a quick rest.

"Speak for yourself," said her sister joining her, trying to summon a little spirit, but the rain was coming down now so hard it was difficult to even hear her speak.

"We can't be too far away," Jenna shouted.

The storm had come from nowhere and the thought that these were the Bone Queen's woods, and she was actively trying to stop them from passing through them, kept coming back to her. Nina Yates's stony certainty had got to her, and it wasn't hard either to remember what had happened in this forest over two decades ago. People had died here.

She was about to turn and resume the climb when she heard something smash down next to her. At first, she thought something had fallen from one of the trees, blown by the gale. She could see a dark shape moving, trembling on the ground. When she went to inspect it, she could see more clearly now that it was a crow, its feathers soaked and bedraggled. Its beak was open wide, but no sound was coming out, or if it was, Jenna couldn't hear anything in the storm. It seemed to be gasping for air, its lungs laboring against the relentless wind.

"Jesus . . ." said Hattie joining her. "Is it dead? I hate crows . . ."

Jenna peered at it. "No, but I think it's dying."

Hattie screwed up her face. "Then let it die, come on—I don't want to stand here looking at it."

"We can't just leave it, Hat."

Hattie looked sick as she realized what Jenna was implying. Jenna began to look in the gloom for a rock or a branch, and then they heard another dull thump. They both turned and saw a second crow lying prone and shaking a few feet away. Above, lightning forked through the dark sky and as the wind gusted again, the crows plummeted—one by one—spiraling downwards into the forest floor.

"What the hell?" shouted Hattie.

"Take cover," Jenna yelled back at her, pointing at a cluster of trees ahead. They ran and took shelter and watched as the macabre sight continued. Puddles formed around the fallen crows, maybe seven or eight now, a mosaic of broken wings and dark blood just about visible in the moonlight. Finally, the onslaught seemed to stop.

"What just happened?" said Hattie staring at the dying creatures in horror.

"She's trying to stop us," whispered Jenna.

"It was the storm—something to do with the storm, that's all."

Jenna gritted her teeth. "Let's keep moving."

After another ten minutes or so the incline finally began to level out. Initially, to her dismay, Jenna thought the woods around the base of the rock face were too densely clustered to pass—that any natural cavern would be hidden behind them. Instead, the woodland began to thin and then they saw them, like the sunken eye sockets of a skull, a cluster of small caves. Jenna ran over to the first one, its entrance framed by moss-colored stones.

"Chloe?" she shouted but there was no reply, no sign of life at all. As if to emphasize the point, the rain turned into a torrential downpour. Jenna turned to Hattie, desolate, almost screaming.

"Where is she?"

Hattie grabbed her by the shoulder.

"I don't know—but right now, let's just get under cover," and she stepped forward into the darkness, taking her sister with her.

In the street, Frank was staring at an impossibility and a multitude of thoughts were going through his head. He'd been lured out here by a text message, and supernatural apparitions didn't use mobile phones.

Surely this was just someone dressed up, messing with him? His eyes told him differently. The thing was moving towards him, and he could hear a strange, slurred dragging sound in its wake. He watched in horrified fascination until they were face-to-face with one another.

"I'm sorry . . ." he said instinctively, the words almost tipping out of his mouth. Clarity came with it—he knew absolutely what he was apologizing for. Lightning flashed around and this time he saw the blade in the creature's free hand. Before he could react, her other hand shot out and spun him around. He felt his hair being pulled back and then suddenly he couldn't breathe. There was pain as his throat was sliced open, filling up fast with liquid—and it felt *familiar*—the same sensation he'd experienced in the cellar of the pub but this time real and terrible. His arms flailed pathetically, and he fell to his knees, choking on his own blood as it poured out around him. The last thing he saw before the darkness took him was that single blazing eye staring down impassively.

"What have you done to me?" said Hattie, shivering as they made their way into the cave. It was at least protecting them from the rain, but that was offset by the fact that they were both thoroughly soaked through. Jenna sighed. Not for the first time in her life, common sense had struck her five minutes too late. Why hadn't she listened and waited until the morning? She pulled out her phone and was glad to see it still seemed to be in working order and even had some signal.

"I'm so sorry, Hat—you were right, we should have waited. Let's just stay here until the rain stops and then we'll go back down. The pub's still there, we'll be eating hot soup and laughing about this in half an hour."

She peered out of the cave mouth, but the rain was showing no sign of respite. In calmer conditions, it wouldn't take too long to get back.

The cave smelt musty, and the darkness was so thick it was impossible to see more than a few feet in front. She took a few tentative steps. There was very little space before the rock ceiling slanted down and then she saw something that stopped her still. Fumbling with her phone she turned the torch beam on.

"What is it?" said Hattie.

Jenna's eyes hadn't deceived her. She knelt and directed the light into the far corner and then they both saw it, the smooth round shape of a child's skull.

Chapter 21

Four days ago

The toilet smelt and made Chloe feel sick. She'd seen the ticket inspector on the platform as the train had pulled in at the last stop. He'd boarded a couple of carriages behind, which had given her a few minutes to come up with a plan and the best she could do was to retreat here. She was also concentrating, visualizing the train carriage she'd been sitting in a few moments before, with a good sense of exactly who'd been sitting where.

The man with the laptop on the adjacent row had barely noticed her watching. He smelt of pungent aftershave and was wearing a crisply ironed pink shirt, his suit jacket hanging from a hook next to him. A middle-aged woman was in the seat in front, ever so pleasantly dripping poison into her phone about a mutual friend to someone who couldn't get a word in. In the seat behind had been a hard-faced young woman who'd given Chloe daggers every time she'd looked around.

And she *had* been looking round at her, periodically making sure her eyes were on all three because no one was what they necessarily seemed. Occasionally, she'd tense as the doors swished open and someone new bustled through. Anything could happen at any time—that was one of the rules of this, she'd realized. She'd deliberately placed herself close to the back of the carriage just in case she needed to move fast, which is exactly how it turned out in the event.

"Tickets from Castle Rose."

The nasal voice had cut through the air like a knife and to her fury, Chloe realized she must have momentarily dozed off as the inspector came through the doors at the other end. She hadn't immediately bolted for the toilet—she wasn't stupid—she knew he'd spot that.

A fussy-looking man further down had started arguing with him about some sort of discount he felt he was entitled to, and she'd used the moment to slip away. Only the hard-faced woman had seen her go and seemed to know why, judging by the smirk on her face. Now as she waited in the small cubicle, Chloe could only hope the inspector would move on through without bothering to knock at the toilet door.

She pulled out the pay-as-you-go phone and checked it again for messages. There was still nothing from *Athelsea100*—just something; *any* kind of contact would be a lift right now. Everything had seemed so clear to her in the comfort of her bedroom, but now that she'd actually committed to this, fear and self-doubt were creeping in with every passing moment.

She'd also started to think about school and what might be happening there. She'd left a brief note for her mum on the kitchen table telling her that she was leaving and warning her not to try and find her. Jenna would have rung one of the teachers to inform them and the news might well be all over the building by now. Her friends would have been quizzed. Had they known she was planning to do this? Did they know where she'd gone? She wondered too if the police were already involved. She regretted now her pink hair; it made her stand out in a crowd. In an ideal world, she'd have dyed it black before she left but there hadn't been time. She just needed to get off this train and catch the ferry to Athelsea. Once she was there everything would be okay.

Chloe leant against the sink and tried to calm herself; at school, they'd just be coming to the end of afternoon break. In her mind's eye, she could see Evie trudging along one of those long gray corridors to her next class. She tapped in her number on the burner and the call connected.

"Clo . . . is that you?" said a familiar voice in a hushed whisper.

"Can you talk?" replied Chloe, trying to sound normal. The sound of Evie's voice had lifted her.

"Yeah, I haven't got long though. Are you okay? Where are you?"

It was hard to hear her through the noise of the train and Chloe put one finger in her ear and jammed the handset against the other.

"I'm fine—I'm on a train, so the signal might cut out. You haven't told anyone anything, have you?"

"No. But it's been mad. The police were here earlier. Someone spoke to the whole class, said if we knew anything we had to tell them. But I haven't, I swear."

Chloe breathed out with relief. She hadn't thought Evie would want to betray her but under pressure, she wasn't the most robust.

"Thanks, mate, I knew I could trust you," she said, sitting down on the metal toilet seat. "So, what have people been saying?"

The was a brief pause and Chloe could hear voices. She guessed Evie was finding somewhere discreet where she wouldn't be overheard.

"No one's really talking about it. Sarah Garland reckoned you'd had a row with your mum though."

"She's an idiot," said Chloe instinctively. "Literally a walking root vegetable."

"Clo—they all think they're going to find you hanging in a wood somewhere. That's what the police were asking about, whether you'd talked about suicide or had been looking it up online."

Chloe was quiet for a moment. She hadn't anticipated that and should have. She didn't care what her teachers or classmates thought, it was her mum she was thinking of. An image crossed her mind—of her mum lying on the sofa nursing a glass the size of a small flowerpot full of red wine. More than that she could remember the things she would say when she was like that, and how cruel she could be. The laughter too—she *never* wanted to hear her mother laugh like that again. There was a very real danger she could return to that, but right now she had no choice but to take the gamble that all this would be resolved before things reached that stage. When she was safe and this was over, then she'd call and let her know that she was okay.

"What did you tell them?"

"That there was no way you were ever going to kill yourself, that you'd never even talked about doing something like that."

"Good."

There were footsteps again outside, and Chloe instantly turned and stared at the lock on the door again. Someone seemed to be hovering, and then she heard the swish of the carriage doors as they opened again.

"Where are you going?" said Evie.

"It doesn't matter."

"You don't trust me."

"Of course I do, otherwise I wouldn't have called you. It's me who's got the problem. But where I'm going, I'll be safe . . ."

There was a pause, Chloe could hear laughter in the background and when Evie spoke next it was with a whisper.

"Clo . . . I don't think you're well. And these people you're going to—"

". . . will look after me," snapped Chloe. "They're the only people who can. *Stella*—"

There were more voices behind Evie now, increasing in volume. "Promise me you'll call again."

"I'll try. It's good to hear your voice," said Chloe and meant it.

"Who is this Stella? Just tell me what it is she can give you that you can't get at home?"

"Protection," she said and hung up.

The distance from Penzance railway station to the ferry port proved to be a mercifully short walk and she found herself on the boat to Athelsea just after four o'clock. The journey was long, nearly two and a half hours through gray, squally conditions. Beautiful as the Cornish coastline was, now she was on the final leg of her journey, the decision to do this felt irreversible, and the realization was unsettling. She found herself in Athelsea harbor by early evening just as the light was beginning to fade. The last of her cash had been spent on a taxi to Ravensgate village and she was now cold, wet, and out of both money and food. Even worse, she was lost.

The dark woodland she was walking through seemed to go on forever and the directions she'd received had long since stopped making any kind of sense. They'd arrived unexpectedly in a text message on the burner phone. The light from its display was also the only thing helping her to navigate in the dark and she was rapidly running out of battery. The moonlight was occasionally finding its way through the lattice of branches and leaves above like long silver fingers, but she was increasingly finding it difficult to even progress a few yards without stumbling in the knotty undergrowth.

Doubt was also creeping into her mind, which in turn was souring into paranoia. Had she been the victim of an elaborate prank? She'd trusted *Athelsea100,* believed them when they'd told her she'd be safe here. But she could see no signs of life anywhere, no sign of the sanctuary she was so desperate to reach. Even worse, she felt vulnerable and exposed to the very thing she'd been running from. Checking her phone, she read the message on the display again; the battery was down to 15 percent now.

"*. . . when you get to the stream, turn right. Follow it until you come to a large clearing.*"

"What stream? There is no bloody stream," she muttered out loud to herself, and then immediately felt self-conscious. She had a sudden sharp yearning to be in her bedroom at home. Above her, there was a rustle in the trees, birds or squirrels leaping across the branches. She looked around, desolate, and waited for the noise to subside. When it did, she concentrated again. Somewhere ahead was the unmistakable sound of running water. With renewed hope, she walked on.

A few minutes later she found herself standing in front of a narrow strait that just about fit the description of a stream. It was the most welcome thing she'd seen all day. The small trickle told her that she wasn't lost, that they weren't lying, that hope and safety were now within reach. She turned right and carried on; the battery was now down to 11 percent. Another ten, fifteen minutes and it would be exhausted. She'd be alone in the dark and wasn't entirely confident she could navigate her way back out again, at least not until there was some daylight.

She emerged into something that even in the gloom she could tell was a small clearing and re-read the instructions on her phone again.

"Head for the tree directly in front of you—you'll know which one—then reply to this text and wait."

She looked around and shook her head.

"What tree?" she said out loud this time. "There's trees everywhere."

She checked again and saw one, an oak if she didn't know better, that dwarfed the rest and walked over to it, using her phone to provide some light. She could immediately see a marking carved into the wood at around head height, a symbol she knew only too well now. A crudely drawn face with one eye and a crooked smile stared back down at her. Feeling her pulse quicken, she flipped the handset around and saw that the battery was now down to just 6 percent. She needed just enough to send a single message, and her fingers stabbed frantically as she typed out the words:

"I'm here."

The message sat obstinately on the screen, and after a few seconds she realized why it hadn't shifted. There was no signal and she swore. She'd been so obsessed with the power that she'd forgotten about the signal. She took a couple of paces forward and there was a flicker at the top of the display. She held her breath and finally the message went. Breathing out with relief she returned to the tree and, with her back to the trunk, collapsed against it as exhaustion caught up with her.

She woke a little later with a start as water dripped down onto her face. It was drizzling again and to her misery when she checked the phone saw the battery had finally died. The only light source now was the moonlight diffused by the clouds above. She hugged her legs and out of the corner of her eye saw a movement, a flicker of light, and held her breath. Somewhere a twig snapped, and she looked around again, helpless, the darkness making it impossible to focus on anything.

She rose to her feet and something else flashed, on the other side of the clearing and she spun round to look. It was approaching, she could hear it quite clearly now, getting closer. She thought about Jenna, regretting everything, wishing she'd tried to explain things better to her, wishing her mother could have understood just a tiny bit more of what had been going on.

"*Mum . . .*" she said helplessly as suddenly it was upon her. Three of them were emerging from different sides of the clearing—she was about to scream when she saw that they were very much human. Two girls and a boy holding torches, and by the looks of them not much older than she was.

"Oh, thank God," she said with relief. For an instant, she became aware of someone behind her and then she was gagging, a cloth stinking of chemicals was wrapping itself around her nose and mouth and she couldn't breathe. And then there was darkness.

Chapter 22

Today

Frank Archer's body was found ten minutes or so after his life had ended on the cobbled street of Addison Lane. Ben Markham had run out of patience and gone looking for his friend and then almost literally stumbled upon him. Frank's jumper and shirt had been removed, and he was lying on his back staring sightlessly at the stars, naked from the waist up. The Bone Queen's sigil had been carved on his chest—an approximation of the familiar round face, with the single eye. Ben had checked for signs of life but there was no question his friend was beyond saving. The ugly slit in his throat was still leaking inky-colored blood out onto the pavement.

The implication of what he was looking at wasn't lost on him. He was staring at his own future—he knew that, a fate that over the years he'd become complacent about. If the discovery of Adam Nicks's bones had been a warning, then this was more of a promise. Everyone who'd gathered in that pub would understand what those markings cut into his friend's flesh signified. His mind was clutching at straws, trying to find some rational explanations—but it was the expression on his old friend's face which sold it. Frank Archer had died terrified, and he hadn't been a man who scared easily. Ben had looked around nervously, but there was nothing there except the wind and rain. Once he'd gathered his thoughts he'd called the emergency services—even though they were now utterly redundant—and then he'd run back to the saloon.

As he'd burst in through the doors, the first face he saw was Debbie looking up in surprise from behind the bar. At his age, Ben had experienced most things life could throw at you, but in that moment, he was completely bereft. It was only when she put her hand to her mouth and her face crumpled in anguish that he realized his soaking clothes were covered in her husband's blood. Katrina, Ruth, and Sheelagh immediately went to her aid, but he saw the fear behind their eyes even as they comforted her. He told them what he'd found, the words gabbling out less sensitively than he'd intended, and felt their collective terror. They knew what this meant too—for all of them.

Liam Tandy arrived in Ravensgate a short time later, and Addison Lane had quickly been converted into a crime scene. He spoke to Ben and the others at the pub as Frank's last few moments were retraced. It hadn't taken long to find the anonymous text message on the publican's phone and none of them genuinely had a clue about who could have sent it. The inspector stayed on the scene, marshaling his people until the early hours. The conditions made things even more difficult; the heavy rain likely washing away crucial forensic evidence. Anywhere else in the UK, CCTV cameras would immediately have been found and checked, but not here. Apart from a few that belonged to some local businesses, there were none to be found on Athelsea.

But of far greater concern to Liam was that there was a direct link between Adam Nicks and Frank Archer. Archer had been there up in the woods the day Nicks had murdered Lily Yates and so had all the other people in that pub. It was also not lost on him that they all had a cast-iron alibi for Archer's murder which could be easily corroborated by his widow.

There was also that marking on the man's chest and, despite himself, Liam couldn't help but remember the conversation with Jenna earlier that day.

In the months since he'd been living on Athelsea he hadn't heard the Bone Queen mentioned once—now there'd been two references to her in the space of a day. It felt like Pandora's box had been opened when they'd found those bones in the sea, a sense of something set in motion that he didn't quite understand. As he looked up at the dark sky, he couldn't help but wonder what Jenna Tipton was going to make of this. Somehow, he didn't think she'd be boarding that ferry to the mainland anytime soon.

The following morning was mercifully drier. In the B&B, Ben Markham paced his kitchen like a caged animal while his wife poured coffee from a cafetiere.

"Do you want some more?" she said. He pursed his lips and shook his head. Neither of them had slept.

"Why's this happening now? After all these years? It doesn't make any sense," said Katrina, sipping mechanically from her mug. Her face was devoid of color and like her husband, the scale and implication of this was only just starting to hit her. "Adam's remains turn up twenty-two years after he died and then this happens in the same week; that can't be a coincidence."

"Of course it's not a coincidence," snapped Ben, looking out of the window. The rain may have stopped but there was a somber atmosphere as the morning slowly emerged from the storm's grasp. "Nina Yates has been saying it for years." Ben turned to look at his wife. "It's begun."

"What do we do?" she said, looking him in the eye.

Ben bit his bottom lip. He thought about the look on Frank's face when he'd found him and shook his head.

"I'm scared, Ben. She's *hunting* us. She's been waiting all these years and now she's coming, and you can't say we don't deserve it . . ."

Her voice tailed off and he wheeled around, genuine fear in his eyes now.

"We need to hold our nerve before we do anything else," he said. He was about to add more when there was a knock at the door. They both exchanged a tired look, and he opened it to find Jenna standing in front of him. Her night had been as rough as theirs, judging by the state of her. She was pale as a ghost and looked like she'd visibly aged in the last twenty-four hours.

"I'm sorry to interrupt but I couldn't find anyone. I don't suppose there's any chance of some breakfast is there?" she said.

Jenna and Hattie had waited in the cave until the rain had finally eased off before making their way back down to Ravensgate using their phones to illuminate the way. It was an hour or so of her life that Jenna would never get back. Just the two of them, soaked through in the cold and dark, next to the bones of a dead child. They'd both assumed immediately that they'd found the body of the missing Josh Nicks. But then Hattie had reminded her of the children of the prison staff who'd died on the island.

"Is this where they were buried, like some sort of tomb?" she'd whispered in the gloom.

There was another explanation too. That Nina Yates had been right, that they'd stumbled upon the cave where the Bone Queen buried her victims. She hadn't been able to stop thinking about those dying crows hurtling out of the sky, or the severity of that storm which had whipped up out of nowhere. It had felt like the Bone Queen had been there with them from the moment they'd set foot in those woods. Worst of all it had been for nothing. There'd been no sign of Chloe, or any human life for that matter. Nothing alive, at least.

As they'd listened to the staccato rhythm of the rain falling outside, Jenna had tried to think things through dispassionately. It was either a murder scene or a burial ground, and a thought had gone through her head:

"This isn't a place where children are safe."

Hattie had read her correctly again.

"Don't overthink it, Jen. Those remains could be hundreds of years old," she'd said, and Jenna had felt a flash of envy. Her sister possessed a natural intuition and knew her better than she was ever able to return. She'd stared back down at the sightless eyes of the skull on the ground and shuddered.

As they'd made their way back to the guesthouse, they'd heard sirens coming from Ravensgate, the flashing lights of emergency vehicles strobing across the night sky. Jenna had assumed it must have been damage related to the storm. She'd also seen enough cop shows in her time to know better than to touch any of the bones they'd found. Her biggest worry was remembering where the cave actually was. Before they'd left she'd looked hard at the small area and did her best to commit it to memory.

It was over breakfast the next day that she learned what those emergency vehicles had been dealing with. She'd been genuinely horrified as Ben told her what had happened to Frank Archer. She remembered the poster of Chloe on the wall of the pub and the small acts of kindness Frank had shown her, which now felt incredibly poignant.

"What does it mean?" said Hattie.

"I've no idea, but as far as I'm concerned nothing's changed," said Jenna. "Chloe's on this island somewhere. We find her and get on that ferry and then get the hell back to London," she said, draining her tea. Frank's death was shocking but Jenna had never seen a dead body until she'd come to Athelsea and the sight of those bones—those very *small* bones—wouldn't leave her. That child must have been about three or four, and it made her remember Chloe at the same age and her eyes began to sting.

"We've still got the same problem though," said Hattie. "We don't know where Chloe is." Jenna's small moment of resolve crumbled as the reality of that hit home. "And there's what happened to Frank . . ."

Ben had told them about the marking that had been found on the publican's body. He'd been skittish when Jenna had tried to push him on who he thought might have done this. Jenna hadn't forgotten too that Ben, Frank, and Katrina had been up in the woods the day Adam had died. What had struck her most about the conversation though was the look in his eye, the expression on his face. The man had been terror-stricken. She'd seen it before when she'd been talking to Nina.

"They were all marked and one day she'll collect."

"What if Nina's right?" said Jenna. "You really believe this thing's real then?" said Hattie.

Jenna remembered the apparition that had materialized in front of her in the woods that had seemed so real, to the point where she could even remember the *smell* of the thing. She remembered too the way Hattie's face had given way briefly to the image of a skull. *Bones*, always bones since they'd come here. Now people were dying on this island—Nina Yates had said Frank Archer had been marked by the Bone Queen and now he was dead—the damned thing's face carved onto his chest.

"Yes," she said slowly. "I really think I do." Jenna glanced across the lounge at the kitchen area and could see Katrina and Ben silently cleaning the dishes in there. Their body language told her everything. What the hell had happened here once?

Chapter 23

2003

The kid was crying again, and Ben looked over at Frank and rolled his eyes. It was too hot, and the shriek of the bawling toddler was echoing around the trees. Even worse it was drowning out the sound of Beyoncé's "Crazy in Love" which he'd been enjoying on the small radio that they'd brought up with them. Lily should have left Josh with her mother for the day, it was too hot up in these woods for a screaming child. He adjusted his sunglasses and took a swig of warm beer from the can he'd been trying—and failing—to keep chilled in the shade.

"Don't you want to take him for a walk, Lil?" said Frank. "It might cool him off a bit."

Lily glared at him. She was a bleach blonde in her early twenties who'd always turned men's heads. It's just a shame she'd turned one particular head Ben thought, as he watched her ruffle her son's thick mop of blond hair.

"He'll be fine in a minute. Perhaps if you want to come over and play with him that might help?" she retorted.

"Some chance of that," said Katrina, smiling sympathetically. She was lying in her bikini, slowly turning a shade of lobster next to Frank. "Frankie's got an allergy to kids, haven't you?"

"That's not true," he replied indignantly. "I'm a big fan of the whole baby-making process. As well you know, Kat," he leered. She blushed and smiled shyly as Frank absently reached out a hand to grab hers. Ben watched the exchange with a little jealousy that he kept hidden. The smell of suntan lotion and sweat hung in the hot air. There was a burst of laughter, and they turned to see Sheelagh and Ruth emerging from the woodland together.

"Where have you two been?" called Ben.

"Just two girls together having some private time," said Sheelagh demurely and Frank grinned again.

"Gossiping then?"

Sheelagh threw him a glare sharp enough to cut steel, but Ruth's poker face gave way to a guilty grin.

"Maybe a bit . . ." said Ruth, and Sheelagh shook her head despairingly.

"Do you want some orange juice, Joshy?" said Lily to her son, leading him over to her beach bag. She pulled out a crumpled sun hat from the bag, plonked it on his head, and then found a small carton of juice. She poked a small straw into it, handed it over, and he began to merrily suck away.

"Boys, look what I found?" said a voice cutting across them. Ben sighed. Everything Adam did was loud. He only had two modes: loud or silently morose with no in-between. Josh wasn't the only little boy he wished Lily had left in Ravensgate. Adam strode across clutching what seemed to be a long white cane. He shoved it in Frank's face and cackled as his friend winced.

"Bloody hell, what the hell's that? It stinks," said Frank

Adam grinned. "A bone of some sort. It must be from a deer or something."

"Yeah, because there's loads of deer up in these woods," said Frank. "I've lived here all my life and never seen one." There was a barely disguised edge to his voice. He'd never liked Adam and along with Ben, he'd never held back from showing it. Adam shrugged.

"An *animal* then," he said as if talking to an idiot. He shoved the end of it into Josh's face.

"What do you reckon Joshy? It's a dinosaur bone, isn't it, mate?"

He'd thrust harder than he intended and hit the boy in the face, knocking the hat off his head and causing him to drop his orange juice. Almost in stages, the child's face went from startled to crumpled to enraged and he began to bawl again.

"Do you have to?" said Lily, furiously. She stormed over towards him, and his infuriating grin grew even wider.

"He's all right," said Adam, and Lily began to try and wrestle the long bone from him. For a second they battled each other but she couldn't loosen his grip, and in frustration she slapped him across the face sending his sunglasses flying. They fell onto the ground and snapped apart and finally Adam's smile evaporated.

"You silly bitch, now look what you've done."

Josh was red-faced and screaming hard and Frank's patience had ended. He sprang to his feet and strode across towards the warring couple.

"What are you going to do then?" said Adam squaring up to him.

If it came to a fight, they were evenly matched, thought Ben. Both were young men in their prime who did their share of working out. Katrina glanced over at him, and he caught the message she was sending, and stood up too.

"Let's all just calm down, shall we?" he said opening out his palms. "We've come here to relax, so why don't we do that."

"Sorry, Dad," said Adam and pushed the bone into Ben's face now and cackled with laughter. Frank grabbed it, pulling it from his grasp and then threw it to the ground. Josh was in full tantrum mode now, and Lily looked almost as furious.

"Why can't you just grow up?" she said to Adam, grasping her son's hand. She walked off into the woods, dragging the boy with her. Adam watched them leave with genuine astonishment.

"Where are you going?" he called but she didn't turn back.

Chapter 24

Three days ago

Chloe was lying on a hard bed somewhere unfamiliar. Her head felt woozy and she could feel the temperature dropping fast. As she sat up, the thing was already upon her, one bony finger extending towards her eye. The creature smelt of stagnant water, and slowly its fingertip touched the skin of her cornea, pushing forward into the aqueous humor. It stung and Chloe desperately wanted to reach up and swat it away but couldn't move. The finger pushed in further, through the pupil with a wet pop and into the ciliary body behind. She began to scream and then woke in a pool of sweat, panting as if she'd been running.

For the first time she took in her surroundings. The last thing she remembered were those people in the woods. Now, she was in a small bedroom that smelt of damp. There was a wooden table with a chair and a door to what appeared to be an en suite bathroom. It looked and felt like a hotel room, but one that hadn't seen any maid service for a very long time. She was lying, still in her clothes on a single bed, with a thin gray blanket over her. Sunlight was pouring in from a narrow window above her head. She looked for the burner phone and her backpack, but there was no sign of them. As she stood up, her mouth tasted of old socks.

She was about to make for the door when she stopped. On the wall opposite someone had crayoned a familiar symbol. A rudimentary face, with a single hate-filled eye, glaring out from under the brim of a cowl. But it didn't scare her, quite the opposite. That told her she'd arrived at her destination and for the first time in ages, she was genuinely safe. She ran across to the door, but found it locked. That was a mistake, surely?

And then she remembered the hand around her face in the woods, the smell of chemicals—she hadn't been sleeping, she'd been drugged. She banged at the door.

"Hello?" she called out. "I'm awake—is anyone there?"

She tried to make out what was going on outside but couldn't hear anything. She spun round in frustration and went over to the window, standing on the bed to get a better look out of it. She could see woodland close by, presumably the forest she'd been walking through when they'd taken her. Beyond it was grass, a field of some sort, and then beyond that she could see water, blue and beautiful in the sunshine.

The door opened behind her, and she whirled around to see a girl, who looked roughly around her own age, coming through it. She had long blond hair and was wearing a thick dark jumper and jeans. In her hand was a tray with a steaming bowl of what looked and smelt like a chicken curry. It was unexpected and the scent of the spices made Chloe's mouth water. It seemed like forever since she'd last eaten hot food or had even been hungry.

"Hello, I'm Grace. I thought you might want something to eat after your journey," she said with a warm smile and Chloe nodded rapidly.

"That's an understatement, I'm starving."

Grace put the tray down on the wooden table. "I'm sorry we had to drug you. We have to be very careful who we let in here—*really* have to be sure about them." She glanced instinctively at the graffiti on the wall as she spoke.

"Of course, I completely get that," said Chloe. Seeing someone who looked and sounded so like her was reassuring.

"And we don't know you yet either—that's why the door's locked. It's nothing personal, we do this with everyone new. Don't worry, it won't be for long."

"Are you *Athelsea100*?" said Chloe uncertainly, wondering if this was the person she'd been communicating with. "Stella . . ." she began.

"Relax—you found Stella. Everything will be explained to you. Stop worrying about these things for now." Grace sat down on the end of the bed and motioned at the steaming plate of food. "Please, eat."

Chloe crossed the room, took a seat, and began gratefully shoveling the food into her mouth. Rich and creamy, the chicken was almost falling off the bone and it tasted divine.

"What made you reach out to us?" said Grace.

"You know why, she marked me," said Chloe through a mouthful of food.

"You're absolutely sure about that?"

Chloe wiped a stray grain of rice from her chin and then rolled up her sleeve. Her arm was still raw from the scratching, small lines of scabs, bleeding from where she'd been picking at them. Grace stared at it without saying a word as Chloe explained what the last few days and weeks had been like.

"Then you did the right thing coming here," said Grace.

"What happens next?"

"I'll introduce you to Aaron."

She said the name as if it was obvious who he was. There seemed to be a nervousness about the girl. She was being helpful, but avoiding any direct eye contact and there was a distinct lack of any warmth too.

"Aaron?" said Chloe.

"*Athelsea100*—and he's the person who can do it," said Grace, her face broadening into a reassuring smile. "The man who can remove the mark of the Bone Queen."

Grace left her to eat and afterwards, with a full belly, Chloe dozed fitfully on the bed again. She was woken by what felt like water dripping down her forehead into her eyes. Blearily, she wiped it away, sat up, and immediately retched. She realized to her surprise that the moisture on her face was her own sweat and that her stomach was cramping like someone was slicing through her guts with a hot knife. The pain had come from nowhere and she could feel vomit beginning to rise in her throat. She dragged herself out of bed and crawled into the tiny en suite shower room.

She'd worked out earlier that she was in some sort of disused hotel. There was a battered No Smoking sign on the wall of the bedroom, together with an equally frayed diagram of the evacuation points in the event of a fire. There was damp on the walls and the taps in the sink didn't seem to work, only releasing a trickle of brown sludge. There was a smell too, like yogurt that had been left out for too long. Chloe lifted the stained toilet seat and retched again. After a few moments, her stomach settled, and she gingerly hoisted herself back to her feet.

The remains of the chicken curry were still on the table in the bedroom, and she thought it must be food poisoning. The chicken had seemed cooked but that didn't mean a thing. She'd wolfed it down so fast that she hadn't really stopped to look at it properly. She could still taste a residue in her mouth and the memory of it produced another wave of nausea. She'd been overheating in bed, but now she was freezing, something more than just the shivers too, her whole body was juddering violently. The room began to spin, and she sank to her haunches, stretching out one hand and grasping the table leg to steady herself. This was a living hell, she thought. Exhaustion and pain combined and as she thought of her mother began to cry.

A key turned in the lock and Grace entered, holding another tray with a jug of water and a glass this time. Her eyes widened in alarm when she saw the state Chloe was in. She put the tray down and immediately went over to help her.

"What are you doing out of bed?" she said as if talking to an errant child. Chloe tried to speak, but her throat was dry and sore. She was shaking hard, and the sweat was pouring down her face. A nasty thought was beginning to form in her mind.

"Come on, you need to rest," said Grace, helping her to her feet.

"You drugged me," Chloe croaked.

"Yes, we did—but it's for your own good," replied Grace without hesitation. She led her to the bed where Chloe gratefully collapsed onto her back. Grace pulled the blanket over her and then poured a glass of water out from the jug and brought it over for her to sip from. "Drink this, you're dehydrated, and it'll help."

Chloe could hear the tempting clink of ice in the glass but turned her head away.

"It's safe," said Grace.

Chloe couldn't resist any longer and grasped the glass with both hands before greedily gulping down several mouthfuls.

"Why would you poison me?" she stammered.

Grace looked at her soberly.

"We haven't *poisoned* you. You wanted protection from the Bone Queen and that's what we're giving you. We need to get all the toxins out of your system first."

"I don't understand, what toxins?"

Grace smiled. "Did you think we'd just wave a magic wand?"

Chloe took another long drag of water, splashing some down onto the bed. "I suppose not."

"There's a reason for all of this," said Grace. "We won't keep you in here forever but think of it like quarantine. When you're ready we'll let you out."

Chloe was about to reply when she felt a sharp new wave of pain in her gut and gasped.

"What the hell did you give me?"

"Just an herbal compound, nothing that will do any permanent damage. If you can get through the next day or two then we'll release you. Did you tell anyone at home that you were coming here?"

"How do I know that I can trust you?" she said, deliberately ignoring the question. So, far she'd taken a lot on faith and for the most part she'd accepted what she'd been told. But she'd been locked up and drugged without her permission, and her trust had its limits. Her change in tone didn't seem to throw Grace in the slightest.

"You'll understand soon enough. Where you are is special. No one knows we're here and it's about the only place on earth you can truly be safe."

Chloe felt dizzy and took another big gulp of water. "Why here?"

Unexpectedly, Grace reached out and stroked the top of her head. Briefly too, she caught sight of what looked like scars on the other girl's wrist.

"Because this side of the island is where Eleanor Aubney lived three hundred years ago. This is the cradle of the Bone Queen."

Chloe was finding it hard to concentrate. "So, you're saying I'm safe just by *being* here."

Grace shook her head. "Not yet. When the time comes, Aaron will remove the mark. But you need to follow our rules until then—for your own good."

Chloe could feel drowsiness beginning to overtake her.

"Were you marked?" said Chloe, still trying to make sense of what Grace had been saying, wondering too about those scars on her arm.

"Everyone here has been. We're all in the same boat, Chloe, and we all want the same thing—to be free of this. You're safe for the moment and that's all you need to know."

"For the moment"—the words rang like an alarm and Chloe began to shiver once more; she'd drunk the water too quickly she realized. Her nausea was rising again too. Grace went into the bathroom, returning with a plastic bowl which she placed by the bed.

"Aaron calls this the *ordeal,* and it won't kill you; it'll just make you stronger. Because that's what you have to be when you come out of this room—stronger than you were before, so you can handle what's to come. Do you understand?"

Chloe didn't even have time to respond. She leant over the bed and vomited into the bowl.

Chapter 25

Today

Ruth O'Brien allowed herself to bask in a brief moment of sunlight before a cloud moved across and darkened the sky once again. She wandered down past the pub and could see several police vehicles parked at the end of the street. As she got closer, she saw Liam Tandy directing operations at the scene where Frank Archer had died the previous night.

He was on his mobile phone having what looked like an animated conversation as the Scenes of Crime Officers worked diligently behind him. Curiosity made her peer past the cordon, and she saw several numbered cones laid out across the bloodstained pavement. Her eyes alighted on a small patch of sticky liquid that had pooled in the gutter. A memory resurfaced of a summer's afternoon over twenty years ago. She was running with blood dripping from her hands, and she was screaming too. Ben and Frank were asleep in the sun, their eyes widening as they woke and realized what she was yelling.

"Are you all right, Ruthie?" said a voice bringing her back into the present. She turned and saw Sheelagh Deeney standing behind her, her eyes also drawn to the police activity in the middle distance.

"What do you want me to say to that?" she said. "I'm as fine as I can be in the circumstances."

"You heard what was carved on Frank's chest?" said Sheelagh and Ruth nodded.

"People are saying the Bone Queen killed him as retribution for Lily," Ruth said, and turned to look at her friend. "Because *we* let her die that day."

Sheelagh dropped her gaze to the ground. "Why now?"

Ruth smiled, almost condescendingly. "We can always ask her when she drops by . . ."

Sheelagh looked up sharply.

"You think this is funny—after what we went through back then?"

Ruth's smiled vanished almost as quickly as it had appeared.

"No, I don't think it's funny and I knew Frank for as long as you did, remember? But what can we do? If she's coming for us then it was set in motion years ago and there's nothing we can do about it now. There's nowhere to run."

They both stared again at the grim scene on Addison Lane.

"He died alone," said Sheelagh. "Nobody should die like that."

Ruth closed her eyes and exhaled. They'd both left the island after the events of 2003 only to return to Athelsea later in life. Ruth had rebuilt her life in a small community not dissimilar to Ravensgate while Sheelagh had come back relatively recently when a vacancy had opened up at the church.

"Do you regret returning?" said Sheelagh, genuinely curious, and Ruth considered the question for a moment.

"I never thought I *wouldn't,* put it that way. If the Bone Queen's really coming for us, then I want to face her here. With you—with my friends. Do you regret it?"

"No," said Sheelagh flatly. "It began here—it's right that it should end here too."

A look passed between them and then Ruth delved into her bag and pulled out a small metal thermos and poured out some hot liquid into its cup. Sheelagh watched her and sniffed the air.

"What's that?" she said. "It smells like a flowerpot."

Ruth's eyes softened. "Homemade lavender tea; it's calming. Do you want some—it might help?"

Sheelagh found a small smile. "I'd prefer something a bit stronger, but then you were always into that stuff."

"If you mean by *'that stuff,'* taking a holistic approach, I'm not going to apologize. It helped me to cope back then and it's helping me now."

Sheelagh nodded. "Whatever gets you through," she said taking in a deep lungful of air. More police vehicles were pulling up at the crime scene.

"How well do you remember what happened?" said Ruth quietly and Sheelagh glanced across at her.

"I can see *every* single moment of it in my mind's eye. I don't think a day's gone by when it hasn't gone through my head at some point. You?"

Even after all these years they'd rarely talked about it. It was a part of their past they'd curtained off, tried to banish as they'd got on with their lives. An illusion of safety that had now been shattered. Ruth cupped her hands around the steaming cup.

"Every time I think about it . . ." she whispered. "It's only the *images,* fleeting sights and sounds that I can remember. It's like there's a part of that day that I just can't access."

Sheelagh looked at her closely for a moment and squeezed her friend's shoulder.

"I can understand that; why you might have blocked that out," she said, then turned and walked away.

Chapter 26

Jenna felt defeated; worse than that, she was terrified. She'd come to Athelsea in search of a disaffected teenager. Now she was up against something that she had no idea how to fight.

"Everything that's happened here routes back to the Bone Queen, but we still don't know enough about her," said Jenna. "I just don't know where we go next with this."

With fear came another emotion. She desperately wanted something stronger to drink than a coffee and beat the feeling down. She could feel it gnawing at her though, with each passing day here, that burning desire for alcohol. In any other circumstances, she would have cracked by now—gone on a bender like no other and obliterated the fear with numbness. That was the other worry at the back of her mind, the one that she didn't dare think too hard about. What she would do to herself if they didn't bring Chloe home.

"You're a journalist—think this out," said Hattie, bringing her back into the moment. "What if this was a story you were working on, what would you do now?"

Jenna nodded. That was exactly the way to approach this and instantly the answer presented itself to her.

"I'd get up off my backside, put my foot in a few doors, and start talking to people," she said, and Hattie smiled.

They continued with a renewed sense of purpose but there was already an immediate obstacle. Ravensgate wasn't just a small village, it was also currently flooded with police following Frank Archer's murder. It was as if the place had gone into lockdown. Nothing was open, and judging by the empty streets the residents had chosen to stay indoors until this was over. It was hard not to feel that the markings on his body were supposed to convey a warning. One that had apparently been received by the local community.

There was a small convenience store not too far from the guesthouse. The shopkeeper had lived on the island all his life and they decided to see if his local knowledge might give them a useful steer. But as they passed the Black Horse Inn on the way they saw a familiar figure walking towards them. Sheelagh Deeney looked lost in thought, and it seemed to Jenna that she'd aged even in the twenty-four hours since they'd spoken to her in the Rectory.

"I'm so sorry for your loss," said Jenna immediately.

Sheelagh looked up slightly surprised at first and then gave them a sad smile of recognition.

"Thank you. It's all a bit unreal. I thought I'd see how Frank's wife was doing, but the police say she's under sedation." She checked herself, remembering why Jenna was here again. "How's your search going—have you had any luck finding your daughter?"

Jenna shook her head. "No, but I have had a few interesting conversations since we spoke yesterday. I met Lily Yates's mother . . ." Sheelagh stiffened ever so slightly. Just enough to tell Jenna that she knew what Nina had probably told them. "You know she predicted this . . ." she continued, motioning at the police cars further up the street.

Sheelagh nodded. "She always thought the Bone Queen would come for us all one day."

"She told us about the caves too. We went up there and found bones inside one of them." Sheelagh reacted again, almost with an involuntary flinch and Jenna had to remind herself that this woman had just suffered a bereavement. "Why didn't you tell us about them?"

"Because they're not relevant," said Sheelagh. "People have been finding bones inside them for centuries. The residents of this village leave them be—as a mark of respect. Like the Gallows Tree, they're just part of the fabric of the island's history."

"Shouldn't they be identified, receive a proper burial?" said Hattie.

There was a peal of laughter in the background. Two of the gowned forensics officers who'd been working in Addison Lane seemed to be sharing some sort of joke as they walked to one of the parked vehicles.

"There's a legend about those bones, if that's the right word for it," said Sheelagh. "That if they're ever removed . . ."

". . . the person taking them will be marked by the Bone Queen?" said Jenna cutting across her. The explanation suddenly seemed obvious.

Sheelagh nodded.

"So, who do you think they belong to?" Jenna asked. "You are the island historian after all."

"I've no idea. Perhaps the children of the prison staff who died in a plague outbreak."

"Nina said it was where the Queen buries her victims."

Sheelagh looked desperately uncomfortable now, like she wanted to end the conversation and be on her way.

"Tell me honestly—do you think you *were* marked by the Bone Queen?" said Jenna. "Because I think Chloe thought she was too. I don't want her to end up like Frank Archer."

There was a sadness that seemed to have overtaken Sheelagh. She looked up at Jenna and for the first time met her gaze head-on.

"Listen to me, carefully. I don't know if your daughter has been marked or is even on Athelsea, but you need to understand something important. There is *nothing* you can do. You can be as defiant as you like but can't help her—you can't affect this situation, and you can't change anything. I know that better than anyone."

Chapter 27

Ben Markham had taken a walk to clear his head. There were too many things spinning around it, and he'd started snapping at Katrina. They were both in shock and he was a man used to dealing pragmatically with whatever problems life threw at him. He and Kat had been through a fair bit over the years too. They'd faced and survived financial difficulties and health scares, but they'd never had children, despite the fact he'd wanted them badly. She'd always been firm that it wasn't going to happen.

It was now nearly half past eleven and usually he and Katrina would be up to their eyes in work. A normal morning meant cleaning up after breakfast, washing dirty bed linen, going through emails, and responding to queries about forthcoming bookings. Even in the relative quiet of the winter season, keeping the business ticking over was demanding, so he was surprised to find the place deserted. The lounge, which was converted into a dining area for the breakfast service, was untouched. Dirty plates and half-drunk cold cups of tea were still there next to scrunched-up napkins. Something was wrong, he knew that instantly. His wife couldn't bear mess, it's what made her so good at her job.

"Kat?" he shouted but there was no reply. There was a silence about the entire place that he didn't like and even before he began to look properly he knew the building was empty. He went upstairs and checked each bedroom but there was no sign of Katrina. Coming back down he stood—both bemused and concerned—in the hallway, then pulled out his phone and tried calling her. Immediately he heard a familiar ringtone coming from the kitchen and still holding the handset to his ear he marched through and saw confirmation. The phone was on the table, his name lit up on its display.

He stopped, trying to think this through rationally. There was no reason to jump to worst-case scenarios—this was, after all, not an ordinary morning. They'd lost someone dear and he himself had needed some time to clear his head. Katrina had known the man as long as he had. Was it that strange that his wife might have needed some space as well, that even she couldn't carry on with her normal routines just hours after such a loss? She had been very spooked over breakfast, after all.

The only problem with that was Katrina wouldn't leave the guesthouse in such a state, and she certainly wouldn't leave her phone behind. He took some deep breaths and tried to rein in his paranoia. If anyone had wanted to hurt her, they would have killed her on the spot, like poor Frank. As he weighed it up, he noticed a piece of paper on the table that he hadn't seen before. It was a single sheet of white A4, and he swiveled it around to look at the image more closely.

It was a charcoal drawing, almost perfect in its detail. In any other context, it might have been beautiful. The light and shade, texture and fine lines captured perfectly the gnarled hand clutching the long staff-like bone. The dark contrasts around the head and cowl accentuated their shape. The distinctive single eye seemed to stare up at him accusingly and all his fears collided.

Chapter 28

Three days ago

Chloe's stomach was sore from vomiting, and she felt dehydrated as she lay on the bed and stared at the ceiling. It was worth it though, if what Grace had told her was true, that this was somehow helping to draw the Bone Queen's toxins out. It *felt* right because that's exactly how it had seemed over the last few weeks—as if she had been poisoned. It reminded her of something her mother had once said to her—back when she'd been drinking—*"you have to hurt before you can heal."* She'd been in her room trying to do her homework when they'd had that conversation. She wasn't the most diligent with her schoolwork at the best of times, but she'd never been more on it than during that period. When her mum was drunk, retreating to her bedroom and burying her head in books had kept her sane.

It was the pain that came out when Jenna drank that made it so difficult to cope with. The worst of it was that Chloe knew what that was and where it came from, and it had nothing to do with her parents' divorce. It was the great unmentionable—the thing that no one could *ever* help Jenna with. She guessed it would torment her mum to the day she died. Understanding that, even sympathizing with it, didn't change the ugliness of her behavior though.

After Jenna had lost her job, she'd sat around the house trying to use her time to find a new one. Boredom and frustration would creep in though and by the time Chloe got home from school, her mother would have already been deep into a bottle of Rioja. *"Don't judge me"* she'd welcome her with as Chloe came through the door.

That particular night, she'd been in her room working quietly when Jenna had joined her and attempted to apologize for her behavior. She'd been less bitter and more emotional on that occasion.

"Everything I do is for you, love. You're my world. I know you hate me sometimes, but I love you. You're my best mate and I want you to remember that. Because if I didn't have you, I'm not sure I'd bother with any of it."

The morning, as it always did, brought more apologies. Chloe hadn't been sure Jenna even remembered what she'd said, but now here, in this strange place in this awful situation, she could remember the exact look on her face, and the tone of her voice. It felt less like the ramble of a drunk and more a truth that the alcohol had brought to the surface. She'd *meant* it. It didn't take much to break her mother's fragile hold on stability and Chloe felt a surge of guilt as she thought about what might be going on at home right now.

She looked up at the graffitied one-eyed face on the wall opposite and bit her lip. She went through the last few weeks since she'd first seen that image of the Bone Queen on her phone and couldn't see a single thing she could or would have done differently.

"I had no choice," she murmured to herself and could feel the tears begin to well. A key turned in the lock of the door and she propped herself up as Grace came though holding another tray. On it was a bowl of steaming soup with a large wedge of bread alongside it.

"Relax, this is safe and that's the truth," said Grace as she saw the way Chloe was looking at it. "We need to build your strength up now. It's something nice and simple that won't upset your stomach."

"How do I know that?" said Chloe.

Grace picked up the spoon from the tray and helped herself to a large mouthful of the thick green liquid, followed by a bite of bread.

"See, it's fine," she said with a warm smile, putting the tray down on the small table by the wall. "So don't let it go to waste."

"Wait, I've got some questions . . ." said Chloe, attempting to sit up. She felt disgusting. She hadn't had a shower since she'd left home, and the smell of her own breath almost made her gag.

"I'm sure you have but eat something first and give your body time to recover. I'll come back later and if you're feeling stronger, we'll get you out of here and I'll answer everything. You can wash, put on some clean clothes, and then I'll show you around."

Grace smiled again and then left, locking the door after her once more.

Chloe felt ridiculously weak, but the soup smelt too good to ignore while the bread, thick and doughy, made her mouth water. If it was drugged, then she was beyond caring. She pulled herself out of bed and went over to the table, collapsing onto the rickety chair next to it. With a trembling hand, she picked up the spoon and took a mouthful. It tasted as good as it promised, and she devoured it with indecent speed. Afterwards, tiredness overtook her again and she fell into another deep sleep, though this time untroubled by nightmares.

When Grace returned a couple of hours later, Chloe felt stronger and although a little unsteady on her feet, she was judged finally fit enough to release.

"What day is it?" she asked as they walked out into a dark corridor. The drugs and the time spent in confinement had left her feeling completely adrift.

"Wednesday," said Grace. "And it's just gone four o'clock in the afternoon, in case you're wondering."

Chloe was mildly shocked, it had felt like early in the morning for no particular reason. She glanced at the peeling walls around her and the filthy carpet they were walking on. It all looked like something from another era. The place smelt too, the same dank odor that had been in the bedroom, but stronger and more pungent out here.

"What is this place?" she said.

"It was a hotel once, but it closed years ago. They never got round to knocking it down. Some businessmen tried to develop the land on this side of the lake, but it didn't work out. It's got its own generator though, which we've managed to fix, and that's why there's light and power."

There was something abrupt about the way she spoke, and Chloe recognized it immediately—it sounded just like the way she'd been with her mother before she'd left. The same subdued tone, which came from the same fear.

They began descending the stairs, which were lined with dusty hand-drawn sketches of Athelsea over the years. Chloe could see that even in its pomp the hotel had been a relatively small-scale establishment, rather than some opulent five-star affair.

"We use the kitchen to cook our food and there's enough bedrooms here for all of us to sleep in," said Grace. "The only thing it hasn't got is running water, but we've got a solution for that too."

The steps creaked as they went down, and as they passed what had once been the reception desk, Chloe could see old-style iron keys with large plastic fobs hanging on a board behind it. Faded posters were pinned up next to it offering sea lion tours around the coast of the island together with *"The Original Athelsea Ghost-Walk."* Something Grace had just said belatedly sank in.

"What did you mean by *this* side of the lake?" she said.

She had no memory of what had happened to her after she'd been captured in the clearing. She could be anywhere now, and the sense of dislocation was faintly disturbing. If she wanted to leave, she had no idea how.

"You'll see," said Grace.

"How did you get here?" said Chloe, genuinely curious.

Grace stopped.

"Like most people, I only stumbled upon the story of the Bone Queen by chance, but it felt like an answer to a question I didn't know I'd even been asking."

The words resonated with Chloe immediately.

"The effect of the mark . . ." She faltered for a moment. "I'd felt like that for years, that sense of *otherness,* you know?" She held up her wrist and showed Chloe the scars on them. "I saw you looking at these earlier . . ."

"How did you get them?" said Chloe, nodding, immediately feeling clumsy—it was blindingly obvious how she'd got them. "I mean—*why*?"

"I was always a lot closer to my mum than my dad, but she got cancer, died relatively young, and I had a difficult relationship with my dad."

"When you say difficult?" said Chloe.

"Not like that," said Grace. "Mum brought me up and Dad was always more interested in his work than me. I fell apart when she died—had a proper mental breakdown—I tried to kill myself, but he just didn't seem to care. Then I found the Bone Queen and realized why I'd been marked."

Suddenly it made sense to Chloe.

"Your dad?"

Grace nodded.

"I found the links online and came here and met Aaron. He's *seen* the Queen with his own eyes."

Chloe felt the goose bumps rise on her skin.

"When? How?"

Grace smiled.

"He'll tell you himself. Come on, I want to introduce you to everyone."

Outside the sun was shining brightly and Chloe could hear a roaring in the distance. She turned and saw the ocean on the other side of some woodland. They were high up, standing in a bald plot of land where the grass in front of the old hotel had worn away. Ancient old terra-cotta pots containing long-dead plants stood on either side of the doors. Knee-high broken white fences surrounded what had once probably been a well-tended garden area. It reminded her of a holiday she'd been on as a child when her parents had rented out a villa in Spain. It felt more Mediterranean here than British, though she did wonder if that was purely because the sun was out.

It felt good to be free of that musty old building though, the air was fresh and invigorating in her lungs and helped with the slight grogginess that she was still feeling. She turned and saw a sight that momentarily took her breath away. As she gazed down there was a vast expanse of water unfolding before her. A majestic lake nestled in the embrace of towering, wooded hills on either side. The sun cast a shimmering path across the surface, turning the water into a canvas of sparkling blues and greens.

"It's amazing, isn't it?" said Grace, her own long blond hair looking golden in the sunlight, and Chloe could only nod. It also suddenly made sense to her why this hotel hadn't lasted. It offered some beautiful views for sure but there was barely any land here, just the hill and the hotel miles from anywhere.

"Do you know where you are?" said Grace.

Chloe felt slightly disoriented. *"Stella—"*

Grace shook her head. "No, that's not what I meant. This was where Eleanor Aubney's house once stood three hundred years ago."

Chloe looked out onto the water again. This view of the lake, of Athelsea, the ocean—even the trees blowing in the wind around them would have been more or less the same. All of this, untouched by time. She was literally treading in the footsteps of the Bone Queen.

"This way . . ." said Grace.

As she followed, Chloe could imagine the hotel working once as some sort of honeymoon retreat with excited young couples climbing these same steps to their island paradise. They came to a tall, incongruous statue of a woman in a robe. It looked passably like one of those old Greek or Roman ones Chloe had seen in museums until she noticed the crack in its fiberglass plinth. Grace stopped in front of it and turned.

"Prepare to have your mind blown," she said. She led her along a winding path until the hill plateaued out. Chloe stared with open-mouthed astonishment at the sight before her. They were standing in front of a large Italian-style piazza, roughly the size of a small football pitch. It was paved with gray herringbone slabs and one side was dominated by a spectacular domed Baroque building. To the naked eye, it was a mass of colonnades and windows, intricate cream and gold marble adorned with elaborate sculptures and embellishments. But at the angle they were approaching, she could also see it was purely two-dimensional—the rear, a completely flat surface supported by rusting girders and scaffolding. "You can be yourself here, Chloe—who you really want to be. I've felt like a prisoner all my life, but it was only when I came here that I really felt free."

In the middle of the piazza was a large ornate fountain that seemed as if it had long since stopped working—the base, full of stagnant green water. On the other side of the fountain was a semicircle of around half a dozen old-fashioned caravans. At the center of them was a prominent gold one, noticeably larger and grander than the rest. On its side, someone had spray-painted in black the Bone Queen's emblem. The remains of a bonfire lay between the horseshoe of caravans and the fountain. There were one or two people, perhaps only a few years older than Chloe, sitting on the steps of some of the wagons, watching their arrival with curiosity. Grace turned to her proudly.

"This is *her* land and now you're one of us."

Chapter 29

Today

"Think like a journalist."

Jenna was trying to do just that but wasn't getting very far with it. At work, she was calm, logical, and focused but right now she was feeling none of those things. The speed at which events were moving was also unnerving her. Frank Archer had been butchered, while the image of those bones she'd seen in the cave wouldn't leave her. She'd been trying to assemble her thoughts into some sort of rational order, but she was finding it difficult. She'd also disregarded Sheelagh Deeney's warning that she couldn't affect the situation—that may well be true, but there was no way she was meekly just going to go back to London. There was nothing that said Sheelagh was right either, the future could still be written—she had to believe that.

She was back in "The Raven" café now with Chloe's laptop and phone on the table next to her. Hattie had left her to it, perhaps sensing that her sister needed some time to herself. Jenna was glad of the space because there was something that she'd wanted to try. She tapped in the password and watched as the laptop booted up, connected with the café's Wi-Fi, and then opened Google. She entered some of the information they'd accumulated since arriving here as search terms. She wasn't sure what she was looking for, but the sense that she already had some useful pieces of the puzzle wouldn't leave her. Something bound them together, she was sure of it, but she couldn't see what yet.

As the results came up, she tried different permutations. In 1981 a man called George Denton had murdered his wife in Ravensgate and then killed himself in a prison cell in Plymouth before it went to trial. Jenna stared at the screen, taking in the words.

"Think like a journalist," she muttered to herself like a mantra and then clicked on the next link. In 1959, a young man from Ravensgate, Frederick Calloway, had killed a married woman on her way home from work. He also died in prison a month into his sentence. Two killers, both of whom hadn't spent much time paying for their crimes. Or had they? Had the Bone Queen exacted some sort of revenge on them too?

She ran a hand through her hair and took a sip from the glass of tap water next to her. Both murders had occurred in Ravensgate. She couldn't see any of the other villages mentioned anywhere—or the harbor for that matter. It all centered on *this* village. There was an article from 2014 on Cornish myths which included a passing mention of the Bone Queen, but the writer clearly didn't think it was one of the more significant legends. As Jenna skimmed through it, she saw a reference to a navy serviceman who'd died here in 1937 and remembered Sheelagh Deeney mentioning it when they'd first spoken to her.

Something familiar was starting to beat a drum at the back of her mind. She knew that feeling, it was the same small burst of excitement she used to feel when she'd cracked a story, and the adrenaline was starting to flow. It was as if her body was telling her something, but she couldn't see the connection yet in the words. She trusted her instincts though—something *was* there. She reread each of the articles again. They all involved men murdering women but that wasn't unusual in itself. You could find stories like that all over the world at just about any point in time. The killers had died in prison and briefly that made her think of Ravensgate Jail. Had the Bone Queen picked off its inmates too?

And then she saw it.

As if on cue, Hattie came through the café door. She'd changed yet again and was wearing a bobble hat with a stylish brown scarf wrapped around her neck.

"How's it going?" she said brightly, taking the seat opposite. Jenna explained what she'd found, and Hattie looked back at her perplexed. "I don't understand—so, there's a history of men murdering women on this island? But just in Ravensgate?"

Jenna shook her head. "It's not just that—look at the dates—2003, 1981, 1959, 1937 . . ."

Hattie still didn't seem to get it, and Jenna snorted with frustration. "Each time it's *twenty-two* years. Even now—Frank Archer was the first person to be murdered here since Lily Yates in 2003. That's *exactly* twenty-two years ago . . ."

Hattie stared back blankly.

Jenna slumped back in her chair. "I've been trying to work out why all this been happening *now*—I don't know why that number is so important, but I think the Bone Queen returns here every twenty-two years. Not just to Athelsea—but to Ravensgate village, where it all began. *That's* why Chloe came here—she wants a showdown with this thing . . ."

Chapter 30

Ben Markham had resorted to searching the streets of the village himself for his missing wife. He'd tried all the obvious places first; the shops she liked to frequent, the café, friends and acquaintances, even headed into the hills on some of the walks he knew she enjoyed, all to no avail. It was possible of course she wasn't in Ravensgate and had got a lift to one of the other villages. She might have even taken the ferry to the mainland, but she surely would have told him if she was planning to do that.

There was also that picture he'd found, the sketch of the Bone Queen on the kitchen table. He still didn't know where that had come from. Was it possible the creature itself had left it as some sort of calling card? It was a message as clear as the marks carved into Frank Archer's body, and it had been well and truly received.

"Why now?" he thought once again. It was as if some sort of grand chess game was underway, working to a strategy that he didn't understand. He recalled Debbie Archer's expression when he'd walked into the pub the previous night, the horror in her eyes. Now it was his turn to know what that felt like.

"Ben—what's the matter?" said a concerned voice and he turned to see Ruth walking towards him.

"It's Katrina," he replied and told her what had happened. "I'm almost at my wit's end, Ruthie," he said, and she put a hand on his shoulder.

"Come back to my place and let's try and work this out," she said, and with a heavy heart he nodded.

A short time later he was sitting in her front room sipping at a mug of hot lavender tea which was doing little to calm his nerves. The whole place smelt slightly of patchouli and combined with the scented drink was making him feel slightly sick. There was a yoga mat on the floor next to a set of French doors that led out to a large, beautifully maintained garden. On the shelves next to the fireplace were what appeared to be a gold Buddha in classic meditation mode, with a pair of large amethyst crystals carefully placed next to it.

"I'm scared, Ruthie, I don't mind admitting it," said Ben. "We can't stop this now. Aren't you worried as well?"

She met his gaze head-on, knowing full well what he meant. "Of course I am, but what can we do? This was set in motion years ago."

"Who do you think sent Frank those text messages?" said Ben, looking her in the eye now. "That's the bit I don't understand . . ."

Ruth shook her head. "Does it matter who sent them? We both know who . . . *what* killed Frank and why." She put her tea down carefully on the coffee table in front of them. "There's something I need to tell you." There was a silence with just the ticking of the clock on the mantelpiece, the only sound as she considered her next words. "When I try and think back to the day Lily died," she shook her head trying to find the words, "it's as if I can't even *access* it anymore. The memory is there, but I just can't pull it out. Does that make sense?" she said. "I don't know if it's the trauma, but I can barely recall what happened after you and Frank had that argument with Adam."

"What did you tell the police?"

"The story that we all agreed together, but there's something else. Since they found those bones in the ocean I keep having these visions, seeing the most appalling things."

He looked at her warily. "What sort of things?"

"Dark disturbing images. Burnt flesh, children screaming in agony. Melting skin and bone." She shook her head again. "You don't believe me, do you?" she said, as she saw the way he was looking at her.

"Of course I do. It's *her*—it's always her, reaching into your mind."

Chapter 31

2003

It was the heat, Adam thought. It was making everyone tetchy. He was walking through the woods, not really through choice. He felt like crap to be truthful, there was very little wind to provide a breeze, and he had back pains for some reason. Lily had wanted space, and he wasn't feeling a great desire to hang out with the others after their earlier stupidity. But then these islanders didn't really have a sense of humor. He'd noticed that about them since he'd moved here. Even Lily hadn't been the same since she'd had Josh.

Sometimes he wondered if she hadn't just used him for that purpose. She'd wanted a baby big-time, but he was increasingly far from convinced she'd also wanted a father for the boy too. Now that he'd done his part, he got the sense that he was welcome to leave if he wanted. Sod that. He was Josh's dad, and he wasn't going anywhere. The kid needed toughening up too. Already, he was showing signs of being soft, just like Frank and Ben were. Neither of them could take a joke. He stopped and leant against a tree and took some deep breaths.

The pain in his back was unpleasant, and unusual. It was probably the result of too much walking after all that beer.

Adam had grown up on a council estate in East London. He knew what poverty felt like, knew what closeted lives these islanders led on this rock. At first it had been what had attracted him to Athelsea, but now the appeal of the place was seriously wearing off. A twig snapped behind him and broke his concentration. He turned but couldn't see anyone and resumed his walk. The trees at least were providing some shade, and he was finally starting to cool off a little.

Guilt was also starting to set in now. After he and Lily had left the others and walked up here their argument had continued and got even more unpleasant. She'd embarrassed him when she'd broken his sunglasses in front of them and slapped his face. The trouble with Lily was that she had a temper almost as bad as his. He hadn't *wanted* to hit her, he *never* wanted to hit her, but she'd made him—that was the truth of it. At least the others hadn't seen *that* part of the row. The look on Josh's face wouldn't leave him either. The boy was definitely getting soft. Adam's own parents had got up to much worse back in the day.

Adam was near the edge of the woods now and he thought he could hear the sea just beyond them. But as he listened more carefully, he realized it wasn't the ocean, it was something different, a rolling, dragging noise in the distance. Was it machinery? But there was nothing up here that could make a sound like that. It was more organic, like something large and slow grinding its way forward. He shook his head, and it seemed to die away, the squawk of seagulls above replacing it instead.

He stopped and decided to turn back. He didn't like rows to fester, and he didn't want this one to continue into the evening. Lily could be a pain when she was really fed up with him. One thing he did have in his armory was his sense of humor. He knew how to make her laugh, Josh too. A few smiles, a few jokes, and the earlier unpleasantness would be forgotten.

He found them both where he'd left them. Lily was stretched out on a towel in a small clearing where the sun was shining unimpeded through the branches. Josh was playing with a small blue ball and seemed happy again. They seemed a *lot* more cheerful when he wasn't around, he noticed. He walked up to her and called out loudly.

"Lil, are you awake?"

She looked up tetchily at him.

"I am now, thanks."

He rolled his eyes. Josh had stopped playing with the ball and was watching them both nervously.

"Don't worry," said Adam with a friendly grin. "Mummy and Daddy had an argument earlier and now they're going to make up." He turned to Lily. "Aren't we, love?"

A gust of wind blew through the trees around them, which was odd because there hadn't been so much as a hint of breeze all day.

"There's something in the trees," said Josh fearfully.

"Yeah. They're called birds and squirrels, mate," said Adam. "Why don't you go and look for some so that Mummy and Daddy can talk alone."

"You stay right where you are, Joshy," said Lily immediately.

"For fuck's sake," said Adam. "I just want to talk to you. Properly. Why do you always have to make it so difficult?"

"Talk?"

She rubbed her jaw gently where he'd struck her earlier. The telltale signs of a bruise were already starting to show, and he wondered if she'd tell the others the truth about how she'd acquired it. She rose to her feet and slipped into her shoes, then gathered up her towel.

"Where are you going?" said Adam.

"Back to find the others," she said, avoiding his gaze.

"Why would you do that? Stay here. Stay with *me* and Joshy. We're a family, aren't we? So, let's spend some time together."

The words got louder and angrier as he said them, and he could feel his temper going again. *He'd* been the one looking to try and build bridges, and she didn't seem to want to know. It clearly wasn't fair.

"Come on, Josh," she said brightly but the boy didn't move. Adam positioned himself in front of her.

"He doesn't want to go. Stop running away all the time and spend some time with me."

"Move out of my way," she said, but there was a flash of fear behind her eyes too and he smirked.

"Make me."

She tried to push past him, and he moved his body to block her again. She stood still and he kept the smirk on his face. One way or another she would do as she was told, he decided. For her own good.

There was a look of pure rage on her face now and out of nowhere she bunched her hand into a fist and threw it into his face. He stood for a moment in disbelief and then put his hand to his nose and saw bright red blood dripping onto his fingers. With a roar he punched her back, his fist connecting with her face and sending her tumbling. There was a sickening crack, which didn't make any sense because she'd landed on a soft patch of earth. Then, Adam saw the blood leaking around her head. She made a strange gurgling sound and rolled over, revealing a granite-gray piece of rock embedded in the ground underneath.

Josh looked confused, staring first at Adam and then back at his mum. She trembled and then made what sounded like a slow, sad wheezing noise and her body went limp.

"Mummy?" said Josh in a small voice as the wind swept through the woods again. Adam was standing paralyzed, his nose still dripping with blood, and then he heard that low moan again, the same as earlier. This time it was louder and nearer. Both he and Josh turned instinctively, because something seemed to be emerging from the shadow of the trees.

Chapter 32

Two days ago

More people were living in the hotel than Chloe had expected—six altogether, now that she'd arrived—including Grace and the mysterious Aaron whom she'd yet to meet. They'd somehow found a way to exist unnoticed by the rest of Athelsea. Food was obtained by stealth—a rowing boat dispatched after dark with supplies either bought or stolen from the shops and homes in the nearby villages. There was safety in numbers here, however illusory that might yet prove to be. Everyone had also been marked by the Bone Queen. There was Marcia, a rather bossy girl from North London, Jack, a teen from Nottingham, who couldn't stop scratching himself either, and Tariq, a terse older guy who'd shown little interest in getting to know her.

As it turned out they'd each been locked in the same bedroom at the hotel and gone through the drugged food routine as well. If nothing else, it made for a good bonding story over the campfire that burnt permanently in the piazza. It was there that Chloe had asked about the bizarre surroundings.

"What's your knowledge of Italian cinema like?" said Marcia.

Of all the things she could have said, that hadn't been what Chloe had expected.

"I don't understand," she said, glancing at the others, who seemed in on the joke.

"Back in the nineteen-eighties, some Italian film company wanted to make a movie here using the lake as a backdrop," said Grace. "They'd already built half the sets when their funding collapsed, and the film never got made. They didn't even have enough cash to take it all down, so it's been here ever since."

"What was the film about?" said Chloe, looking at the palazzo with renewed wonder.

"I've no idea; something to do with a group of travelers, I think," she said. "They'd constructed half a Mediterranean village and then abandoned it. That's part of the reason why there's nothing else here—all this stuff needs demolishing first."

". . . which costs money," said Tariq, rubbing his fingers together. "No one's been over here in years."

Chloe thought about the view across the lake she'd seen earlier, and she could understand what the producers must have had in mind. There was certainly a generically Mediterranean feel about it, especially in the sunshine.

As she got to know the others, she noticed there was an awkwardness about each of them. They were different to the people Chloe had hung around with at home. It was a stilted quality that she couldn't quite work out, like they were each slightly broken in some way, nursing invisible wounds. She felt a sense of walking on eggshells, as if pushing any of them too hard wasn't a good idea. It was only when the subject of the Bone Queen arose that they truly came alive. As they recounted how they'd each been drawn into this, Chloe nodded with recognition, their experiences chiming closely with her own.

Like her, none of them had wanted to hurt anyone close to them. They'd each followed the same online trail she had, and they'd all come to believe that Athelsea was the only place where they could truly find any refuge. The future was uncertain and for the moment the only thing that mattered was surviving day to day and not returning to the lives they'd left behind. Fear made for a strong bonding agent though. Strangers they may be, but Chloe found their mutual terror strangely comforting.

Much to her relief, there was also a shower and a working toilet. Behind the piazza was an old, rusting motor home that had belonged to the film production company. Once, it must have been intended as a trailer for one of the stars who'd never been cast and inside were both a water pump and basic bathroom facilities. Chloe had been intrigued as to who'd help them repair it. Most of the others weren't much older than her, but someone had clearly worked on the generator at the hotel and managed to restore the motor home too. Grace had been evasive on the subject other than to say they'd had some assistance and Chloe hadn't pushed it.

She'd washed and changed into some clean clothes and for the first time since she'd left home was starting to feel a bit more like herself again. While she'd been locked in the hotel room, they'd taken her burner phone away, and Grace had politely but firmly insisted it wouldn't be returned. If she wanted it back, then she'd have to leave. That was one of the few rules they'd insisted upon. She'd had a momentary pang as she thought about Evie and the promise made on the train that they'd speak again. She'd also wanted to ring home at some point, just to put her mother's mind at rest but that too would have to wait.

Her first sight of Aaron came the following afternoon. She'd been allocated a room at the hotel, which she was trying to make a little more habitable. It wasn't much better than the one she'd been locked up in before, coated in dust with a cloying dampness in the air. She'd opened the window to try and get rid of the ever-present smell when she'd heard voices outside. She saw a thin, wiry figure with spiky blond hair walking towards the entrance alongside a second older man carrying a toolkit. Despite the cold weather, the younger man was wearing just a white T-shirt and jeans. In his mid-twenties or so, he possessed sharp, intense eyes that even from a distance gave him an unnerving quality. Briefly, he looked up, saw her, and then carried on talking.

Curiosity took her downstairs and as she walked round looking for the pair, she found the spiky-haired man on his own, by the open door of what appeared to be some sort of cellar. He was leaning against the wall and when she approached him, he smiled languidly.

"Are you Aaron?" she said, and he nodded.

"You're Chloe, aren't you?" he replied, and she waited for him to extend a hand, but he didn't. She peered down through the door where the other man she'd seen seemed to have gone.

"Who's the guy down there?" she said.

"That's Garth, don't worry about him. He just helps us out from time to time."

She could hear clanking now, iron on iron somewhere. "He's having a look at the generator, it wasn't used for years, so it's pretty unreliable." That wide-eyed stare of his was even more unnerving close-up. When he spoke, there was unnatural calm about him.

"You've got questions, haven't you? What's going to happen? How are we going to protect you?"

He had the same tension about him as the others, but if anything seemed even edgier. She could imagine he had a temper on him too.

"Come on, let's take a walk and I'll answer some of them."

He led her away from the hotel and towards the woodland behind it.

"Are you in charge then?" said Chloe.

He laughed. "Not really, that's not how it is here."

They'd entered the woods now, which were muddy and dense. Although it was only mid-afternoon the light was already beginning to go, and Chloe felt rather vulnerable alone with this man.

"Can you take the mark away?" she said, in a smaller voice than she'd intended.

He looked at her like a doctor humoring a patient.

"Of course—that's why you came here isn't it?"

They'd emerged from the trees and were approaching what appeared to be a cliff top, a rotting wooden fence silhouetted by the setting sun separating them from its edge.

"Takes your breath away, doesn't it?" he said motioning at the vast ocean beyond. "It's nothing like where you've come from. Of school, your mum and dad, chips and beans, and Instagram." He was pointing now with the palm of his hand and there was a rhythm and passion to the way he was speaking. "This is a special place, Chloe, and you've come here at a special time."

"I'm sorry," she said, "but that's not good enough," and his eyes flared with surprise. He'd clearly thought a pretty view and a few smooth words would do. "I've run away from home, been locked up, poisoned, and chucked my guts up, and I'm *still* terrified about what's going to happen. How do I know I can trust you?"

He turned to look out at the sea again. The sun had turned crimson red as it made its final descent into darkness, its last rays daggering across the water towards them.

"Because I've *seen* the Bone Queen and I know what she can do, and you *should* be scared."

She turned to Aaron, a silhouette now against the red sky.

"Prove it," she said.

He nodded and ran a hand through his scalp. When he spoke, the confident, almost messianic tone he'd used earlier was gone. He seemed to be genuinely trying to find the right words.

"The first thing you notice is the sound, like something being dragged along the ground slowly, sucking in the air around it." Immediately Chloe knew *exactly* what he meant. She'd heard that noise but couldn't be sure where; in her bedroom at home, on the train to Athelsea, or in that room while she was retching in pain, but she had heard it.

"When she appears, there's a smell, like barbecued rancid meat . . ."

She nodded in fascination. That too she'd experienced, the faint trace of it in the air, but again she couldn't identify when or where.

The clouds seemed to be scudding at speed, and Chloe could feel the wind blowing harder around them as if it were responding to his words. The outline of something was starting to bubble into shape behind him, taller than a man, dark and misshapen. "She has long red hair," he continued, "but her face is scarred. *Really* scarred. Black, blistered skin, hanging off the bone, and those hands . . ." He faltered and she was quite certain now that he *was* remembering, not inventing. ". . . they can tear a man apart."

The thing behind him was now starting to solidify, and Chloe could see licks of what looked like black fire as if it were alight. It was as though the words were powering it, summoning it into being. There were razor-sharp teeth too, smiling hungrily back at her. She tried to speak but couldn't, paralyzed by both his words and the image. It almost looked like it was *part* of the man in front of her. Aaron smiled, oblivious, and the thing winked out of existence.

"Trust me. She's real and I've seen her. Do you believe me?"

"Yes," she whispered and meant it.

When they got back to the hotel, Grace had returned from a foraging trip to Ravensgate. To Aaron's visible delight, she'd also managed to procure some alcohol from somewhere, together with food and toiletries. Later they ate tinned soup by candlelight inside the hotel and then spent the evening on the piazza in front of the bonfire drinking cans of supermarket beer and cider. Grace noticed that Chloe seemed reluctant to join in.

"Don't you want a beer?" she said.

Chloe shook her head.

"My mum drank a lot . . . it's kind of put me off the stuff," she said.

"It'll help you relax," said Jack and tossed her a can anyway.

"He's right, it'll help you to sleep," said Grace.

Anything that managed that was worth a try, Chloe thought, and she snapped open the can and took a sip. It was cold and went down easily. Marcia smiled and threw her another can.

"You'll need more than one."

As she took another swig, she looked again at the slightly larger gold caravan at the center of the horseshoe of wagons, her eyes drawn once more to the spray-painted face of the Bone Queen on its side.

"Who does that belong to? None of you go near it," she said.

"That's because it's off limits," said Aaron, joining them from nowhere.

"Why?" said Chloe. He ignored her and looked around and she could see something important was coming.

"I want to be as honest as possible with all of you about what happens next." He left a dramatic pause. "The Bone Queen comes to Athelsea on the anniversary of her death. When she returns to the cradle of her birth that's the moment when the mark can be removed. That time is almost now, and you all need to start preparing yourselves."

"What do you mean by *preparing*?" growled Tariq.

"Because the only way to remove the mark is by confronting her." There was silence and Aaron looked around again, the smell of alcohol heavy in the air now. Chloe felt sick. She hadn't anticipated this. The idea of actually facing the Bone Queen was terrifying. The only sound in the night was the crackle of the bonfire and Aaron smiled.

"And that's exactly what we're all going to do."

They were out there for another hour before the cold became too much. Aaron waited for them all to go back to their rooms and then made his way to one of the caravans. Inside, the once vibrant red and green colors and intricate patterns on the curtains and upholstery had long since faded. Grace was sitting on a battered chaise longue and greeted him with a smile. He went over to a wooden cabinet, pulled a key from his pocket, and unlocked it. Grabbing a half-drunk bottle of vodka from inside, he unscrewed the top and took a long swig before offering it to Grace.

"We'll be safe, won't we?" she said uncertainly as he sat down next to her.

"You know how it works. The only true way to appease her is by making a sacrifice."

"How do you mean?" she said, and he smiled grimly.

"How do you think I mean—*blood for blood . . .*"

Her eyes flared with fear, and he leant to kiss her before she could speak.

Chapter 33

Today

Clancy Bird had lived on Athelsea all his life. For as long as he could remember his day had begun with a walk by the sea with his dogs. And then when the last of them had died, and he'd become too old to take on a new one, he'd come down here anyway. This little stretch of shore took some accessing, partly through the woods and then a clamber down across some steep rocks, but was always worth it.

His leg ached as usual. The effects of a silly fall off a ladder over thirty years ago. He'd had any number of jobs in his time: handyman, taxi driver, gardener, but somehow he'd always got by. There'd never been a wife. An early heartbreak had left deep wounds, but he'd been close to his sister and then when she'd died, he'd rebuilt himself down here, alone with his thoughts.

There was none of the noise of the summer tourists, just this rugged landscape and the pastel palette of the sun on the sand. He could feel his stomach rumbling as it always did this early. He didn't mind that, didn't mind walking long enough to properly feel his belly cramping. It made breakfast—thick porridge made with water, and a coffee black as midnight—all the sweeter.

He was about to turn back when he saw it. At first he tutted, unsure if it wasn't just a large piece of detritus dropped from a boat that had washed up. But as he got closer, his walking stick patting down on the wet sand with increasing urgency, he felt the bile rising in his throat. At the age of sixty-seven, it had been a long time since Clancy Bird had felt this scared.

The girl's head had come to rest on a small piece of rock jutting from the sand. The flesh on her face and arms was peeling away. Fish, crabs, and sea lice had picked away at her and the remaining skin had become translucent pearl white. Sightless hazel eyes stared out impassively and he could see a cluster of maggots wriggling from her nostrils. Behind, the water lapped gently, foaming, then evaporating around her. A pale hand was stretched out as if grasping for help, and it was only as he got closer that Clancy saw the shattered mess where the top of her forehead used to be.

Chapter 34

Liam had quickly rung Jenna and explained what Clancy Bird had stumbled upon on the island's eastern shore. He'd asked her to come to the morgue to make a formal identification and had sent a car to Ravensgate to pick her up once the body had finally been moved. The place looked more like a small workingmen's club from the 1970s. It was a narrow breeze-block of a building with a low flat roof and frosted windows. Immediately after she'd heard of the find, all the fear Jenna had felt watching those bones being brought ashore came back to her like a cruel joke. Had her daughter's body been out at sea all along?

The journey there had seemed to take forever. As the car swung round the island's narrow bendy roads she'd veered between plunging depression—the certainty that it *was* Chloe's body that she was about to see—and desperate optimism. The belief that nothing was set in stone yet and that it could be anybody they'd found out there. When she arrived, there wasn't so much a waiting room as a tiny reception area with two solitary plastic seats next to an unmanned hatch. She rang the bell by the hatch window and when nobody came, took a seat and waited.

She'd clung tightly on to Liam's description of the body and that the hair color was wrong. Chloe's natural color was brown, not black—but she was also aware that she may well have dyed it again. The neon pink look would have drawn obvious attention, so it was a possibility, a percentage chance that was now tormenting her. She hadn't brought Hattie with her for this or even told her about it yet. There was a good reason why but that was also something she'd need to address later. Right now, this felt like a journey she needed to take alone.

She'd almost cracked in the car though, wanting to call Tom, needing to talk to *someone*, because in that twenty-minute drive to the morgue, she'd never felt so lonely. Her fingers had gone as far as pulling the phone from her pocket and hovering above the screen, but she hadn't gone through with it. It wasn't fair to make him share the next hour, whatever it might bring. For all their differences and arguments, even he didn't deserve that. So, she was here, alone in a small space not much bigger than the size of a bathroom, waiting to learn whether she was too late and if her daughter was already dead.

She looked up and saw her reflection in the dirty window opposite. Heavy-lidded eyes, carrying the shadows of prolonged weariness, stared back at her. There were new unfamiliar lines of fatigue across her forehead, and then they seemed to blur. She could hear a noise too—it sounded distant, which was odd given the confined space she was in, like something heavy being dragged slowly through mud. There was a smell too, like a really bad barbecue. When she looked up, the reflection opposite had *changed.* She could see long auburn-red hair now, dropping around her shoulders, a single eye staring up like it knew exactly what she was thinking. Her skin felt on fire and when she looked down the flesh on her hands was blistering, pus-filled boils bubbling up and bursting.

"Jenna?" said a familiar Irish accent, and she turned to see Liam watching her with some concern. For a moment she didn't know where she was, had no memory of anything since getting out of the taxi, and the feeling was disorienting.

"Are you okay?" he said, as she remembered why she was here. *"Get a grip,"* she thought.

"Yes, sorry—I must have dozed off for a second."

He gave her that small-little-boy smile of his.

"Is this really necessary?" she said. "There must be something you've found that rules this girl out. It *can't* be Chloe. How long has she been in the water, do the dates even match?"

Liam looked like he wanted a hole in the ground to open and swallow him, which didn't help.

"The forensic pathologist has done a brief examination. He can't narrow it down yet, so we won't know for sure until the postmortem is done. But his early estimate does fit into the timeline of your daughter's disappearance, I'm afraid."

He'd offered Jenna the opportunity of identifying the body via a photograph and she'd thought quite hard about it before declining. If it *was* Chloe then she needed to be there in person and that was the only way she'd wanted to do this. For her, the idea of her daughter's dead face popping up on her phone was marginally worse than seeing it in person. She took a deep breath and rose to her feet.

"Let's get this over with," she said, and Liam looked even guiltier.

"I'm afraid I'm going to have to ask you to wait for a few minutes more. I just need to check that they're ready for you, first."

She sat back down without even looking at him as he opened the door by the hatch and disappeared inside. It was one wait too many. The tears crept up upon her unexpectedly—first a sting in her eyes, then a sniff, and finally a full torrent. She swallowed, determined not to let Liam see her like this, took some deep gulps of air and regained her composure almost as quickly as she'd lost it. The door opened again, and Liam rejoined her.

"Are you sure you're okay?" he said, noticing her slightly more flushed appearance.

She turned away and nodded.

"I'm fine," she lied.

He led her down a narrow corridor to a plain white door at the end. Again, Jenna steeled herself, prepared and simultaneously totally unprepared for what was on the other side. He opened the door to let her in and there was an immediate drop in temperature as they stepped through. They were in another small bare room with just basic furniture and a few medical charts adorning the walls. Some sort of antechamber she guessed, with yet another door opposite.

"Just so you know, the body's been in the water for a while, so we've covered her up from the neck down," said Liam. "There's a serious head injury that we've also tidied up. You'll also notice one hand that isn't covered—if you want to hold it." Jenna looked at him in surprise. "It's standard practice," he added. "Some people find it a comfort. Are you ready?"

She took a deep breath—this room smelt unpleasantly of chemicals—and nodded. He led her over to the final door and opened it.

Jenna could see instantly before they'd even reached the mortuary table that it wasn't Chloe. She couldn't stop herself whimpering with relief. Liam was watching her with concern, but she continued to walk over to the body. Regardless of who this was, she felt an instant bond with the mother of this girl who wasn't here. There, but for the grace of God and all that—and there was guilt too—because she knew something that woman didn't.

She looked down at the face. She was pretty. The eyes were closed now, the expression serene. A large bandage covered a section of her forehead. Who was this girl and how had she got here? Was this connected to Chloe? Had they met and spoken? It felt that way even if she didn't have any concrete proof. She saw the hand, palm facing upwards, and instinctively grasped it. She couldn't believe how cold it was but couldn't let go of it, either.

"Jenna?" said Liam and she realized she hadn't told him yet.

"No, that's not my daughter. I don't know who this is."

They stood there for another few seconds until, finally, Jenna released her grip on the dead girl's hand.

The morgue wasn't too far from the harbor and Liam drove her there where another taxi was waiting to take her back to Ravensgate. The whole experience had left her deeply shaken. It may not have been Chloe on that table, but next time she might not be so lucky. Liam seemed to sense she wasn't ready to leave just yet.

The skies seemed almost white, the sea frothing restlessly beneath as the pair walked along the harborside.

"I'm sorry, I found that really difficult," she said. "Not just for the obvious reasons, but because it also brought back some unpleasant memories for me." Liam looked at her quizzically and she shook her head apologetically. "Something that happened when I was a kid. I try not to think too hard about it."

He looked up at the sky.

"Do you think you'll be able to identify her?" she asked him.

"Chances are—yes. We'll run DNA tests, dental checks—all the usual. It may take a while, but we'll get there." There was a fluttering of wings, and he paused as some gulls flew off, heading out towards the ocean. "How's your search going?"

Jenna took a deep breath and then exhaled. "I know a lot more about *why* Chloe came here and what she might have been looking for—but I just don't know where she is on this island. People keep telling me it's a small place, but it feels the size of Australia at the moment."

He nodded sympathetically. "The only consolation I can offer is that the ferry terminal has Chloe's description, and they haven't seen a teenage girl matching it leave. She's still here somewhere—you've got to keep the faith."

He meant well, but it was no consolation at all.

"I'll try, thank you," she said mechanically.

"How are you coping—it must be difficult dealing with this on your own?" he said.

Jenna looked out at the restless sea again.

"I have my sister. If she wasn't here, I don't know what I'd do." He was watching her closely now, and she shook her head. "When I was looking at that body, I couldn't lose the feeling that whatever killed her is also connected to Chloe's disappearance. That they were both drawn here by the same thing," she said carefully, and his eyes narrowed.

"Connected in what way?" he said.

She glanced at him sharply. "What if that girl believed she'd been marked by her too?" Liam opened his mouth to respond but she cut him off. "Don't you understand? Time's running out—I have to find my daughter before whatever's on this island finds her."

Chapter 35

Katrina Markham had been missing for just under six hours now, and as far as Ben was concerned it felt like six days. He'd driven out to the harbor and asked people he knew there whether they'd seen her, but there hadn't been so much as a trace. The only scant consolation was that nobody at the ferry terminal had seen anyone matching her description either, so she had to be still somewhere on Athelsea. Was this her destiny—just to be *taken,* her fate, never resolved? In its own way that felt worse than what had happened to Frank. He knew not just what he'd seen with his own eyes, but also what the Bone Queen was supposed to have done through the centuries. The bones of her victims were up in the woods, littering the caves in the rock face there. The idea that Katrina had joined their number now made him nauseous.

As he returned home, he noticed the front door to their guesthouse was ajar. In his heightened state, even the smallest thing out of place was alarming and the sight stopped him in his tracks. Tentatively, he pushed it open and stepped inside.

"Kat?" he said hopefully but there was no answer. He walked through into the hallway but couldn't hear a sound and knew from experience that the place was empty, their few winter guests out and about somewhere. Had one of them left the front door open?

"Katrina?" he called, louder this time but there still was no reply.

He went through into the dining area and saw the light on in the kitchen behind and felt a rush of relief. He strode on, ready to tell his wife exactly what he thought about the stress she'd been causing him when he saw her.

She was sitting on one of the oak chairs surrounding the kitchen table. Slumped back, it was as if she was dozing, but he could already see the blood dripping down into a sticky pool beneath her. As he moved closer, he saw the open slit in her throat and as he finally reached his dead wife, saw too the sightless black sockets where her eyes had once been. Cupped in her hands, as if proudly holding a trophy for a photographer, was the sketch he'd found earlier of the Bone Queen.

Chapter 36

2003

Adam was staring at the trees, while Josh stood behind him. Lily's body was where it had fallen, but neither of them were even looking at her now. Their eyes were transfixed on the woods, and it was hard to even explain why. They both just *knew* something was there, the feeling so oppressive, they couldn't *not* look.

"Frank—is that you? Come out of there and show yourself?" barked Adam. The sun was beating down so hard now that even breathing felt different. That slow, distant sound was there again, and he glanced briefly down to check where Josh was.

A twig snapped and the noise stopped. A woman dressed incongruously in a long dark cloak with a cowl over her head stepped forward and at first Adam thought it was some sort of bizarre fancy dress gear. Whoever they were must be boiling underneath all that. They were carrying a long staff but as the figure got closer, he could see it was a gnarled, elongated old bone not dissimilar to the one he'd been waving around earlier. It was hard to articulate but everything about this thing made him want to run, the feeling almost primal.

There was something about the silhouette that was familiar too, an old myth Lily had told him about when he'd first arrived on Athelsea. But that was impossible. What worried him more was whether this individual—he couldn't even tell whether they were male or female—had seen what had just happened. They must have heard the struggle, he realized. This was some sort of New Age hippie type who'd been up in the woods meditating and had come to see what was going on. That was it, everything else was just his imagination. He wasn't thinking straight because of Lily, and he needed to get his shit together fast.

"It was an accident," he stammered. "She needs medical attention," he said, pointing at his dead girlfriend. The thing just stood there. Adam could feel that sharp pain in his back again, the one he'd felt earlier. There was complete silence around him, he couldn't even hear the ubiquitous seagulls overhead or the roar of the sea in the distance. It was as if time itself had stopped.

"Say something," he shouted and slowly it lifted its head. He saw an eye from under the brim of the cowl blazing with fury. Its hand moved up and lifted the hood away.

To his astonishment, the face underneath was that of a beautiful young woman with long rust-colored hair, which tumbled free onto her shoulders. Now that he could see her properly, she had piercing blue eyes and porcelain white skin. But it was only there for a second and then it shimmered, the hair graying, the nose widening, the skin cracking with age, and then there was an old Black woman staring at him with undisguised hatred. It had barely settled when it blurred again, the crocodile skin smoothing out, the gray hair turning brown above oval, searching eyes. A middle-aged white face this time. Her mouth curling into a cruel smile, flashing sharp white teeth.

Adam started to back away and grabbed his son by the hand, but the creature—the woman—raised its arm and pointed the long bone at him, and he froze on the spot, his legs unable to move of their own free will.

"Daddy?" said Josh but he couldn't even reply, his larynx as paralyzed as the rest of him. The thing's face changed one more time, back to the first one it had worn, the young woman with the rust-colored hair. Something was happening to her though, the skin blistering, turning red, bubbling and melting into something horrific and burnt. It raised its free hand and slowly turned it, and Adam felt his head turning without his control, his spine slowly twisting in the opposite direction. The pain in his back was excruciating—exactly where he'd felt it before. Still his head kept on turning and for a moment he locked eyes with his son and then something snapped with a popping sound, and like a puppet whose strings had been cut he fell to the ground.

Chapter 37

Today

A taxi had brought Jenna back from the harbor and dropped her in the center of the village where she caught up with Hattie. After explaining where she'd been they headed back to the guesthouse to consider their next move.

"You really think this girl was killed by the Bone Queen too?" said Hattie.

"I'm sure of it," said Jenna. "I can't prove it, but my guts tell me she's like Chloe—not from this island, but someone who came here because she thought she was marked as well."

"Don't you think you're jumping ahead?"

They'd reached the entrance now and Jenna pushed the door open.

"No, anything but—" She was about to say more when she stopped. Something immediately didn't feel right. There was a noise too, a low moan coming from what sounded like the lounge. Jenna and Hattie exchanged a look and walked through. The sound was clearer as they entered the room—it was of a man sobbing and was coming from the adjacent kitchen. Jenna could see the door open and called out:

"Ben—is that you?"

There was no reply and cautiously they walked through. Jenna saw Katrina first, slumped back almost decadently in her chair, two black sockets where her eyes used to be, long streaks of blood streaming down her lifeless face. The gash in her throat, grinning at them like some sort of distorted smile. Ben was sitting opposite her, his head in his hands sobbing uncontrollably. Jenna stared at the scene, horrified, with only one thought going through her mind. The Bone Queen had been here, under the very roof where she'd been sleeping, and had now taken someone else.

"Ben . . ." she stammered, and he looked round, seemingly only now aware of their presence.

"Get out . . ." he said. Now Jenna could see the picture of the Bone Queen on the table next to him.

"I'm sorry," she said.

"Just get out!" he screamed, and they turned and fled.

"You need to call Liam," said Hattie as they stood outside the front of the building.

"What's the point—what can the police do now? You can't slap handcuffs on this thing," she said. "We need to find Chloe—time's running out."

"How? We've still got the same problem; we don't know where she is."

Jenna took a deep breath, more than ever she needed to think clearly now. She was almost feeling desensitized to the horrors this island was throwing at her. First the girl on the mortuary table and now Katrina in the space of an hour. She wondered how long Ben, Ruth, and Sheelagh had left and what was going through their minds and then banished the thought—she didn't have the luxury to dwell on anything but Chloe.

"We need to know more about this thing—what bits of this island are associated with her because that's where Chloe must be. It's the only thing that makes any sense to me."

"Before you went up to the morgue you were onto something—that twenty-two-year cycle," said Hattie.

This is what Jenna loved about her so much. Hattie had been underwhelmed by the discovery, but it hadn't stopped her chivvying and pushing her. She was keeping her active, moving her along when she got stuck and frustration threatened to paralyze her. If she did find Chloe, it would be because Hattie hadn't given up on her sister, so that she wouldn't give up on her daughter. She owed her more than she knew. She looked up and saw the tip of a tree, swaying in the distance.

"I have an idea . . ." she said slowly, remembering something she'd seen before.

Hattie smiled. "I thought you might."

Five minutes later they were back walking through the clearing where the Gallows Tree stood just above the village. A large black crow was squawking loudly, strutting around near the trunk as if it were on guard there. It reminded Jenna momentarily of the dead flock in the woods and their crumpled broken bodies. She approached the tree, stopped in front of it, and took in the sight again. Her heart was still pounding from what she had seen in the guesthouse kitchen, and she forced herself to concentrate again, trying to banish the sound of Ben Markham's sobbing from her mind.

The surface of the tree trunk was etched with a tapestry of writing which she guessed must span centuries.

"There's something I saw when we were here before. It didn't mean much then, but we know more now."

"What?"

Jenna looked again at the different version of the Bone Queen's sigil that had been carved onto the wood. The tree may have been planted on the site of the old jail, but it was clear that somehow over the years it had also become associated with another of the island's icons. She walked around it and frowned, wondering if her memory had been playing tricks on her. The wind blew hard through the clearing and not for the first time it didn't feel coincidental, as if the force that inhabited this island was expressing its displeasure. And then she saw it: *"In thy name Eleanor Aubney born 1761 'til thy death in fyre 1783."*

"That's it," she murmured.

"What?" said Hattie, exasperated. "Jen—just tell me what's going through your head."

"So, remember Sheelagh told us the legend of the Bone Queen is based on someone who lived here once called Eleanor Aubney?"

Hattie nodded. "Yes, an abused woman who was burnt alive and left for dead?"

"That's right." She pointed at the tree. "That looks like it happened in 1789."

"So?" said Hattie.

Jenna glanced up at her sister. "Look at when she died. If those dates are right, Eleanor Aubney was *twenty-two* years old when she died." Her words hung in the air for a moment as Hattie absorbed it. "I'm sorry, but I'm not going to accept that word *coincidence* again," she said.

She pulled her phone from her pocket and opened up a browser. Hattie watched her and then began rubbing her hands together to keep warm. "Can't we do this in the café, it's freezing out here."

The light was also starting to go, but Jenna was too engrossed in what she was reading.

"Chloe wanted to come to Ravensgate specifically," she said. "Not just Athelsea, but this village. We also know Eleanor Aubney came from Ravensgate too. The one thing we're missing is a location because I think there was somewhere very specific Chloe was searching for."

"Probably those woods," said Hattie pointing at the trees above the clearing. "She's up there somewhere if you ask me. Where else *could* she be? I'm sure if we did a proper search we'd find her."

Jenna looked up from her phone. "Maybe. But where did this legend begin?"

"Legend? You're talking like it's a fairy tale," said Hattie and Jenna realized she was right—the words mattered.

"Where was this creature *born*? And where did she die?" I think that's the answer, Hat. Find that, and we'll find Chloe."

"And you think you can do that with Google?" said Hattie and Jenna scowled at her, then looked back down at the screen.

There was a forum she'd got into the habit of checking regularly. It was a fairly innocent one for people planning a holiday on the island during the summer months. Most of the threads talked about mundane stuff like the tide times, recommended restaurants, and which hotels to book or avoid. She'd kept an eye on it because it had helped her build up a sense of the place. As she glanced through it again, she noticed there were a few new posts there since the last time she'd looked.

One particular thread caught her eye. It was simply titled *"Stella"* and had been posted three hours ago and so far, hadn't received any replies. The post was brief and rather oblique by a user called *kmac14*:

"Has anyone been to Athelsea and found Stella yet? Does anyone know who she is? If you have any info—DM me IYKYK."

"If you know, you know . . ." she murmured, staring at the acronym. Something about the name Stella stuck in her mind because she'd seen it somewhere else.

When she'd searched Chloe's bedroom in the immediate aftermath of her disappearance, there'd been a notepad open on her desk. The top page had been covered in random jottings which had included train and ferry times intermingled with doodles. Jenna had a feeling some of it might be important and she'd taken a photo of it just in case. She brought the picture up on her phone and expanded the image with her thumb and forefinger. Most of it was still incomprehensible, but she studied it closely and then found what she was looking for. The name *Stella*—scrawled at the side in red Biro.

Chapter 38

One day ago

Chloe had slept appallingly. Her room was freezing and there wasn't any proper bedding. She'd worn her clothes with just a thin blanket covering her on a yellowing pillow that smelt of mildew. But all that was better than the dreams a full night's sleep had produced recently. Those moments when she did drop off had conjured vivid images that had lingered in her mind. Her father laughing helplessly at her for something or another she'd done, her mother drunk, careering around the kitchen swearing at the world. Aaron's words the previous night had also stayed with her. *"You all need to start preparing yourselves."* She'd tried not to think about that, but it had been almost impossible not to.

She lay staring at the ceiling and felt her stomach rumble. Dragging herself out of bed she went downstairs and helped herself to some cereal and milk from a fridge lined with mold that smelt of rotting cabbage. After she'd eaten, she went outside and marveled at the sight spread out in front of her as the morning sun shone down over the lake. She wondered about the people who lived on the rest of the island and whether they knew the true history of this area. When she remembered all the stories worldwide, it was a funny thought; these people living, oblivious, in the shadow of the Bone Queen.

"That view gets boring after a while, trust me," said a voice behind her and she turned to see Grace walking out of the hotel entrance towards her.

"What time is it?" said Chloe automatically. Without either a phone or a watch she had no idea.

"Just gone half past seven."

Grace didn't seem to have a watch either and it was a bit later than Chloe had assumed. She must have slept longer than she'd realized too. She could still taste the alcohol from the previous night in her mouth, and it made her feel sick. A toothbrush and toothpaste were both things she'd sell her soul for right now. She turned back to face the lake. It was like the perfect Christmas morning. The air was sharp but clear and the sun, creamy yellow against the blue sky.

"It's not boring to me," she said. "You should try living in London if you want dull."

Grace gazed out onto the water with her. It looked inviting enough to swim in today, though you'd probably only last a minute before hypothermia got you.

"No thanks," she said.

Chloe looked at the other girl for a moment, remembering the story she'd told her before about her dad.

"Where will you go—once this is all over?"

She said the words hesitantly, but she had to believe this *would* be over one day, that Aaron would be true to his word. Grace shook her head.

"I'm not sure. But *this* . . ." She motioned at the hotel behind them. ". . . is the only place I've ever been where I've felt like I could truly be me."

Chloe thought about it for a moment. There was something alluring about it all, a safety in its complete isolation. The beauty of the lake didn't hurt either.

"This place is *hers,* Chloe," continued Grace, "and therefore it's *ours* too. Because we *belong* to her. That's how I see it anyway. The mark doesn't have to be a curse, it could be a blessing. Everything you've ever been led to believe that your life would be doesn't matter here—there's no school, no rules, no parents. This is a safe space for people like *us*—there's a different future for you if you choose it, Chloe. You just have to reach out and take it."

The words were coming fast and passionately, and Chloe was struggling to keep up. Her understanding of the Bone Queen was of something so powerful Erin Henderson had murdered her parents to keep it at bay. And yet Grace was talking about her as if she was something almost benevolent.

"So what did Aaron mean last night about preparing ourselves?"

"You'll find out soon enough," she said and then turned and headed back towards the hotel.

Chloe walked down to the piazza and began to explore the area around it on her own, partly to give herself some space to think. Some of that conversation had rung true with her—this *did* feel like an opportunity to step out of the life she'd been living. There was certainly something tempting about it. She wouldn't have to worry about homework or teachers, or the other girls at school bitching about her. Her mum wouldn't be on her case either. That relationship had become so much more strained since her dad had left home. And then there was her dad: with each passing day, he felt more and more like a stranger. An ineffective older brother rather than someone who held any sway over her life.

As she wandered through the long grass thinking about it, she could see plenty of relics that the film production company had left behind. Large wooden trolleys loaded up with huge lamps full of broken glass. Scaffolding, like giant bits of Meccano in the weeds, and there was even an old iron tower which looked like a relic from the Second World War. The sort of thing soldiers shone searchlights down from. Rusting and decrepit, it creaked in the wind. The whole place felt decaying and off kilter and she decided to head back and see if any of the others had woken up yet.

She made her way towards the spectacular domed building which ran adjacent to the piazza. From behind, it was far from impressive, just a flat two-dimensional facade held up by corroding iron supports. Rainwater had pooled at its base and the whole area smelt rotten. Now that she was close, she could hear it rasping like the tower behind her and she wondered just how safe it was. Surely, it hadn't been designed to last this long. As she made her way around, she heard a voice, which she recognized immediately as Grace's. It was a one-way conversation and sounded like a phone call, which was odd because phones were supposed to be banned. It would explain why she'd been up so early, so she could sneak out and do this undetected.

Chloe stepped closer to the back of the fake building to try and eavesdrop. It was hard because of the wind but the exchange sounded almost subservient. Lots of *"I will's"* and *"I'll try's"* and her tone was markedly different to the one she'd used with Chloe. Maneuvering her way around to the side of the fake palazzo she found a small gap behind the first two wagons in the horseshoe. From there, she could see Grace hunched on her own, clearly pocketing a phone before walking back in the direction of the hotel.

Pressing her back against the caravan she thought hard about what to do next. Grace was the person who gathered food and supplies for the group. It would be much easier for her to get her hands on a phone if she really wanted one. But given how committed she was to the cause here it seemed odd. So, who had she been talking to and why? There clearly wasn't any love lost between her and her father.

Chloe didn't mention what she'd seen to any of the others, but she began to think about that phone and where it might now be. Grace probably wasn't carrying it on her person, and the discreet way she'd made the call suggested she hadn't wanted Aaron to know about it either. She might have hidden it somewhere, secreted perhaps in the woods. But there was also another possibility.

The disused hotel was relatively small, with around eighteen rooms spread across three floors. Chloe knew which room was Grace's and picked her moment when everything seemed quiet. The others were either downstairs or relaxing by the caravans. She crept along the long corridor and knocked at the scratched wooden door. The floorboard gave an incriminating creak as she waited but there was no reply. She tried the handle and pushed it open. That it was unlocked wasn't altogether a surprise. Grace had warned her not to lock her own room. Most of the hotel's spare keys had been lost over the years, so if anyone mislaid a key, there would be no way back in.

Chloe saw a room very similar to her own. It was marginally larger and considerably messier. Moving quickly, she searched the place but couldn't find any trace of a phone. She tried under the bed, in the single old, rickety clothes cupboard and the shower room but there was nothing. She was about to give up when she had one last thought and grabbed a small wooden chair from the corner. Lifting away some of Grace's clothes she took it over to the cupboard and used it to stand on. There, at the top, just out of sight, she found what she was looking for.

She retrieved the handset and then coughed as she was enveloped by a cloud of dust. Waiting for a second in case anyone had heard her she sat back down on the chair. Switching the device on, she waited as it came to life and then smiled when she realized her luck was in. This was a cheap burner, not Grace's own phone and it wasn't locked. She could use it to call anyone she liked. More than that she could delete any evidence of using it afterwards and Grace would be none the wiser.

It was now or never; she could phone home if she wanted and tell her mum she'd made a huge mistake. Then the words came back like a sharp whisper in her ear:

"The moment you know about the Bone Queen, she knows about you."

She felt a chill run through her, a familiar nagging itch on the skin of her arm. There could be no question of leaving, not until this was over, however it played out. Slowly, she stood back up on the chair and put the phone back where she'd found it.

Chapter 39

Today

Liam Tandy poured himself a cup of coffee from the machine in the corner of his office and collapsed into the chair behind his desk. He took a sip, scowled, and put the cup down. He didn't really care about the quality of the coffee, but after the afternoon he'd just endured the only requirement was that it be hot. Instead, he swallowed a mouthful of tepid liquid and sighed.

The girl they'd found washed up on the shore was called Kayla McDonnell. She came from Dumfries in Scotland and had been missing for sixteen days. Identifying her, as it turned out, hadn't been too difficult. She'd had a large birthmark on her right upper forearm that looked a bit like the shape of France. When they'd searched the system, cross-checking distinctive birthmarks against the current roster of missing teenage girls nationally, it hadn't taken long to pull up a picture of Kayla. From there he'd been certain that they'd solved the mystery of who she was, if not how she'd come to meet her death.

The next task had been to inform her parents, and Dumfries and Galloway police had supplied him with the relevant contact details.

There were some uncomfortable similarities to Chloe Tipton. Kayla, it emerged, had also been obsessed with the story of the Bone Queen and even Liam was now starting to acknowledge a pattern. Unlike Chloe though, she'd left little clue that she'd intended to travel to Athelsea. Nevertheless, somehow that's where she'd ended up and now her distraught parents were en route to the island.

That was two deaths now in quick succession in a place where these things were rare events. He'd also now received formal confirmation that the bones they'd found in the sea did indeed belong to Adam Nicks. Their discovery seemed to have been the catalyst for all this, and Jenna had been right about one thing—the Bone Queen was the common denominator.

At the back of his mind, he felt guilty about Jenna. There was a very real danger that whatever fate had befallen Kayla McDonnell might also have happened to Chloe. The sea around Athelsea had already given up two bodies this week, and he hoped that was the end of it. There was something else she'd said that was also nagging at him.

He did a quick search of her name on the internet and a fairly long list of results appeared. Most were stories she'd worked on as a journalist which carried her byline. She'd done some seriously impressive work over the years. Her career seemed to have peaked in 2018 with a much-publicized exposé of abuse at a London care home for a national newspaper. But instead of kicking on, she then seemed to have disappeared, resurfacing a couple of years later as an online journalist.

He tried her social media next and found her on LinkedIn, Facebook—which she didn't seem to use much—and Instagram. She'd also been on Twitter but appeared to have stopped posting once it had rebranded itself as X. Her Insta was public and there wasn't too much there, but he began scrolling through it anyway. There were some pictures of an overweight tabby cat, a younger version of Chloe before she'd dyed her hair pink, but very few of Jenna herself.

Right at the bottom he found what he was looking for. There were two pictures that had been posted together in 2022. They were of a well-tended cemetery on a sunny day. The first was a wide shot of the place, the second a specific grave with a fresh bunch of purple flowers laid on it. Underneath, Jenna had posted *#hattie #annualpilgrimage.* The words written on the headstone read:

BELOVED DAUGHTER AND SISTER

HARRIET TIPTON

Dec 18th 1983
July 18th 1996

Chapter 40

"Just tell me what you're thinking?" said Hattie. Jenna was once again striding into the woodland surrounding Ravensgate, heading up to the church. She turned to her sister and stopped.

"I want to know who Stella is—and what her connection is to the Bone Queen. And I think Sheelagh might have the answer. There's not much about this community she doesn't know."

Hattie was struggling to keep up, literally and metaphorically.

"So, do you think she's with Chloe? This Stella person?"

"I don't know—but I want to know where it happened, where Eleanor Aubney was either born or killed because I think that's where Chloe's gone. If the Bone Queen comes back to Athelsea every twenty-two years, then where else is she going to go?"

As if on cue, the patter of raindrops began to fall around them, and the firs and pine trees began swaying in the wind. Jenna smiled grimly at her sister.

"See."

"What?"

"She knows . . ."

Hattie looked around as the rain rapidly began to increase in intensity. "She's trying to stop us again, isn't she?"

Jenna nodded. "Just you and me now, Hat," she said to the sister who wasn't there and then turned and marched on with renewed determination.

Sheelagh Deeney listened as the wind howled around the building outside. It felt like everything was falling apart. The Bone Queen was coming, had always been coming, and now it seemed Judgment Day was upon them all. They deserved it too because they'd let Lily down. She'd been one of them, part of their group of friends and they'd failed her. In her mind's eye, she could see Adam's dead body lying in the dirt, could see also what happened next . . .

She began to tidy the church for want of something to do—she was certainly in no rush to return to the Rectory and spend her evening waiting for the inevitable. There was a strange desire to put her house in order before the devil came a-calling. When the moment arrived she wanted to look the creature in the eye because she wasn't going to die carrying guilt and regret.

Walking over to the utility cupboard at the back of the church to fetch a broom, she felt a dull thudding pain in the back of her head. As she began to sweep up, it quickly developed into an absolute skullcracker of a headache. The more she tried to move around, the more it seemed to pulsate and in the end became too painful to ignore. She found some painkillers in her bag, collapsed onto one of the pews, and began massaging her temples with her thumbs. She heard a noise underneath the wind whistling through the broken windows and looked up, her head spiking with pain at the sudden movement.

"Hello?" she called out, but no one answered.

The wind died down and then she heard it again. It was like an old man sucking slowly on a sweet. She'd heard it before too on a hot, sunny day a long time ago and she wondered if she was imagining this, manifesting the damned thing into existence. But the sound hadn't gone away and if anything, she could hear it even more loudly now, ominous and close.

Her heart was starting to beat faster, almost in sync with the thumping pain in her head. She walked over to the entrance. Another blast of wind swept through and made her jump. She pulled the door open. It was only mid-afternoon, but the sky outside was dark charcoal gray, the rain tipping down into the cemetery.

"Is there anybody there?" she called, looking around but couldn't see anything. Then, in front, she thought she saw a cat staring up at her. She stepped closer and understood with horror what it actually was. On the weed-strewn path were two disembodied eyeballs, nestling in a viscous pool of dark liquid.

Behind her, she heard that slurred, dragging noise again. She turned and realized it was coming from the graveyard. It seemed to be everywhere now, loud like something heaving itself from the very depths of hell itself. The wind blew once more and a loose bit of masonry smashed down next to her making her jump. Briefly, out there in the gloom, she saw it—the outline of a woman, white teeth bared and a stare of accusation that had been over two decades in the making. The shape began to advance as the gale whipped up.

"I swear I'm not hiking up this hill one more time," said Hattie as they walked through the graveyard of St. Hugh's church.

Jenna smiled. "I couldn't have done this without you. You know that right? I'd be on my own, I'd have no one."

"I know," came the reply, the whinging tone dissipating. "That's why I'm here. To the end—wherever this takes us."

Jenna stopped and closed her eyes, dismissing a memory from long ago and forced herself to focus on the present. She could see the lights on inside the church and quickened her pace.

It was only as she approached the entrance that she saw she was too late. Lying on the ground in front of her was the prone form of Sheelagh Deeney. A huge chunk of masonry was lying next to her, and she was quite dead. Her head had been split apart. Blood, bone, and brain matter were spilt out onto the mildewed flagstones. As Jenna stopped in horror, once again the reedy voice of Nina Yates came back to her.

"They were all marked and one day she'll collect."

Chapter 41

2003

Ben had visited the mainland on many occasions. When he was a child, his parents used to take him over as a treat to see the Christmas lights at Mousehole Harbour. He'd dated a girl from Plymouth when he was eighteen and had frequently traveled across to see her. But he'd only been to London once and he'd hated it. It had been so *full*—all human life spilling out of its buses, tube trains, and shops. Streets full of gridlocked vehicles, and a general sense of wary unfriendliness as people passed you on the pavement. Frank often talked with great enthusiasm about leaving the island and building a life there, but it wasn't for Ben. As he lay beneath the baking sun, he was certain he'd stay on Athelsea for the rest of his days. It was home, after all.

He glanced across at Katrina. She and Frank were dozing next to Sheelagh. They were lying on their towels, each with one arm extended, gently holding hands. Try as he might, he couldn't stop himself feeling a burst of jealousy and just a little venom too. He was sure there'd been something nice building between him and Kat before Frank had muscled his way in. He instantly felt guilty; he'd known them both too long to hold any genuine enmity. What would be, would be. A shriek pierced the silence, shrill and piercing, and all four of them sat up, instantly alert.

Ben recognized it instantly as Ruth. As they all looked around fearfully, they knew then that something terrible had happened. He'd remember that feeling later—the certainty, even before it revealed itself. Simultaneously, he'd also known that Adam was at the center of it. They heard the pitter-patter of feet and turned to see Ruth running towards them, pulling Josh along with her from the scrubland behind. She was in tears, a wild expression in her eyes and they were both covered in blood. Her yellow T-shirt was soaked through, her arms and hands bright red and dripping.

"They're dead," she screamed as soon as she saw them.

Frank was already on his feet.

"What are you talking about?" he said as Ben, Sheelagh, and Katrina all rose to join him. For a second Ruth couldn't speak and just stood there taking huge gulps of air. The most terrifying thing about the whole tableau wasn't Ruth though, it was the expression on Josh's face. Traumatized didn't cover it. He was shaking hard, the look in his eyes far away and distant. He'd seen *something*—that much was obvious.

"Adam and Lily," said Ruth finally.

"Show us," said Frank.

As she led them through, part of Ben was hoping that Ruth had got this very wrong. Maybe someone had just hurt themselves and she was overreacting. A few moments later, he knew without any shadow of a doubt that she wasn't mistaken. Lily was lying on the ground, face up. Her expression was strangely quizzical as if she was searching for something in the sky above. Blood was leaking out of the back of her shattered skull and Ben could see bits of white bone mingling with the leaves and dirt. In the heat, the flies were already starting to congregate.

Adam was lying a few feet away and they all stopped when they saw him. His head was resting on the back of his shoulders staring at them from an impossible angle. Frank immediately leant down and checked Lily's pulse. It was a sensible thing to do, but utterly pointless. Ruth was now holding back, still holding Josh by the hand. For obvious reasons, she didn't want to bring him any closer. Ben turned back to them and forced a smile from somewhere.

"Did you see what happened, Josh?" he said.

For a second it looked like the boy was too far gone to answer and then his eyes centered on Ben. He tried to speak, but his mouth quivered, and he couldn't find the words.

"It's okay mate, take your time."

The boy looked up at Ruth uncertainly, then suddenly yanked his hand from hers and ran into the woods. The suddenness of it took them all by surprise.

"I'll go," said Sheelagh, immediately setting off in pursuit. Ben turned to Ruth as Frank and Katrina came over to join them.

"What happened?"

She looked confused now, wearing almost the same dazed expression as Josh. She scratched absently at her arm. It was only then that Ben noticed how raw the skin there looked.

"I don't know, I can't remember. I was lying in the sun with you and then the next minute I was here . . ."

"You're going to have to do better than that, Ruthie," said Frank, but she was shaking again, as if only suddenly now aware of just how much blood she had on her.

Ben tried to rationalize it. They'd all seen Adam getting physical with Lily before over the last few months, had all pretended that it wasn't going on. Had it got out of hand, escalated into *this* somehow?

"They must have got into a fight," he said, looking around. "Adam pushes her, and she hits her head on that rock. He's so shocked by what he's done that he backs away, then falls and . . ."

Katrina stared at Ben as if he was mad.

"Look at the state of him Ben, how do you fall and do *that* to yourself?"

He stared at the body and at its unnatural shape. He had no answer to Katrina's question and a terrifying thought struck him.

"No one's going to believe that *we* didn't do this. Think about it—there's no other explanation."

"Except there is, because we *didn't* do it," said Katrina.

"Then maybe someone else is here," said Frank.

"Where? There's nothing here," said Ben, but they all looked around nervously anyway. Katrina was staring at a patch of ground by Adam's hand.

"What's that?" she said, pointing.

They all came over to look. In the dirt, Adam had drawn something resembling a circle. The tip of his finger caked in earth had been in the process of trying to complete it when he'd died.

"Why would you do that with your dying breath?" said Ben.

"To try and tell us something," said Frank. "About *who* did this to them."

"I know what it looks like. I've seen it before," said Katrina, glancing around at them all. "We all have—it's the face of the Bone Queen."

Frank snorted with derision.

"Don't be ridiculous, Kat. You're reading too much into it. It was the last twitch of a dying man's hand."

They all turned as they heard Sheelagh walking back with Josh.

"I'm going to take him back down to the village, away from here," she said quietly, and Ben noticed the way the boy was staring at Ruth now. Something seemed to pass between them as Sheelagh led him away.

"Ruth—are you sure you don't know what happened?" said Ben. "That's a lot of blood you've got on you . . ."

Ruth looked haunted.

"When I found them, I checked to see if Lily was still breathing. That's how I must have done it. I didn't notice."

Katrina was still staring at the circle in the dirt.

"The Bone Queen's meant to be a spirit of vengeance. We all saw what Adam was doing to Lily, and we did nothing about it, and now look what's happened," she whispered.

Frank glared at her.

"This wasn't the Bone Queen and Ben's right: people *will* think we did this. No one's going to believe we were asleep."

"So, what are we going to do?" said Ruth.

Ben opened his mouth to speak and then stopped.

"Can you hear something?" he said, and they all tensed. There was a noise. Something slow, deep, and primal. It didn't seem to be coming from one place, it sounded close and yet distant at the same time. Some great machine? A boat perhaps on the ocean, or something else altogether? Katrina let out a small scream and pointed at Adam and they all swiveled round to look.

His body was twitching. As it moved, blood began to stream from its nostrils and mouth. The eyes remained closed, and the head was lolling uselessly onto its shoulder. The twitching turned into full-on juddering as if there was an electric current passing through the body. With a jolt it pushed forward, giving the impression of sitting upright. Its left arm lifted drunkenly, one finger clearly pointing at the group for a moment. And then for a second time that afternoon, Adam Nicks collapsed and was still.

Chapter 42

Today

Jenna had been surprisingly calm after finding Sheelagh Deeney's body, or at least she had thought she was. She'd immediately called Liam and told him about both Deeney and Katrina Markham. It was only when she heard her own voice out loud, small and childlike, that she'd realized how terrified she was.

"It looks like someone smashed her head in with a brick, but the wind's blowing really hard and there's a lot of fallen masonry around here," she'd heard herself saying.

"Stay calm and wait until I get there," Liam had said, which was easy enough for him to say. She'd felt like she owed it to Sheelagh to stay beside her and then she'd seen those eyeballs, rolling gently in their own mucus, and retreated back into the church. There could be no doubt who they belonged to either.

As horrific as this was, her mind was whirring as she stared at the deserted nave. Another of the circle of friends who'd been there when Lily Yates died was now dead, and that twenty-two-year cycle was repeating again. It was a wheel she was convinced had been turning ever since Eleanor Aubney had died and returned as the Bone Queen. That meant Ben and Ruth were probably next—more than that—they must both know that too. She could only wonder what they were thinking, or what she would do in their shoes because you couldn't run from this thing. Chloe had run *to* it. Where in this gruesome pecking order did her daughter come? She thought again of the girl on the mortuary table, and whether Chloe was already dead, her body waiting to be found in the same terrible state.

When Liam arrived, there was something different about his demeanor. There was little of the warmth she'd received before from him. He'd brought two uniformed constables with him, and his overworked forensics team were now in the process of transferring from the crime scene at Addison Lane to the graveyard. Without a road up to the church, everything seemed to take an age. He was brusque, almost terse, but she put that down to the fact that he now had another dead body on his hands.

"Why were you up here, anyway?" he said as he began inspecting the scene. He'd looked over the detached eyeballs with the studied curiosity of a surveyor checking a wall for damp.

"I wanted to talk to Sheelagh—ask her something. Does the name Stella mean anything to you? Chloe wrote it down, and I think—"

"Were you on your own?" said Liam, cutting across her.

She looked him directly in the eye. "Why? Am I a suspect?"

It hadn't occurred to her that she may be, but these deaths had only taken place after she'd arrived on Athelsea. Even she could see why that might be giving him pause for thought. He asked the two constables to stay with the body and motioned at Jenna to join him inside the church.

"I'm asking you because you're the only potential witness here," he said.

"When I got here the place was . . ." She was about to say *quiet as the grave* but stopped herself. ". . . silent and I didn't see anything either." Liam's mobile began to ring, interrupting them, and he put the phone to his ear and listened for a moment.

"Ben Markham's taken an overdose," he said tonelessly.

When they went back outside a pair of SOCOs were emerging from the path in the woods and beginning to get to work. Liam went over to the two constables who were guarding the body and spoke to them briefly before rejoining Jenna. He breathed out, his breath visible in the cold afternoon air.

"Is he okay?" said Jenna.

"He was found in time—he's been taken to the local hospital, where they'll pump out his stomach."

For a moment Jenna felt guilty at leaving Ben alone with his wife's corpse. She'd been so desperate to find Chloe she hadn't even thought about him. Then she remembered what had killed Katrina, and most likely Sheelagh too and wondered if it wouldn't have perhaps been better if he'd succeeded in taking his own life.

"Come on, I'll walk you back down to the village," said Liam.

"I need to find Chloe—" she began.

"Jenna—you were at both these crime scenes, and I need to take a statement from you. Right now, that's my priority."

There was downright hostility in his voice.

"You can't really believe I had something to do with this?"

The look on his face said otherwise.

"I've taken a lot on trust from you so far—but I'm also starting to remind myself that I barely know you."

"Why would you even say that?"

He looked her hard in the eye. "Do you want to tell me about your sister?"

The question took Jenna by surprise.

"*Hattie?* What about her?"

His eyes were boring into her now and she imagined this was how he viewed a suspect just before he arrested them.

"Back at the harbor you said she was with you, here on Athelsea."

"She is—I couldn't have got through this without her."

"Except she isn't, is she?" Jenna was already shaking her head. "She's dead. I know that she died a long time ago."

"No." Jenna looked around the windswept graveyard for Hattie but couldn't see her.

"She died in 1996," said Liam, more gently now.

Jenna closed her eyes and felt her heart break all over again.

Chapter 43

Côte d'Azur, 1996

"You can't go! Mum *said* you can't go. I'll find them and tell them where you've gone if you do," shouted Hattie.

"You won't," said Jenna, grabbing her straw sun hat. "And you sound like a whiny little brat," she added for good measure. For the third day in a row, the sun was too hot, and the glare was bouncing off the white flagstones around the pool, bright to the eye even in sunglasses. Their parents had left them alone for the afternoon at the villa they were renting while they caught up on some souvenir shopping. The humid air hung with the heavy smell of suntan lotion.

"Those boys on the beach—" began Hattie.

"Étienne and Raphael, you mean?"

"They weren't interested in you; they were *laughing* at you."

Jenna decided she'd had enough. She was sixteen and the three-year gap between them had never felt so wide.

"They told me they'd be at La Fabrique by the beach and also what time they'd be there today. Why would they do that if they weren't interested?" She reached underneath the sun lounger for her flip-flops and slipped them on. "You wouldn't understand anyway—you're just a kid." Hattie was now removing her headphones from her portable CD player, realizing that Jenna was serious.

"You can't go."

"So you keep saying—watch me."

"You're supposed to be watching *me*, remember," she shouted, and Jenna grinned.

"I am watching you—watching you disappear. *Au revoir* baby," she said with a wave and deliberately skipped towards the villa's gates.

"Jenna!" screamed Hattie, but by now her sister was out onto the floral-scented street and heading away without a care in the world.

The precise timbre and pitch of Hattie's final yell had never left her nor the pouting expression on her face. She'd heard it accusingly many times since, in dreams and unguarded moments. The boys hadn't been at the beach when she'd got there and later when she'd returned to the villa, she'd understood the catastrophic mistake she'd made. Hattie was lying facedown in the pool, her long black hair drifting around her, the water tinted dark with her blood. Later they'd find her portable CD player at the bottom of the pool. The assumption had been that Hattie had dropped it, then slipped, smashed her head open, and drowned while trying to retrieve it. All when her sister should have been there with her, watching over her—because that's what sisters do.

What Jenna would remember later was how alone she'd felt in those minutes afterwards. There was no saving her and there was no one else around in the immediate vicinity to even call. The eerie quietness of the scene would never leave her, nor would that image. Later she'd lied, telling her parents she'd felt sick in the sun, gone inside to lie down in the shade, and fallen asleep. It had taken over a year before she'd confessed the truth to them.

In the end, she'd needed to, the shame had been eating away at her from the inside out. She thought it would help to tell them—that they'd understand why she'd lied—but they hadn't. Her father didn't speak to her for months afterwards, simply sitting in his chair in front of the television periodically sighing. Later, they'd diagnose it as catatonic depression, but it wasn't Hattie's death that caused it; it was Jenna's lie. Not long after she told them, she started to find solace in drinking.

Her dead sister had literally haunted her since she'd arrived on Athelsea—a kind supportive sibling who'd been there for her in her hour of need. And now Liam had punctured that bubble, and she was completely alone again.

Chapter 44

Today

Chloe thought she was looking at some sort of sculpture for a moment.

"What is it?" she said, and Marcia smiled. They were standing on a small patch of bare earth at the side of the lake. It hadn't been easy getting there. There were no pathways through the woodland here and they'd had to clamber down through thick bramble to reach it. Marcia had promised her that the effort would be worthwhile and now that they were there, Chloe was far from convinced. They were standing in front of a rotting wooden structure, rising out of the water in front of them. Overgrown vines draped over it like ghostly fingers, trying to drag it back under. Chloe's first assumption was that it had something to do with the old movie set. Something else that had been built and abandoned a long time ago.

"What you're looking at is special, Clo," said Marcia. Chloe bridled at the abbreviation of her name. The only other people who used it were Evie and her parents, and it was jarring to hear it coming from someone else's mouth.

"It doesn't seem that special to me," she said.

"Look at it carefully. It used to be a bridge a long time ago. That's all that's left of it."

Chloe stared again, her eyes alighting on the crumbling timber supports that disappeared into the dank green water around them.

"Am I missing something?"

"This is where it happened," said Marcia as if it were obvious. "It's where Eleanor Aubney was attacked by a pack of men. They set her alight here and threw her into the lake to drown."

Chloe suddenly realized the significance and stared again in awe. Occasionally the soft plop of a small fish broke the surface of the water nearby punctuating the stillness.

"Oh my God, this was where she rose, wasn't it?" she said. "Where it actually happened?"

Marcia nodded. "It's over three hundred years old. It's amazing anything of it still exists."

Every time the wind blew the structure seemed to sway gently, the water lapping quietly against it. A dance the two must have been doing every day for centuries, Chloe thought.

"Can I touch it?"

Marcia smiled. "It doesn't bite."

Chloe scrambled down the final few yards, reached out and placed a hand on the damp wood. It felt like living history under her palm. The act was strangely moving too, the legend now tangible—quite literally in her hand. That the setting was so peaceful made the whole experience even stranger.

Marcia climbed down to join her. The thing itself looked like a skeleton of sorts.

"I've come here a few times now and it never gets boring," said Marcia, and Chloe immediately understood why she felt like that. The most terrifying part was that you could so easily picture the Bone Queen rising from these waters, ready to take her revenge on the world. If Chloe had been here on her own, then she almost certainly would have been scared out of her wits. Marcia's presence and the quietness of the scene made it feel different though. There was something reverent about it, beautiful almost.

"I still don't understand how Aaron's going to remove the mark. What does he actually *do*?" she said.

Marcia shrugged. "I don't know, but I believe him when he says he can. Don't you?"

Chloe considered it, idly studying the decaying, majestic thing in front of them. Now that they were close, she could see carvings all over it, different versions of the Bone Queen's sigil visible despite the decay.

"But why *Aaron,* what's so special about him?"

Marcia looked round to check they were alone, which was absurd given how difficult getting down here had been. They'd have heard anyone else approaching way before they even got close.

"Because he's *seen* her with his own eyes. She came for him once but didn't take him. No one else has ever done that and survived without making a sacrifice."

Chloe remembered the way he'd described his encounter with her. She hadn't doubted the truth of it then and still didn't. "I think there's a good reason for that, and it's just my theory," continued Marcia, "but he had a difficult childhood, I know that much. There are a few things about it that he's told me, but he gets really touchy when you ask him about it." She broke off and stared across the water.

Chloe followed her gaze and saw what had caught her eye. A small rowing boat was making its way over. She could just about see Grace in the middle of it, pushing the oars in a steady rhythm, creating a small ripple around her as she edged forward.

"Where's she been?" said Chloe thoughtfully.

"Gathering more supplies probably," said Marcia.

Momentarily, Chloe wondered whether to tell her about the call she'd seen Grace making earlier, but her instinct told her not to.

"Do you trust Grace?" she said probing carefully, and the other girl shot her a look, instantly alert.

"Of course. Why do you ask?"

"Because sometimes I can't tell what she's really thinking, I suppose."

It was a deliberately neutral statement, enough there though to develop if Marcia wanted to, but she simply smiled.

"She's been marked, just like you and me and wants it removed the same way we do. It makes her jittery sometimes, that's all. Why, what is it?" said Marcia, watching her more closely now. Chloe furrowed her brow, aware she needed to get this right.

"Everywhere else the Bone Queen has been, the only way people have escaped has been by offering her someone in their place, right?"

"So what are you trying to say?"

"Just now, you said Aaron was the only person who'd seen her and lived without doing that. So, what did *he* do that saved him?"

Chapter 45

Katrina Markham's body was still in the kitchen where her husband had found it. The guesthouse was now a crime scene or at least it would be in due course. A constable stood protecting the entrance, which was the extent of the police response that Liam's meager resources could manage so soon after the discovery at the church. When they arrived, Liam forbade Jenna from entering the building. She waited patiently outside with another officer as he went in to inspect the scene for himself. Truth be told, she'd had little appetite to follow him in anyway.

"You need to start going on the front foot, Jen," urged Hattie. "Whatever's going down has begun. You need to *do* something."

It was good to hear her voice again, even if the emotions it brought were bittersweet. So much of the pain in Jenna's life had come from losing Hattie. She'd always known her drinking had been rooted in that loss too. That her sister was here—in some form anyway—when she most needed her, had been important. She hadn't been lying when she'd told Liam that she couldn't have managed without Hattie. She watched as the detective marched out of the front door of the guesthouse. He stopped to mutter some words to the PC manning it and then came over to join her.

"I'm going to be tied up here for a while. My colleague will sort out a room for you at one of the harborside B&Bs."

She could tell he was trying to sound calm and businesslike but wasn't fooled. Whatever he'd seen in there had shaken him, she could see it on his face and hear it in his voice too. She was beginning to get a sense that he was just a little bit overwhelmed by what was happening and couldn't blame him. Hattie—or at least that part of her subconscious she represented—was right. Events were now moving at speed.

"You don't want to put me in a prison cell then?"

Liam looked guilty for a moment.

"Judging from the way the blood's congealed around the wound her throat must have been cut a few hours ago before she was brought here. If you'd done it, you'd be covered in blood, and you also have a cast-iron alibi: *me*—because we were at the morgue together then."

Jenna nodded. "Thank you."

"I'm sorry if I was a bit harsh with you earlier."

"What about her eyes?" said Jenna, ignoring his apology. It was the question that had been silently stalking her; whether the mutilation had occurred before or after death. In her mind, she could still see the cheerful smile on Katrina Markham's face when she'd first arrived here—the natural warmth in those chestnut-brown eyes. Liam shrugged helplessly.

"We won't know when that was done until the autopsy's complete." He shook his head. "Ben must have decided to take matters in his own hands after he found her."

Whatever else had gone on here, Jenna could see how much Katrina had meant to him and she felt another pang of sympathy.

"I think this is all about silencing witnesses," he continued. "Someone's clearly targeting those people who were with Lily Yates on the day she died. I know she had some cousins on the mainland—in the

Hampshire area I think—I'm going to talk to my colleagues over there and see what they know," he said confidently.

"Good luck with that," said Hattie.

"I'll get someone to run you to the harbor and book you into a hotel," he said. "We need to clear the area now and let my people get to work."

Jenna was already shaking her head.

"I'm not going anywhere. They're nearly all dead now—can't you see it? The Bone Queen is collecting these people, and my daughter might be next."

She could see straightaway that she'd taken a step backwards with him again.

"Jenna—"

"You didn't answer me earlier. Do you know anyone in Ravensgate called Stella? Does that name mean anything to you?"

He shrugged helplessly.

"No, I don't know what you're talking about."

"I told you—it's a name Chloe wrote down, why I think she came here. I need to find her."

She turned and started walking towards the road.

"What are you going to do?" he called out to her.

"Whatever I have to," she replied without turning.

Chapter 46

The Lady Magdalene Hospital was a small twenty-bed building situated roughly at the center of the island, only a few miles from Ravensgate village. Its first foundation stone had been laid in 1901 although it was believed the hospital was built on the site of the original infirmary that had served Athelsea Jail back in the 1700s. A small red car pulled up outside and Ruth O'Brien stepped out and walked calmly up to the main entrance. She smiled at the young woman behind the reception desk and asked where she could find Ben Markham. The receptionist smiled sympathetically, gave her the information she required, and offered her a boiled sweet from a bowl on the counter. Ruth walked through following the directions she'd been given, smiled pleasantly at the bored-looking constable guarding Ben's ward, and then breezed inside.

She pulled a screen around Ben's bed and took a seat next to him.

"How are you feeling?" she said, placing her bag on her lap, her voice oozing with honeyed concern. He propped himself up, pleased to see a friendly face.

"Like I've been hit by a ton of bricks." He sounded like he'd been gargling shards of glass. "But I think that's the sedatives they gave me. Thanks for coming over, it's good to see a friend. It's just you and me now, Ruthie."

He looked at breaking point.

"Why did you do it?" she said.

He swallowed and breathed out, wincing as he did so. The effect of having his stomach pumped had left everything feeling sore. "Why do you think?" he replied.

Ruth nodded understandingly. "You thought you'd end things yourself—before *she* came for you?"

He nodded. "You didn't see what happened to Kat. Her throat had been cut, and she'd been left to bleed out like a pig in a slaughterhouse. And her eyes, Ruth . . ." He put his head in his hands unable to finish. Ruth unwrapped the sweet she'd been given and popped it in her mouth.

"Maybe she deserved it, have you considered that?" she said brightly.

Ben was nonplussed for a moment, unable to believe what he'd just heard as Ruth sucked noisily on the sweet.

"Did you really think there wouldn't be a price to pay?"

She smiled sweetly, still rolling the sweet around her mouth. Absently, she scratched at her arm.

"Who are you trying to convince, Ben? I can see the fear in your eyes. We were *marked* that day and you've always known it," she said. "Adam told us as much, even *after* he'd died. It was perhaps the most useful thing he ever did." She shook her head. "You didn't really believe that you could live on *this* island and think she wouldn't come after you?"

Ben stared at her and didn't recognize the woman he'd known almost his entire life. "Kat always thought you were mad," he muttered.

He felt light-headed and just wanted her to go now. He didn't need this—whatever it was.

"That wasn't the worst analogy you made earlier," she said. "Katrina squealed *exactly* like a pig in a slaughterhouse when she died."

She crunched on the sweet loudly and watched the realization crystallize in his eyes and then started fishing in her bag for something.

"You?" he said. "You did this to—?"

He broke off because something was happening to Ruth. Her face seemed to be shimmering in the half-light, her features blurring. Before he could react, he felt a sudden sharp pain in his midriff. He looked down in astonishment and stared at the small knife handle jutting out from it and wheezed instead. Liquid was bubbling up in his chest, a heat spreading across it and the room seemed to be darkening. He tried to focus on the face leaning over him but couldn't and let out his last breath with a gentle sigh. She pulled the blanket to cover over the blood leaking freely now onto the sheets and from a distance he looked as if he were merely sleeping.

"Hush now," she said, her own face back in place. She picked up her bag, squeezed through the screen, and walked out of the ward. She smiled politely again at the police constable outside and returned to her car. Over the last few days, the blackouts she'd been experiencing had stopped. Where once she'd been confused by these moments, now she had perfect clarity about who she was and where she needed to go next. She scratched her arm and as she buckled up, was aware she didn't have much time and pulled her phone from her pocket.

Chapter 47

Jenna found a bench in the middle of the village and sat down. She literally had nowhere else to go, but was beyond caring. She imagined Ruth O'Brien would be the next to die and then the only person left on Athelsea who'd been marked was Chloe. It was now or never. She had to find her and protect her, somehow. She pulled up the picture she'd taken of the piece of paper Chloe had left in her bedroom and expanded the image. Her imagination hadn't been playing tricks on her—it was definitely the word *"Stella"* written at the side. As she looked again there seemed to be a second word next to it. It had been scribbled over, so was hard to decipher.

At first, she thought it was a surname. Stella Norris, perhaps? She racked her brains. Why was this person so important—was she the individual who'd lured Chloe here with some promise of lifting the mark? Jenna exhaled with frustration. So much seemed to rest on this and she was sitting on a bench in a cold, dark village trying to decipher a single word under her daughter's scrawl.

Eventually, after a few false starts she thought she'd identified the first letter as an "M."

"Stella Morris?" she wondered out loud. The size of the word made it look a decent fit and she tried googling that in combination with "Athelsea" and "Ravensgate." She didn't find anyone by that name and swore. She tried some different combinations—Stella Marie, Moss, Massey but all to no avail. It was when, more in hope than expectation, that she entered Stella Marris that she got some joy.

At first, it wasn't immediately obvious and then she saw it—not a name, but a phrase and it stopped her in her tracks. She found Liam's number and called him straightaway.

"Slow down," he said a few moments later. "And say that again."

"Not Stella Marris—Stella *Maris,*" said Jenna urgently.

There was a pause as he processed what she'd just said. "I don't understand, who or what is that?"

"It's Latin; it means The Star of the Sea."

"I'm sorry Jenna, I'm not sure what you're trying to tell me and I've kind of got my hands full in case you hadn't noticed."

She could hear the tick of irritation in his voice and ignored it. "It's the name of a yacht in Miami, a beach house in New Zealand, and a restaurant on the Greek island of Kos . . ." she said.

"Brilliant," said Liam, his patience sounding like it had almost reached its limit. "But do you want to explain to me how this is relevant?"

She could hear voices in the background which she guessed were members of his forensics team. "Because it's also the name of a hotel that used to be on Athelsea a long time ago. I found a record of a winding-up order online. It's by a lake somewhere—"

"The *lake*?" cut in Liam. "Nobody lives up there. It's just a wilderness, and it's miles from the village."

"It's called *Ravensgate* Lake despite the distance. I think that hotel's still there, and more than that, I think it's where the legend of the Bone Queen began."

"In a hotel room?"

Jenna looked up at the café's ceiling light. "Of course not, but I should have put it together before. The legend always talks about Eleanor Aubney *rising*—but rising from where? What if she rose from *that* lake? I want to go over there—now."

"Jenna, just wait—"

But she'd already hung up.

Jenna could hear her footsteps echoing across the cobblestones as she strode through the deserted village. The woods loomed above her, a wall of twisted trees and shadows that sounded like they were whispering secrets in the blowing wind. The hill with the Gallows Tree felt increasingly like a dividing line separating more than just the two physical worlds of Ravensgate and its surrounding forest. Her phone was giving her a rough idea of the route up to the lake, but it was going to be another long hike in the dark. She also had no idea how she was going to get across the water either. She'd cross that bridge when she came to it, she thought mirthlessly.

The hum of an engine made her look up and she saw a car coming towards her. As she moved to let it pass, it slowed to a halt and the driver's window glided down.

"If you're going to go up there, at least let me give you a lift," said Liam in his soft Irish drawl. Jenna found a tired smile and gratefully walked round and jumped in.

"You don't have to do this," she said. "You've got two murder scenes on your hands."

"I've also got a duty of care. I can't just let you go up there on your own when there's a killer on the loose. I also know I can't stop you."

"No. You can't," she said. "You don't think I'll find Chloe there, do you?" she added, looking across at the policeman. There was no street lighting, just narrow twisting country roads now that they were clear of the village.

"Even if that hotel is still standing, why would anybody be living in it? There's no power, no water, no food. It's freezing and it's dark and it makes no sense."

"It makes sense because that's where the Bone Queen rose," said Hattie and Jenna nodded in agreement almost imperceptibly.

"I think it's the only place left she can be," she said.

"And if she's not, then what will you do?"

Jenna exhaled. "I honestly have no idea."

They carried on driving for another ten minutes or so. Finally, the road crested into a rise and there, unfolding before them, was the vast expanse of the lake. Jenna leant forward to take the scene in. In her mind's eye, she'd imagined something much smaller in scale, but even at night, it was spectacular. Ringed by silhouettes of distant hills, a bright silver moon hung in the sky above, its light cutting across the water like an invitation.

He brought the car to a halt and they both got out. Immediately, Jenna saw a group of small rowing boats moored at the water's edge.

"They belong to some of the people in the village, it's not proof of anyone living over there," said Liam guessing what she was thinking.

"No—but it *is* a way of getting across." She stared over at the landmass on the other side but it was too dark to make anything out. All she could see were the outlines of yet more hills. "I take it there isn't a road that goes round?"

Liam shook his head.

"No, that side of the lake is only accessible by water, and on the other side of those hills is the Atlantic Ocean." Even Jenna's conviction was starting to crack a little—was Chloe really over there? "It would make more sense to wait until the morning. I might have a few extra officers freed up to go with you then too," he added.

Jenna thought about Ruth again. Privately, she very much doubted Liam's morning was going to be any easier than his evening had been.

"No, this is the perfect time. I'll take a quick look around under the cover of dark and then come straight back. If people are living there, then they won't see me, will they? I can get a sense of what's going on and then give you a call. How does that sound? A reconnaissance trip, that's all."

"Liar," said Hattie and she wasn't wrong.

Liam nodded and Jenna walked over to one of the rowing boats and peered into it for a moment.

"Any sign of trouble—and I mean *any*—you get the hell out of there and call me," said Liam.

She smiled back at him. "Do you need me to salute?"

"Just be careful."

He helped her push the boat onto the water and watched as she stepped into it. Sitting down, she picked up the oars and he gave the small vessel another shove to get her moving. Tentatively she began propelling herself backward. She turned briefly and raised a hand, and he waved back, watching her slowly inch forward into the inky blackness.

Chapter 48

Jenna felt a strange calm as she slowly progressed across the lake. She knew full well that she may be placing too much faith in the idea, but she was certain now she was finally heading towards a reunion with her daughter

"You've got this," whispered Hattie as Jenna focused on the landmass ahead. So far there had been no surprises, no storms, or birds falling from the sky, just a cold breeze as the boat moved forward. She had a fair idea of what to expect now—a disused hotel and more of the seemingly endless woodland that encircled the whole island. What she didn't know was *who* else was over there waiting for her. She was certain the Bone Queen had killed Frank, Sheelagh, and Katrina and if she was right then she was rowing into the belly of the beast.

As she approached the shore, she could see a small wooden jetty coming into view. There was a narrow patch of land there before the incline of the steep hill behind it. She'd been on undercover investigations as a journalist in her time and decided she needed to channel that experience if she wanted to bring Chloe home.

"Think this out rationally," advised her dead sister.

She reached the jetty and jumped onto the wooden boards. Grabbing the boat, she pulled it ashore and stowed it safely away from the water. She could see a well-worn path leading up into the woodland.

"She may not want to come back," said Hattie. "You still haven't addressed that."

"You're not helping," said Jenna.

Before, her sister had been a source of support, but since she'd confronted the subject with Liam, Hattie seemed to have morphed into the sum of all her fears, nagging at her when she least needed it.

"There is no Hattie," she said to herself. "Hattie's gone," and this time there was no reply.

She shivered. It seemed even colder on this side of the water than it had been in Ravensgate. The type of cold that cuts through clothing and chills you to the core. The canopy of leaves above wasn't helping either. In the murk, she couldn't see the odd stray branch until it struck her head, and each step seemed to get steeper and steeper.

As the hill finally plateaued out, she emerged from the woods to see a final row of trees in front of her. She'd been thinking so pessimistically that she hadn't considered what else might happen; that her daughter may be *pleased* to see her, might be cold and hungry and more than ready to leave.

As she walked towards the trees she saw a rusting sign in front of them. Fading red letters on a cream board that said:

Stella Maris—The Star of the Sea
Where dreams come true!

Underneath, someone had graffitied the ubiquitous face of the Bone Queen. It gave her a burst of renewed hope—the hotel *was* here then, or at least had been. She followed the path through the trees and the sight that greeted her on the other side was extraordinary. She'd been expecting a small crumbling building, not this. In the moonlight, her first view of the huge Baroque facade of the palazzo completely took her by surprise.

"What the hell?" she muttered.

She stared at the bonfire in the center of the piazza and felt another surge of adrenaline. *Someone* had lit that fire recently, people were here. Simultaneously, there was excitement at the thought of just how close Chloe might be now, and fear too—Liam's final words of warning ringing in her head. This place looked crazy. For a moment she thought she could be anywhere, at any time. Nineteenth-century Florence, or medieval Annecy. She could see a horseshoe of caravans behind the flames and heard the creaking of iron as the wind rustled up once again.

There was no sign of the hotel, and she wondered if Chloe might be in one of the wagons. As she got closer to the bonfire, she could see the detritus of discarded beer cans and empty crisp packets nearby. There was a sudden movement behind the flames, and she saw a tall figure step forward from the shadows. It was a boy, perhaps no older than Chloe, tall and gaunt and for a moment they locked eyes. He looked as shocked by her presence as she was by his.

"Hi . . ." she croaked, her mouth dry, and the youth turned and ran, disappearing into the darkness. She stood still, unsure of what to do, and could only hear the crackle of the fire and the distant sound of the sea somewhere. She looked up at the palazzo—surely that wasn't the hotel?

She steeled herself and walked closer to the huddle of caravans. There were more signs of life now. Blankets were laid out, weighed down by supermarket bags filled with snacks and cans of drink.

"Hello?" she called out but there was no reply. Behind, she could feel the heat of the fire on the back of her neck and let it warm her for a moment.

"Hold your nerve," said Hattie.

Again, she remembered Liam's advice to leave at the first sign of trouble. Except there was no chance of that now—not when she was this close. Something flashed and she saw a torch beam flickering from behind the wagons. A wiry figure in a hoodie strode out towards her, the tall boy she'd seen before struggling to keep pace behind him.

"Who are you?" snapped the newcomer. His voice was harsh and there was something about his eyes that unnerved her, his gaze severe and unblinking.

"My name's Jenna Tipton," she said courteously. She thought she sounded like she was at a cocktail party and hated herself for it. It was the fear creeping in, and she'd already seen enough to know that she didn't want to show these two that she was scared.

"Chloe's mum?" said the young man with the torch, even as she was already reaching into her bag for one of the flyers. Hearing her daughter's name spoken aloud made her heart jump. She was *here*—she'd found her. The blood rushed to her head and for a moment she forgot about the Bone Queen and everything that had happened in Ravensgate.

"That's right, and I'd very much like to see her."

The man considered her request, the glow of the fire on his face exacerbating that stare of his and she held her ground. Unexpectedly, his stern expression gave way to a laconic smile.

"Yeah—sure, I reckon she'll be pleased to see you too."

Jenna breathed out.

"Thank you. What's your name?" she said.

"I'm Aaron and this is Jack," he replied. There was a slight singsong quality to his voice that she found unsettling. Everything about him was unnerving. He was making her flesh crawl, but she just wanted to see Chloe again and she was so close now. "Come with me," he said. "I'll take you to her. You stay here Jack, in case there's anyone else."

"There's just me, I promise," she said but he ignored her and had already begun walking. She followed him through the caravans and off the piazza onto the long grass behind it. Not far on from there, she saw the small rectangular shape of a building slowly take form. She could see the words *Stella Maris* written on a sign above the door. Some of the letters had faded and in the dark it was almost illegible.

Jenna thought of those scribbled words she'd seen on Chloe's notepad and now here she was. She'd found her, traced her, followed the clues, and got the reward for her persistence. The place was a wreck though. Some of the windows were smashed and broken shutters hung open. It looked like a death trap, and she just wanted to get her daughter out of there. Aaron led her inside—which impossibly seemed even colder—leant over an old wooden counter, reaching for something, and then walked towards a staircase. A yellow light was flickering above them, and Jenna thought she could hear voices from a room behind the counter and held back. Aaron turned, his face impassive.

"She's upstairs."

Jenna peered at the staircase and hesitated. A filthy red oriental runner seemed to lead up into darkness.

"Do you want to see Chloe, or don't you?" he said, then turned and skipped up the steps. She followed him and he led her down a pitch-black corridor before stopping at room number seven. The place smelt of damp and was freezing. Aaron knocked at the door and called out Chloe's name, then turned the handle to open it.

Jenna couldn't stop herself, the smile already spreading across her face, but inside was just darkness. Aaron shoved her and she fell forward. Reaching down he snatched her bag and then slammed the door shut. She heard a key turn in the lock and realized that's what he must have grabbed from behind the counter when they'd arrived.

"Hey!" she yelled but could already hear him marching away down the corridor.

"What have you done, Jen?" said Hattie.

Chapter 49

Alone in her room, Chloe's fear of what the night was about to bring had returned with a vengeance. She thought she'd heard a door slamming somewhere in the building. There was shouting too, a voice that just for a moment seemed familiar, but that was impossible. She was hallucinating, she realized—she must be. The nightmares that had begun when she'd been marked were bleeding into the day, that feeling of reality bending again. She rubbed at her arm and winced in pain, the skin was red-raw to the touch now. She was feeling desperately lonely and didn't trust any of these people—wasn't sure she even *liked* any of them. She felt a longing for connection but there was nobody on this island who could provide it, and she only had herself to blame for that. She was quite alone now, she understood.

Her breaths were shallow, quick gasps of air that were doing little to calm her racing heart. She almost wanted the Bone Queen to arrive now and end this. She buried her head in her hands and felt something wet to her surprise. She was crying and hadn't even noticed. There was a knock at the door, and she quickly wiped the tears away. Grace let herself in and smiled that awkward smile of hers.

"Just wanted to see how you're doing?" she said.

"What was that noise earlier?" said Chloe, turning so that she couldn't see how red her eyes were.

"What noise?" said Grace.

"I heard shouting—a woman. It didn't sound like either Marcia or you."

"You're imagining it. There's no one here but us—how could there be?"

There was silence in the room for a moment—just the wind outside and the usual creaks and rattles the old building made. Grace shrugged. "See?"

Chloe shook her head. "I heard you talking to someone earlier, this morning after we spoke. You were alone on the piazza, and you were using a phone. I saw you with it."

"You were spying on me?"

"Who were you talking to?" They locked eyes and then Grace shrugged.

"Someone on the island. A friend, I suppose—they help me with food and supplies. They know we're over here and are sympathetic."

Chloe looked at her suspiciously. The explanation *sort* of fitted what she'd heard, but Grace had sounded nervous then and looked even more skittish now.

"You're lying," said Chloe, surprising herself as the words came out more from instinct than thought. Instead of getting angry at the accusation, Grace seemed to shrink even further.

"It's the least important thing now. The Bone Queen's coming tonight, Chloe, and I've got a message from Aaron: he wants you to stay in here and when he's ready we'll all go out onto the piazza to face her together."

She was shaking, Chloe noticed. The accusation about the phone call suddenly didn't seem to matter anymore. The reality of what she was saying was penetrating. The moment was drawing close, and the thought of that was paralyzing.

"Promise me you'll stay in here?" said Grace and Chloe nodded.

Jenna was lying on the bed of the small room, furious with herself. She'd been stupid, so keen to see her daughter again that she'd thrown all common sense out the window. Instead, she'd blundered into this situation like a naive teenager and paid the price. She'd thought about shouting for help but it seemed pointless. There was no one who'd come to her rescue and she began to wonder if Chloe now knew that she was here and simply didn't care.

Her thoughts were unexpectedly disturbed when she heard the key turn in the lock . Aaron came through carrying a cup of tea in one hand and what appeared to be a supermarket croissant in the other. The way she was feeling it might as well have been dinner at the Ritz. He put them both down on the side table by her bed.

"Room service now, is it?" she said.

"We're not animals," he replied. She stared down suspiciously and then picked up the tea and took a sip. It was tasteless but hot and that was all that mattered. She tore open the wrapper of the pastry and took a large bite of something sweet and rubbery. Aaron was back to that strange staring inscrutability he'd shown her on the piazza.

"Chloe doesn't want to see you and you need to understand that and leave," he said. The words were like a hammer blow and Jenna put everything into not letting it show.

"I'm not going without her," she replied in the same matter-of-fact tone.

"It's her choice."

He could be lying, but there was a horrible ring of truth to it. The conversation she'd had with Hattie—with *herself*—on the way up from the jetty came back to her.

"I'm sorry for locking you up," said Aaron, "but I need you to accept the truth of the situation."

"And what's that exactly?"

"That Chloe came here for a reason."

"I know," Jenna said. "She'd been marked by the Bone Queen." Aaron just gave her the same glassy stare. "She thought you could lift it from her—but can you?"

"Yes—because I've seen the Bone Queen before—and I survived. She knows me. She has *always* known me."

The way he said the words made her freeze.

"What do you mean? *How* did you survive, what did you do?"

He looked petrified for a moment, the hard exterior suddenly giving way.

"Did you sacrifice someone? Is that what you think will save you?" she persisted.

"No," he said, but the look in his eye was terrifying her.

"Yes, you have—because I saw her on a mortuary table only a few hours ago. That was you, wasn't it? Why you brought my daughter here?"

The pieces were starting to fall into place now for Jenna and even as she asked the question, she wasn't sure she was ready for the answer.

"Blood for blood—that's how this works," he said as if it were obvious, but Jenna shook her head.

"Is my daughter even still alive?" she was shouting the words now. Those large eyes centered on her, and his mouth spread into a leery grin.

"I suggest you think hard about what you want to do," he said and turned to go.

"Don't run away. Tell me what happened to you!" she shouted after him. "Why did you get marked, Aaron? Because there's always a reason . . ."

He turned his head sharply and she wondered if she'd gone too far.

"Chloe's *staying*," he snarled, visibly controlling himself.

"Then let me see her, I want to hear her say that to my face."

His anger gave way to a smile and the speed of the switch chilled her to the bone.

"That can be arranged but be careful what you wish for."

Aaron locked the door behind him and saw Grace waiting for him at the top of the stairs.

"What happened?" she said, whispering. Downstairs he could just about hear the muffled conversation of the others coming from the lounge.

"She drank the tea, which should keep her quiet for a bit. Does Chloe know she's here?" he said.

Grace shook her head. "I told her to stay in her room and Jack's been told not to say anything to her."

"Good, because that woman won't leave the island without her."

"So, what are we going to do?"

"We were going to make a sacrifice tonight." She drew in a small, sharp breath when she realized what he meant.

"We can't. The moment Chloe sees her she won't agree to that."

"So we kill two birds with one stone."

Chapter 50

Liam had returned to the church to talk to the forensics team working at the crime scene there. Sheelagh Deeney's body was still where it had fallen but he was relieved to see that Katrina Markham's eyeballs had at least now been removed and placed in a tagged evidence bag. The logistics of moving the body to the morgue weren't going to be easy. There was no way of getting a coroner's ambulance up here and a stretcher party would have to carry her down through the woods in the dark and he didn't envy them the task.

He also knew where he needed to go next. Ruth O'Brien was the only untouched member of the group of friends. He was certain *someone* knew the truth of those events—that could be the only explanation for what was happening. But the sight of those eyeballs by Sheelagh Deeney's crushed skull, the gashed throat of Katrina Markham, her sightless head tilted back onto her shoulders, spoke of something different.

He made his way back down to the village and walked to Ruth's cottage and rang the bell. If he'd still been with the Metropolitan Police, he'd have had someone in a patrol car outside, but he just didn't have the manpower here. Hopefully she'd see sense and come to a place by the harbor so at least no one would find her if they came to her home. There was no reply, and he peered through the living room window. Inside it was dark—but he could see something that looked odd, and a nasty suspicion began to form.

Picking up an ornamental rock from the front garden, he weighed it in his hand for a moment and then smashed the window. Wrapping his hand into the lining of his coat he pushed out the fragments of the remaining glass in the frame and then climbed through it. The French doors to the garden were wide open. He stepped out onto the patio, and looking down he saw a patch of something dark and touched it. It was sticky and when he held his hand up saw it was blood.

His phone rang and it was the officer he'd left at the hospital with Ben. He quickly told him what they'd found there, and that Ruth had paid Ben a visit only minutes before. Even as he was speaking Liam's eyes alighted on the garden shed, its door flapping open in the wind. One look inside clarified instantly where Katrina Markham's throat had been cut. It was a kill room soaked in blood. No effort had even been made to hide it.

"Her car was sighted heading in the direction of Ravensgate Lake," continued the constable on the phone, oblivious. As realization dawned, the full extent of the mistake he'd made earlier was occurring to Liam.

"Jenna," he murmured.

The headache had come from nowhere and so had the nausea. Jenna was leaning over the sink in the small en suite shower room, retching into it. At first, she'd thought it was just an accumulation of all the stress she'd been under, the toxins flushing through her system. Then she realized it was more than that, something almost certainly in the tea that Aaron had given her earlier. On reflection, there'd been a slightly bitter aftertaste to it, and she should have been smarter. The question was *what* had he given her and why had he done it?

She certainly felt weak now and wondered if this was the fate that had befallen Kayla McDonnell. She felt like she was on fire and yet she also knew the room was freezing cold. The awful thought occurred to her that she'd already lost the fight for her daughter before it had even begun. In an hour or two's time, they'd throw her lifeless body over one of these cliffs and she'd wash up on some shore the same way Kayla had.

Before she could develop that grim thought the bathroom door behind her opened and Jenna turned in astonishment to see a familiar face.

"Chloe?" she said, unable to contain her joy. Her daughter's pink hair had been slicked back and she had a jaundiced look about her face. There was no life or even recognition in her eyes. "What have those bastards done to you?" she said, moving instinctively in to hug her and then stopping when she saw the short stubby knife in her hand. Chloe hissed, like a feral cat bearing its claws, before plunging the blade into her chest. She repeated it in quick staccato jabs until Jenna sank to her knees.

And when she looked again, there was no blood or any sign of anyone else. The liquid she could feel on her face and neck was sweat, and the pain in her stomach, cramping from whatever she'd been dosed with. Taking a deep breath, she put two fingers down her throat and forced herself to vomit into the sink. Shaking, she turned on the tap and wiped her chin, then drank greedily at the mud-colored trickle that came out. It had been so vivid; she could have sworn that it had been her daughter standing there. Even worse, she'd got herself to a place where she could genuinely believe that Chloe might do that. That realization was even worse than the hallucination.

"You've got to pull yourself together," whispered Hattie.

"I know," yelled Jenna back at her and for a second her sister was there too—breathing and as lifelike as Chloe had just seemed. Then the shadows took her, and she was alone again.

"I don't know what's real and what isn't anymore . . ." she said to herself, looking at a face she didn't recognize staring back from the broken mirror.

Aaron was now sitting slumped on a chair in Grace's room. They'd checked on Jenna and heard nothing from outside so had assumed the drugged tea had done its work for the moment.

"I'll give it another hour," he said. "When the time comes I don't want her unconscious, just pliable."

"Ruth's coming over," said Grace. "She called me a few minutes ago. Whatever's been happening in Ravensgate must be over."

Aaron nodded but said nothing and not for the first time since she'd met him, Grace wondered what it was that he wasn't telling her about Ruth. The older woman had helped them both since they'd been living in the hotel, but any mention of her name always seemed to produce an uneasy reaction.

Her own relationship with the woman had only developed relatively recently. Aaron had introduced her as a friend—someone who could help supply them with food without attracting attention from the other villagers. She had explained to Grace some of the island's history. She'd shown her the Gallows Tree and told her about the twenty-two-year cycle. She knew only too well what Grace and the others were going through and had come back to the island to face her own reckoning with the Bone Queen.

Aaron stood and grabbed Grace gently by her shoulders, looking at her carefully.

"Are you ready for this?"

She nodded. She felt on edge, terrified but also strangely euphoric at the thought of what was about to unfold.

"I think so," she said. That fierce stare of Aaron's had never made her feel smaller, like something tiny under a microscope. "Are you certain we'll be okay—that she'll spare us?"

He nodded.

"*Blood for blood* remember—that's what removes the mark. If we get Chloe to kill her own mother then we'll *all* be spared—just like before."

Chapter 51

"How are you feeling?" said Aaron, putting his arm around Chloe's shoulder. He'd gone in to check on her for one last chat before they all headed out to the piazza. In his other hand, he was holding a bottle of vodka.

"I've brought this for you, it'll help you to relax."

Chloe shook her head. "I don't need it. I'm fine."

"It's for your own good. Just think about what's going to happen later." Chloe had been trying very hard *not* to think about that because when she did, the fear returned like a tightening fist in the center of her stomach.

He shrugged.

"It'll help take the edge off your fear."

She stared at the bottle, then grabbed it and took a swig.

"I know how scared you must be but remember why you came here in the first place. It's almost time."

Chloe nodded and scratched her arm mechanically. "I'm ready," she said.

He motioned at the vodka. "Have some more."

She lifted it to her lips again and this time he held the bottom against her mouth, forcing her to swallow more than she'd intended. She coughed and wiped the excess liquid from her chin.

"Trust me—you'll be grateful for it later," he said.

She could already feel her head gently spinning. "If you say so."

"Have you thought about what you might want to do afterwards?" said Aaron.

"How do you mean?"

He opened out his palms. "You're not a prisoner here. You can leave if you want tomorrow. I'm sure your family are very worried about you."

He was looking at her closely and she got the sense he was fishing for something. She explained about her parents' divorce, and the state of her relationship with them before she'd left.

"They wouldn't have understood any of this and I didn't want to hurt either of them. Blood for blood, remember?" she said.

"So you live alone with your mum then?" he said. "It must be difficult when things are that strained?"

Chloe nodded. "She's got her own issues. She lost her sister when she was quite young and she's also a recovering alcoholic." He seemed to react to that, and she immediately felt guilty. Whatever she thought about her mother it had been a cheap thing to reveal to a stranger. "She hasn't drunk in a while though. That's what worries me—how she's coping," she added. Things might have been tense between them, but that didn't mean she didn't care about Jenna, and it suddenly felt important to her that he knew that too.

He pointed at the vodka.

"One more for luck?" Dutifully she took another long swig. She felt hot now and even dizzier. "Good girl," he said and took the bottle off her.

“So, what’s going to happen later?” she said.

“We’ll gather out by the fire, and then when she comes . . .” He searched her out with his eyes again. “. . . there’ll need to be a sacrifice because that’s how this works.”

Chloe’s eyes widened with alarm, and he shook his head.

“Not in the way that you think. She won’t hurt you if you do exactly what I tell you. It’s symbolic. What you sacrifice is *yourself*, your loyalty in return for your safety.” He pulled something from his boot. He was holding a small but sharp-looking ceremonial knife. The type you found in gift shops that sold vapes and cheap booze.

“What’s that for?” she said.

“To make the sacrifice.”

Chloe looked confused. “I don’t understand—if it’s symbolic?”

He smiled as if her mistake was obvious. “It’s not uncommon to see things when the Queen appears. I know I did. They can be anything though—phantoms from your past, friends or family maybe—but to prove yourself you must use this.”

Chloe was hypnotized by the blade. She’d never seen steel that shiny before, reflecting like a mirror. “Why? *How?*”

“Because you have to let go of them, that’s the point. Use this—as hard as you can—and they’ll vanish. The Queen will leave, and you’ll be free. Do you understand?”

Her mind went back to the emails she’d received from *Athelsea100*—or Aaron as she now knew. It felt like an eternity ago. *Blood for blood* she thought again. He offered her the handle and she stared at it uncertainly.

Grace had gone down to the jetty to await Ruth’s arrival. Her heart was pumping harder and faster than she’d ever known it to. She liked Chloe and didn’t want to hurt her, but her fear of the Bone Queen overrode everything.

“We’re as ready as we can be,” said Aaron and she turned to see him walking towards her. Grace reached out a hand and took his, felt it tighten around her own. As they stood listening to the water lapping gently around them, the old rhyme on the Gallows Tree came back to her.

In shadows deep the Bone Queen sleeps,
Beware the night when shadows creep,
For in her gaze the lost bones weep.

In the distance, she saw the small outline of a rowing boat making its way across. As it got closer they could see it moving now at surprising speed, almost following the shimmering pathway cast by the moonlight. A few minutes later, Ruth brought the boat up alongside and jumped across to join them. She looked tired but greeted them both with a smile.

"Where's the woman?" she said straightaway.

"Locked in one of the hotel rooms. I gave her tea with some of the compound you mixed," said Aaron. "Chloe also told me something about her that I think we can use," he said. He explained what he had in mind, and Ruth nodded approvingly.

"Then get everybody out onto the piazza now. She's coming soon—I can feel it."

"What's been happening in the village?" said Grace and Ruth smiled.

"What I always told you would happen in the final days: death. Which is nothing new to Ravensgate, believe me."

Grace thought she saw something change in the older woman's eyes for a moment, like a small emerald fire blazing and dying.

Jenna had managed to calm herself down—that was the good news. The bad news was her head was pounding like a bass drum. It had started small like headaches always do and had steadily got worse. She was lying flat again on the small bed, massaging her temples. She'd been thinking about the conversation she'd had with Aaron earlier to try and distract her from the pain. A suspicion had grown in her mind—how he'd survived that encounter, why he might feel now, twenty-two years later, that he was marked.

The door to the room unlocked and Aaron entered holding a bottle of half-empty vodka in one hand. His eyes were blazing, and she immediately sat up. There was nothing of the restrained civility he'd displayed before.

"What did you put in that tea?" she said, trying to show him she was stronger than she was feeling. The way he was looking at her, it was like he was on something.

"Something to shut you up," he said and took a step closer. "But I can see that didn't work."

He took another step forward.

"When did you see the Queen before, Aaron? What happened?"

He looked feral now, but he stopped advancing and smiled, baring his teeth.

"*Here* on Athelsea. When my dad killed my mum, and the Queen came and struck him down."

Jenna realized what he was saying—and what it meant.

"You're Josh Nicks . . ." she whispered.

The cold fury on his face turned into white heat and that was when she knew she was right. His hand shot out, grabbing her by the throat, taking her by surprise. His grip was like iron, and her bravado was exposed because she was too weak to fight back. She made a strangulated cry, and he pushed her down onto the bed. He was still holding the vodka bottle and as he brought it round, only then did she understand what he was intending to do.

"*No* . . ." she screamed with a mixture of fury and terror, but he ignored her and began pouring the liquid into her mouth. She desperately twisted to turn her head away and it splashed onto her face, into her eyes stinging them viciously. She began coughing and could now feel the burn of the alcohol on her lips and in her throat. He put his knee onto her chest pinning her down, forced her jaw open and then tipped the remainder of the bottle into her mouth.

Chapter 52

Liam hadn't wasted any time. He'd pulled together as many of his team as he could, and they'd gathered with him by the lake for an impromptu briefing. They'd found Ruth's car parked nearby and he was certain that she'd taken one of the boats and had gone over to the other side, even though it still seemed as dark and as silent as ever over there. Occasionally, he thought he saw something in the hills above that might have been from the orange glow of a fire, but it was difficult to tell. Too much time had passed since he'd waved goodbye to Jenna from the same spot. If everything had gone as planned, she should have returned by now and called him. The question troubling him was, who else was over there with Ruth?

"I don't know what's waiting for us," he said, looking at his men as he spoke. "We've got reason to believe Kayla McDonnell may have died on that side and then her body floated round to the eastern shore where we found it. It's also where we think Ruth O'Brien has gone."

He talked them through the lay of the land and what to expect, and some of them raised an eyebrow as he described the derelict hotel and the aging film set.

"Sounds like the place is falling apart—just how dangerous is it?" asked one of the younger ones.

"I've no idea to be honest, so tread carefully," Liam replied. "In the first instance, it's a narrow patch of shore followed by a steep climb up a hill. I'm confident we've got enough numbers to deal with whatever's there, but the key thing is to move quietly because we also think there may be at least two potential hostages. It's going to be dark and difficult terrain, so be careful. Anyone got any questions?"

The eight men shook their heads and Liam gave them the go-ahead to proceed. Fortunately, there were just enough boats to squeeze them all into for the short journey across.

Given the manpower he was taking over this should be straightforward, he thought. So why did he feel so uneasy? The image of the face left next to Katrina Markham's body came to mind again, the single eye staring out accusingly at him. He banished the memory and saw one of the older men, watching him.

"Do you think we'll see her then—the Bone Queen? That's where they say she rose," said the man and Liam scowled at him.

"I don't believe in ghosts, sergeant, and neither should you."

He strode towards the boats and stopped. Just for a second, he'd heard something odd, a sound he couldn't quite identify, slow and deep. But when he listened again, there was nothing.

Jenna was in the dark. After Aaron had finished forcing the vodka down her throat, he'd taken what looked like a bandanna from his pocket and tied it around her face to cover her eyes. She'd then been dragged out of the room and taken outside somewhere. Even in her stupor, she knew that none of it had been done randomly; he was trying to disorient her, mess with her senses in every way that he could. She'd kept a tether to reality by focusing on Chloe. In her mind's eye, she could see her daughter across the kitchen table at home and was holding on to that image with everything she could muster.

She was in shock too. She'd spent so long avoiding alcohol—identified it so closely with the worst moments of her life—Hattie's death and the breakdown of her marriage. What Aaron had done had been invasive and humiliating. Worse still, how did he *know*? Had Chloe told him about her vulnerability? She was drunk, reeling in the dark, the demon inside of her enjoying the sensation despite everything.

"Shut up," said a voice, which she recognized as belonging to the scrawny boy, Jack, she'd met on the piazza earlier. She realized she'd been mumbling, vocalizing at least some of this out loud.

He removed her blindfold and stuffed something into her mouth, a dirty rag that tasted of cooking oil which made her gag. She knew now where she was, inside one of the caravans she'd seen before. It was ornate but dusty, broken crockery lining the shelves around her. Jack was there with a young girl not much older than Chloe and they both looked terrified. She'd been waiting for her moment to escape and now that it had come, she could barely stand unaided. Jack pulled her hands behind her back, and she felt something cold and hard—plastic ties she guessed—binding them together. With an effort, she tried to find the words, make an argument that would cut through and get these children to see sense.

"Chloe," was all that she could manage.

Ruth was sitting alone inside the largest of the caravans in the horseshoe. In any other circumstances, she might have admired her surroundings, this one all polished brown oakwood with red velvet trim and intricate stained glass windows. She was staring at a cracked mirror that hung on the wall opposite, almost entranced by her own face. For over two decades her memories of what had happened on the day that Adam and Lily had died had become increasingly jumbled. The others had convinced her that Adam had killed Lily in a fight and had then died himself in some sort of freak accident. They'd persuaded her to leave Athelsea with Josh and the pair had moved to the mainland where they'd lived quietly together in a small Lancashire village that wasn't so different to Ravensgate.

It had been a calm, uneventful life but she'd always known that something about it wasn't quite right. For many years, the boy she'd renamed Aaron had been terrified of her. It wasn't until his early teens that he'd finally shed that, but a residue of it remained to this day. More than that, she could *feel* the passenger she was carrying, had known there was one even if she didn't quite understand it. Athelsea had never left her, the pull of the place so strong that she'd always known she'd have to come back here one day. Aaron had felt it too. Ahead of the twenty-second anniversary of their departure, she'd brought him home to try and free them both of the burden they'd been carrying all their lives. It hadn't been until the last week that she'd truly understood that none of it had been her choice at all.

The catalyst had been the discovery of those bones in the sea. From the moment they'd been brought ashore those occasional memory lapses she suffered from had changed in their nature. She'd *remembered* more each time her passenger had taken control, understood more about their relationship. The truth of what happened in 2003 had begun to come back to her too in fractured images. Memories, from her own mind, long held in check but others too that she was quite convinced *weren't* hers. The same terrible events but from a different perspective.

They'd bled into her dreams too. The snap of Adam's spine, the neck of a serviceman in 1937, a scullery maid in 1893, and so many more before then. When Frank had died, she'd seen it so clearly, could almost feel the rain on her face that night and yet she'd been in the inn, but she'd known he was dead even before Ben had run back to tell them.

It was when she'd taken Katrina Markham's eyes, listened to her old school friend screaming as her hands dripped with blood, that she'd understood who and what she was now: a vessel for something much greater than herself. She'd carried her passenger for so long that they'd now become one. These events, these deaths: Frank, Katrina, Sheelagh, and Ben were preordained and had been for over two decades. And there was still one more to go—she understood that only too clearly. The light from the bonfire outside was shining through the stained glass window giving her face a deathly green glow. And as she looked at her reflection, her features shimmered one last time, and all that had been Ruth O'Brien was gone.

Chapter 53

Chloe's senses were all over the place, she could feel herself sweating profusely, despite the freezing temperature. As she made the short distance with Aaron from the hotel to the piazza, she felt like she was having a panic attack and started scratching at her arm again with claw-like fingers. The moon—not quite, but almost full—was illuminating the entire area. The huge facade of the fake palazzo looked silver and magnificent behind it, while the ever-present bonfire was burning angrier than ever. Grace, Tariq, and Marcia were standing together in front of the caravans and greeted them both with nervous smiles.

"Go and stand in front of the fire and wait there," whispered Aaron into her ear. She could smell weed and alcohol in the air and remembered his comments earlier about "taking the edge off their fear." She walked until she was close enough to see the sparking embers on the ground in front and then turned round to face the horseshoe. There was silence now and she looked across at Aaron wondering what she was supposed to do next.

The door to the big gold caravan swung open and time seemed to stand still as a figure swept out. Chloe saw the shadow of its cowl first, the swish of the purple robe and there was no mistaking that silhouette. A mask covered her face, but she could see jewel-like eyes. Every doubt she'd ever had burnt away in that moment. Aaron and the others dissolved into the shadows too and she felt an unexpected serenity. She'd been *right* all along—the evidence was now standing in front of her. The thing was holding the long staff-like bone she'd seen in all the pictures, and it began shambling towards her one step at a time. Chloe felt nothing but pure adrenaline, her heart beating so fast she could barely breathe.

She glanced over at Aaron—"*trust me*" he'd said earlier—but no one seemed to be doing anything, even Grace looked petrified now. Chloe's hand automatically went to the knife in her pocket. She pulled it out, the blade flashing in the glow of the fire. The Bone Queen jerkily came to a halt. Surely, she wasn't scared of a knife? She seemed to half-turn and Chloe looked over at what had caught her attention.

There was a movement now behind the caravans and a *second* shuffling figure came into view, moving in the same disjointed way. Its face was also covered by a hood of some sort, and then she saw it was wearing jeans and a very familiar pair of dirty white trainers. Jack was behind it, pushing it forward, and the others parted to let them through. Chloe felt the air disappear from her lungs. This *couldn't* be who she thought it was. It was impossible—her mother had no idea that she'd gone to Athelsea. Everything seemed to spin again, and she felt the heat from the fire make the sweat run down her neck.

The Bone Queen motioned at Jack to stop. He brought the figure to a halt in front of Chloe and the Queen reached out and removed its hood. The bleary-eyed figure of her mother stood in front of her, tear-streaked and trembling.

"Clo . . ." she said hoarsely.

Chloe stared at her in disbelief. This was a fantasy, a *phantom* as Aaron had warned her there would be. Killing it would be her salvation. It was swaying and looked pathetic. Chloe felt all her hatred and fear blending together and she ran forward with a cry, raising the knife ready to plunge it into the thing's chest and then stopped.

"Kill it," commanded the Queen, her voice harsher and stronger than she expected. Chloe pictured the knife sinking into this thing's flesh, hearing it scream before it evaporated away. She could do this, needed to do this, and readied herself. She looked at the face once more, met its eyes and there was *familiarity.*

"Drop the knife, Chloe," said someone behind her. It was unexpectedly gentle with a lilting Irish accent. She turned and saw a man in a raincoat suddenly standing there. The voice was warm and friendly, but his eyes were focused on the blade. Men in black fatigues were spreading out across the piazza. For a moment Chloe wondered if these were more phantoms.

"I don't understand," she stammered.

"Please, Chloe, just drop it for me," said the man and she realized he was real and meant it. She released her grip on the blade, and it fell into the mud. Chloe rushed forward and hugged her mother. Long delayed tears began to come now, thick and fast from nowhere as she began to understand what she'd almost just done. She could see Aaron turning to run, but the group by the wagons were now completely encircled by the men in black. Marcia was fighting like a cat, but the life had gone out of Grace. She was standing motionless, almost oblivious to what was going on around her.

Jenna watched as Liam discreetly picked up the knife and used it to cut her free from the ties. She gave him a small nod of thanks, which he returned with an almost imperceptible nod of his own. She hugged Chloe back, feeling the life breathe back into her, the weight of days of worry instantly gone. She was almost crushing her, she realized, but the most important thing was that her daughter wasn't pulling away, her own hands gripping her back almost as tightly.

There was a sudden movement in the corner of her eye, and she saw the cloaked figure move round and stand right in front of the fire. The creature grabbed a stray branch, its end alight, and held it out in front of her as the remaining officers moved to block her escape. Liam motioned at them to stand back and only then did Jenna realize how closely it resembled the picture she'd found in Chloe's bedroom. She watched as Liam moved to confront it.

"What's this all been about, Ruth?" he said, and the name caught her by surprise.

"That's not Ruth O'Brien," she said, slowly disengaging from her daughter. There was a sound now, hypnotic, beneath the noise of the fire. She'd heard it before, but couldn't place where or when, like something slowly heaving itself along wet ground.

The creature lifted its hood and for a second they saw Ruth staring back at them and then darkness seemed to envelop her face. She lifted the branch above her head and Jenna understood what she was about to do before she did it.

"No!" Jenna yelled, but it was too late. She brought it down and the purple robe caught light immediately. The staff-like bone fell to the ground and all they could see was a mass of orange and yellow fury enveloping the outline of something human. For a fraction of a second Jenna saw another face, younger and startlingly beautiful. The flesh began to boil on the bone, a rictus grin spreading across it. Then she staggered back, fell into the fire, and the flames leapt into the night sky.

Chapter 54

To Jenna's initial surprise, Chloe had wanted to spend a few more days on Athelsea before returning to London. The more they'd talked, the more she'd understood why. The idea that they could just slot back into their old lives as if nothing had happened was ridiculous and they both had a few demons to exorcise first. Chloe had almost murdered her mother and they both now understood how close to the precipice they'd each come.

Jenna too had needed time to recover from what Aaron had done to her. The night they'd been rescued, in the hotel—a proper hotel this time overlooking the harbor—she'd been ill. A combination of the drugs she'd been given, the alcohol, and the stress of the whole experience. Her temperature had shot up, and she'd emptied out the contents of her stomach several times over. Chloe had stayed with her, nursing her through until they'd both felt stronger. There, in the small hours—literally and metaphorically getting the toxins out of their systems—they'd reconnected again.

The following days had been spent talking. Whatever spell the Bone Queen had cast over her daughter seemed to have finally dissipated.

Rested and recuperated, they were now waiting for the ferry, and Liam had come to see them off. He'd been in touch, regularly checking in on their progress and updating them as he tied up the remaining loose threads. Chloe was taking one last walk along the seafront as Jenna and Liam waited for the approaching boat to dock.

"So, how are you doing?" said the policeman with an affable smile.

"I'm not talking to an invisible sister if that's what you're thinking," she said, looking at him with slight embarrassment. "I don't usually talk to invisible people as a rule. I just felt—"

He held out a hand to interrupt her.

"You don't owe me an explanation for anything. You had some unresolved issues; perhaps you're not seeing her anymore because you actually found some answers here."

Jenna took a deep breath.

"Maybe."

There was something to that. Her relationship with Chloe hadn't just been restored, it felt strengthened too. Her daughter's forgiveness—if that's what it was—was what she needed to banish the self-doubt and insecurity that had manifested Hattie in the first place.

She looked out at the horizon; the water was deep blue with just a few licks of foam in the morning wind. "Did you ever find out what happened to Kayla?" she said. The girl's fate and the sight of her on that mortuary table hadn't left her.

"We've had a chance to interview all of those kids now. They seemed to think that if they sacrificed someone, then they'd lift this *mark* off themselves. They gave her a hallucinogenic and then pretty much chased her off the end of a cliff as far as I can tell. The toxicology report backs that up."

Jenna was pretty certain it wasn't those youths who'd chased Kayla to her death. She looked at Chloe in the middle distance, grateful again to have got her daughter back in one piece. Her nightmares had stopped, she'd finally started to leave her arm alone, and most importantly she seemed truly to be free of the Bone Queen's mark.

"And Aaron . . . or Josh? Where's his head at?"

Liam shook his head. "I think that's one of the most chilling aspects of all of this. If anything, he seems *happier*. He genuinely thinks Ruth sacrificed herself so that the Bone Queen wouldn't take him. Which is nonsense of course."

"Is it?" said Jenna, turning to him.

"Of course it is. Ruth O'Brien was responsible for the murders. I've got all the evidence I need to prove that."

"You said she was in the pub when Frank Archer died."

Liam shook his head dismissively.

"I think one of the others did that at her instruction. Aaron most probably. We found a burner phone in the hotel which we think was used to send the text that lured Archer out of the pub. We're still talking to them, but I expect to get a confession. Given everything that boy's been through it's hardly surprising he's psychotic."

"Maybe," said Jenna, turning back to the sea.

"You really think that was the Bone Queen you saw at the end?" said Liam carefully and she considered the question for a long moment.

"Put it this way—I think something terrible happened on this island once and embedded itself in the very earth and rock of the place," she said, looking him in the eye.

"You mean the legend of Eleanor Aubney?"

"If you like, or maybe she was just the first documented case, and it predates even her. Perhaps it was something to do with those bones in the caves, or maybe nothing to do with them at all." He didn't reply and she knew he was too polite to argue.

Chloe was walking towards them and looked up shyly. One thing she'd done since they'd rescued her was dye her hair bright pink again and it instantly seemed to brighten her whole demeanor. She looked a very different person to the listless teenager they'd found just days ago. The ferry was starting to maneuver itself into dock now.

"Are you ready?" said Jenna to Chloe, and her daughter nodded.

"More than ready," she said.

Liam held out a hand and Jenna rolled her eyes.

"Don't be daft, come here—thank you for everything," she said and gave him an impromptu hug. "Take care of yourself."

"You too," he replied, and for a second there seemed to be a melancholy about him. He gave them one last wave and then turned to head back to the station.

"Come on," said Chloe watching him go. "Let's get off this rock."

Epilogue

The cell wasn't quite as bad as Grace had feared. It had a desk and a chair, and there was even some shelving with a few books. A small window brought in a little natural light despite the bars, and she couldn't help but notice that it wasn't that much different to the room she'd had at the old hotel. The solitude had been strangely welcome because there was a lot she'd had to reflect on.

Her father had disowned her. He'd been informed of where she was and that she'd been involved in the death of a teenage girl. After that, he'd refused to take her calls and hadn't come to visit, so now Grace was quite alone. Inevitably, she had also thought a lot about Aaron, though she obviously hadn't seen him since the night of their arrest. She wondered if he was okay and was thinking about her too. He'd lost both his parents and now his stepmother. Like her, he had no one. They'd find each other again though; she was sure of it.

The other curious thing was that she should have felt some relief, that the mark of the Bone Queen had finally been removed. There had *been* a sacrifice. She was quite sure that was why Ruth had torched herself, so that the rest of them might finally be free. So why had the disturbing dreams continued? Weird, strange imagery that she could only remember the distant shape of when she woke. They were of other times and places, though Ravensgate Lake always seemed to be at the heart of them. Even more disconcertingly, her whole sense of time seemed to be out of kilter too. She couldn't really remember how the days were passing right now. She'd sleep for a bit and then wake with no idea of whether it was morning or evening.

She kept seeing Frank Archer's face as well. In her mind's eye, it was dark, with the rain teeming down, and he looked terrified. She was holding something, gripping it tightly—a knife of some sort—and there was the sensation of steel cutting through soft tissue. Then there was blood, more black than red, dissolving instantly on a rain-soaked pavement. The image was so clear, and yet she had no memory of the night he died, just of waking up in the hotel room as the storm raged outside.

She scratched her arm. It had started to itch badly since she'd been incarcerated. She shook her head, went over to the sink in the corner and ran the tap. Splashing cold water onto her face she breathed out. When this was over, she would return to Athelsea. Her destiny lay on the island, and she could sense in her bones that there was still an unfinished chapter to her story.

Her bones.

The last line of the rhyme came back to her again.

"For in her gaze the lost bones weep."

She stared at her reflection in the mirror above the sink and, just for a moment, her features seemed to shimmer and blur . . .

Acknowledgments

Most things in life get easier the more you do them, but writing books seems to be the exception to that rule. *The Bone Queen* is a book of firsts for me. It's my first novel to be published in the United States, which I'm incredibly thrilled about, and it's also my first horror novel. All my previous works have been police procedurals, so this was very much a step into the unknown, and it proved to be a real challenge.

So, with that in mind, I must say a big thank you to my UK agent, Hayley Steed, who I worked intensively with on the book you've just read. The genesis of this story came in a small café in West Norwood in south London on a cold morning in 2022 and went through many a twist and turn from there. Without Hayley's diligence and eye for detail I'm not sure I'd have found my way out of Athelsea's woods! But I owe her a great deal for this book, and I'm delighted with the home it's found with Minotaur Books.

Big thanks too are due to Chad Luibl, my US agent, and all the team at Janklow and Nesbit on both sides of the Atlantic. Chad was a calming and reassuring voice while the book was being read by the world and an invaluable guide to the lay of the land in the US.

Enormous thanks as well to Michael Homler at Minotaur—it's genuinely a privilege to be involved in what you do, and I'm so proud to be amongst your stable of incredible writers.

Thanks as well to everyone else involved in the process—to the publicity teams, copy editors, cover designers, booksellers, bloggers, reviewers, and fellow writers who've taken the time to read the book—it's all hugely appreciated.

And a special thanks to my good friend Nishat Ladha, who always reads my books as I write them. Emailing her the latest chapters and waiting for her reaction on WhatsApp has become an integral part of my writing process.

Finally, thanks to you, the reader, for spending some time with me on Athelsea—I hope you enjoyed it and felt it was time well spent. I can't wait to see what's next!

About the Author

Mark Grey

Will Shindler has spent most of his career working as a broadcast journalist for the BBC. He also spent nearly a decade working on a number of British television dramas, working for both the BBC Drama Series Department, and Talkback Thames Television as a writer and script editor. He has been writing novels since 2020, including the five-book critically acclaimed DI Alex Finn series: *The Burning Men, The Killing Choice, The Hunting Ground, The Blood Line,* and *The Cold Case. The Bone Queen* is his first novel for Minotaur Books in the US. He currently combines reading news bulletins for BBC Radio London with his novel writing and has previously worked as a presenter for ITV West, a reporter for BBC Radio Five Live, and as one of the stadium presenters at the 2012 London Olympics. He lives in London.